BALLGAME

THE AMERICAN WHO WATCHED BRITISH MYSTERIES
BOOK TWO

BALLGAME
— ARTHUR JOHN —

— AN —
AMERICAN WHO WATCHED BRITISH MYSTERIES NOVEL

Ainsley Publishing

Text Copyright 2025 by A.J. Rathbun
Cover art & design by Jon Sholly

All rights reserved. No part of this book may be used or reproduced in any manner whatsoever without the written permission of the author.

ISBN: 979-8-9926415-1-6

Library of Congress Control Number: 2025903238

FOR NATALIE AND AINSLEY

1

Slowly turning a dusty 1987 AMC Matador the same sandy brown color as his sports coat into the massive parking lot, Detective Marlowe picked one of a handful of empty spaces near the lot's entrance. He wanted time to consider before entering the controlled chaos of a freshly minted murder scene. *To soak in the atmosphere*, he thought, shaking his head at his own phrasing like a horse bothered by a fly. He believed facts, not fancy, solved murders. But taking stock of the physical area where a murder happened tended to be helpful.

Shrugging his large frame out of the car, he re-tucked the wrinkled, white button-down shirt under his sports coat and settled a royal-blue baseball cap over his bald head as protection against the morning sun. Perching for a moment on the hood, he gave a wide gaze across the landscape. The Hettie Patty High School and Playfields, utilized by kids attending the school as well as a host of other sport teams, families, and organizations, cut a wide swath across one of the City's northeast neighborhoods. The orange-bricked school itself popped to the lot's north. Well-maintained, twenty-foot-tall main building walls glowed in the Saturday afternoon sunshine, while shorter, single-story metal outbuildings spread from it like the arms of a petrified octopus. Stretching skyward, Douglas firs loomed over a wide grassy lawn in front of the school. On the back side, nearest to where he'd parked, a few picnic tables dotted sculptured lawns and a park area, a sidewalk bordered by irregular flowers curving through it and a handful of thick laurel bushes in irregular outposts.

The other side of the 150-space parking lot was bordered by the far edge of the first of four baseball diamonds. Right field was visible, vivid green grass currently empty of kids, occupied by a solitary crow picking at an something unidentified not fifteen feet from first base. There were soccer fields across the street from the school's front side as well. *Horrible spot for a murder*, he thought. Any murder spot is horrible. But here? Worse. "Time to get to work," he whispered, lifting up off car.

At the lot's far end, a host of police cars and SUVs, white vans, and an ambulance clustered, lights flashing, voices rising and falling indistinct as an untuned radio. He'd gotten a few feet when he heard a noise from a grouping of five laurel bushes wide as a bull and tall as a barndoor, curved into a slight U away from the school sight lines. Taking a step off the sidewalk in the bushes' direction, the sweetish acrid smell of marijuana smoke hit him—not an unusual smell since it became legal in the City a few years back. Some cigarette butts dotted the green grass like a rash, the laurel grouping being an ideal spot for high-school smokers. In two more steps, he was around the bush edge and saw three teenage boys looking at him lazily.

They were attired nearly identically: ragged jean shorts, Converse sneakers, short socks, and T-shirts. Each shirt was different, however, and one wore a royal-blue baseball cap with a hand-stitched S, matching Marlowe's. That hatted one—African American, fifteen years at a guess—was tallest, just over six feet, and wore a shirt that said "High Profile." To his right was a Caucasian kid, hair dyed a stagnant pond green, shirt featuring a golden, foot-high sparkling S and the words "Family Values." The third, Asian American and the shortest, had three black plastic bands around one wrist and wore a shirt with a picture of a crab and the words "Mind Over Mussel." He spoke in a voice pitched low, just over a whisper, as Marlowe took another step.

"Detective."

"That obvious?" Marlowe asked.

"The suit coat's a giveaway," the tallest boy replied, scrunching his hat down lower.

"Facts," said the third, not looking up, scratching circles in the dirt with one sneaker.

"Ah," said Marlowe, tugging at his right sleeve. "Should have guessed."

All four were silent as a police car, siren raging, screamed into the lot, passed them, angling at the other end.

"Have any officers talked to you," Marlowe continued once the siren faded, "about this morning's . . . incident?"

Three affirmative nods.

"Okay." Marlowe started to walk off, hesitated, and turned back. "Guessing you told them, but were you here all morning?"

More nods coincided with the three speaking rapid fire, cutting each other off.

"The cops ask—"

"Or demand—"

"And we answered."

"Thanks. For me, hear or see anything out of the ordinary?"

The one with green hair cocked his head. "A scream like a cat mewing. Two screams."

"More like screaming hedgehogs, to me," said the one in the hat.

The third one's head bobbed up and down. "And then someone yelled, 'Time,' loudly."

"Thanks again." Marlowe felt he'd better move on and began walking, before once more turning back to say, "Nice hat," while slightly tipping his.

He got another nod, a smile, and one low-pitched word. "Twins."

He took two more steps before turning a final time, feeling as he did it that he'd turned and returned so much he was like a fictional detective who can't make it through the door. He waved at the laurel enclave the boys were standing within. "Why stay here?"

"Toil and trouble out there, boss," the crab-shirted one said. "Safer here."

Walking away, Marlowe mulled the kids. *High? Just kids talking to a police officer, which had to be off-putting. Kids talking to any adult?* He'd ask the officers on the scene what they made of them, get their names just in case. He wished he'd stopped for a second cup of coffee, help knock the morning's haze back farther into the recesses of night. One cup never equaled enough, even when it was a double espresso grabbed at his favorite coffee stand in the City, Sampson's Sips, run by a jolly red-haired Australian.

Continuing parallel to the parking lot, he skirted up to the crime scene from the back side like a cowboy sneaking up on a herd of wandering cows, hands in the pockets of his also-brown slacks. Once abreast of the second baseball field, the field next to the one where the body was, he cut across the lot, curving around cars. Police tape cordoned off both fields, an area of parking lot nearby, a concession stand, multiple metal bleachers, and sidewalks. Enough police tape to paper a large living room. Multiple uniformed officers, a few white-body-suited CSI staff, plus civilians and non-uniformed officers moved and gestured around him.

A hand on the first line of tape, about to duck under, badge out so the officer keeping unwanted people off the scene could scan, he heard a high-pitched, obviously excited bark coming from behind him. Turning, a mid-sized, blurred tan missel of a dog launched itself in his direction as the man at the end of the dog's leash started talking.

"Ainsley, stop. Ainsley, no jumping. Detective Marlowe does not need you in his coat pocket. There are no treats there."

Marlowe bent as the dog sat, tail wagging as fast as a hummingbird's wing, putting his hand out so she could lick it. *Must have some croissant crumbs still on there,* he decided, taking in the sixtyish-pound Staffordshire terrier's unique tan-with-black-accents brindling, highlighted by a single white streak like lightening up one side of her neck.

"Ainsley. Surprised to see you." He straightened up, keeping his hand down low enough for the dog to reach it, and looked at the man at the other end of the leash. "John. Surprised to see you too."

Sixtyish in age, John Arthur wore a teal baseball cap with the image of two happy dogs on it, a lightweight gold-and-green striped hoodie, brown shorts, bright gold-and-green striped high socks, and nearly round, nearly clear glasses with hints of gold in the frames. Smiling broadly, his eyes twinkled.

"She hasn't forgotten you, Detective. Dogs rarely forget a smell."

"That a compliment?"

"Rarely forget *anyone's* smell, I should have said. Or another dog's smell. Or a neighborhood cat. Or bunnies. Ainsley is wild for bunnies. We have one that's taken up residence mainly around our lavender bushes, driving her mad. Which reminds me of Poirot saying, 'If you wish to catch a rabbit, you put a ferret into the hole, and if the rabbit is there, he runs.' Ainsley would—"

Marlowe held one hand up, palm out, in a motion made by thousands of traffic cops every day.

"A palm stop. The international sign of the police when cars are driving out of order, or when suspects—Witnesses? People in general?—are talking too much. I can go on a little." John's enthusiastic nature was often unbridled.

"You can." Marlowe replied, a wisp of smile appearing, then vanishing like sun behind a persistent cloud. He brought the hand down from the stop motion into a shaking one, and the two shook hands as Ainsley attempted to lick both at once.

"Down, Ains." John laughed, pulling a piece of dried lamb lung from his pocket. "Sit." Ainsley sat, but her tail and head metronomed between the men.

Marlowe first met John during a previous case, one in which John had found the body of a murder victim near a local community center while walking Ainsley. The detective and his team had considered John a potential suspect on-and-off during the case wrangling, then shaded toward him as a witness; a strange one, as he'd seemed overly involved in the case, asking questions and theorizing. Turned out, he brought good insights. It also turned out that the older man, a widower, was a fanatical fan of British TV mysteries. He quoted them constantly, explaining about this crime solving priest and that suspiciously minded spinster, using them in a way to fill the lonely space in his life since his wife had passed away. By the case's end, he'd used what he'd learned during their history of watching those mysteries to help solve the crime. He could be a lot to take, but Marlowe had grown to like him.

"Mind letting me know what you're doing here, John?" Marlowe dried off his hand as he talked quietly. "This particular Saturday, at this school, at this time. Not crime chasing?"

"No, not that. Though if I wanted to start a detective business—"

"Which I hope you don't."

"Which I don't. But if I did, hanging around sporting events might not be a bad business plan. Lots of mystery show episodes circle around sports. In *Midsomer Murders* alone, you have murders on a cricket pitch—tough to follow somewhat for me as I've never understood cricket—at a rowing match, and at a rugby club. Then in the *Brokenwood Mysteries*, there's also a murder on a rugby pitch and on a golf course. Which brings to mind the classic Poirot *Murder on the Links*, where the body is found in a golf course bunker. And that's just the starting gun of sporting mysteries. There's—"

"John?" Marlowe gently interrupted.

"Yes, Detective?"

"Say you weren't starting a sporting mystery detective business. Why are you here this morning?"

A siren started up as a patrol car raced out of the lot.

"Today. Here. With all this"—he motioned to crowd whirling around them—"pointing to a serious crime. I must come clean, Detective Marlowe." He paused for effect, causing a nearly imperceptible eyeroll from Marlowe, as if tracking a flitting sparrow overhead. "I was here when the murder was committed."

"Murder?"

"As Marple once said when talking about a suicide that was actually murder, 'We don't know that for *sure*.' But this has to be murder. For one, would this many officers and SOCO—I mean CSI—teams be here for a lesser crime? Maybe. But two, would your partner, the amiable Detective Morven, be here?" John said of the longest-tenured detective on Marlowe's team. "That brings us to point three." He held up three fingers, causing Ainsley to momentarily jump, then sit back down. "Detective Marlowe himself. Announcing it's a murder. Also point four, I happened to be sitting not too far away when the victim, how can I comfortably say it, expired. And it felt like a murder. I've seen so many—"

"On TV."

"On TV."

Marlowe had nearly forgotten how John could pull the ponies off the trail with his combination of enthusiasm and tangential TV thinking. "John, rein it in. Why were you here, around this school, these playfields on this *particular* day and time?"

"Got you. The background of a potential suspect or, hopefully, witness," John continued as Marlowe breathed in deeply. Ainsley seemed to notice, as she began licking his hand again. John's tendency for the theatrical was another aspect of the man that was both a touch endearing and a touch annoying. "I have a good explanation. Across the street are playfields used more for soccer and Ultimate frisbee. My younger nephew, Coen, was a big Ultimate player and now coaches an Ultimate team, the Applejacks. They were playing this morning, and I decided to come and watch. Lovely day for it."

Marlowe gave a *keep it going* nod of the head.

"Not too hot yet, skies as clear and blue as one might dream about during the dull dreary December hours, probably remaining dry from dawn until dusk. I was thinking about when my nephews used to play baseball here when they were kids, when Marlene and I used to come watch them. Feeling nostalgic, when the Ultimate match ended, I thought:

why not go watch a little baseball? Didn't figure I'd be dropped into another tragedy today, or ever. Unless you called for my assistance; a phone call I keep waiting for after our earlier case. Not that I honestly *believed* in becoming a consulting detective. But if you watch enough shows, the fantasy of solving a crime does start to take hold, even causing you to forget the actual suffering behind the crime scenes."

Marlowe looked up at towering maple nearer the school putting a swath of building and lawn in shadow. A Steller's jay perched high up on one branch took flight.

"Makes sense. Picked this second field randomly?"

"There were unoccupied spots on first bleacher. Easy sight lines of the action, as well as the people, if you pick a high corner seat. I'd heard a cheer when walking up, so felt it might be a swell game to watch. Why, do you think, are kid's baseball bleachers the most uncomfortable seats in the world? Do they make them that way to keep parents' attention on the game? Or to keep anyone from dozing off?"

Marlowe pulled off his hat and scratched his head, saying nothing.

"Sorry." John pulled his eyes back to Marlowe from gazing at the bleachers. "Back on track. Sat down, watched a couple innings. The cheer I'd heard was for the team whose bleachers I was on, the Reign. The other team was the Torrent. The latter led six to one when I walked up. That cheer was for a two-out, three-RBI Reign triple. There were a few scoreless innings. Then the sixth. First batter struck out. Second batter walked. Third batter hit a single. Next batter up took the first pitch and hammered it. A half-second after the whack of bat on ball, a horrendous scream broke through the chatter and cheers, followed by a second scream. Slightly different in pitch but achingly loud. Then a man yelled, 'Time!' twice. I and others headed to the front of the bleachers, where a man was on the ground, not moving. I overheard someone saying he'd had a fit. Then it got very chaotic. Parents grabbing kids, disordered talking, crying, people gathering, making it hard to get nearer. But even from a few feet away, he looked... looked done, to me."

"Not pleasant. Hope the kids were kept away. Next?" Marlowe prompted.

"I felt I should get closer, check his pulse, while not contaminating the scene. But a tall man, I'd say six one, Caucasian, oval face, probably only 160 pounds, balding dyed black hair, black shirt, dog collar—"

"Hold up. First, no need to bring in the line-up particulars yet. Second, dog collar?"

"Roman collar, priest's collar. You know, the white band around the neck but under the shirt line?"

"Sure. A priest."

"He was bending over the body, and a woman, long straight dark hair, well made-up for a baseball game, leather bracelet, black bangles—" He checked himself, continued. "She said loudly, 'Nobody touch him, I've called 911. I tried to help gently herd people, without much luck even with Ainsley around their ankles. The calvary arrived quickly in the form of firetrucks, ambulance, and police. More rapidly than our last case. They asked us to move back but not leave the area. And here we are."

"Got it. Good summary. Helpful. I should be moving on, but stay if you can." He grabbed the police tape, pulling it up to duck under. Before he could make the duck, John spoke again.

"Detective Marlowe? Sorry, one more, two more, actually three more quick things."

"Quick?"

"Quick."

"Okey dokey. But I'm late, and it's important."

"Quick, I promise. Though I fear, as Mrs. Marple said, 'I am very inclined to rambling. One wanders from the point altogether without knowing one is doing so.' First, I spoke to Detective Morven briefly when she arrived."

Marlowe ducked under the tape as John talked.

"Second, one point about the scene. Not getting close, I didn't see many details. However, and I'm sure the folks in white will pick up on it, I did notice a magenta stain the size of a small footstool. I initially surmised blood. Not to be morbid, but that seemed off in coloring in retrospect. And the smell was boozy, fruity. I didn't hear a shot or see a weapon, but did see a partially crushed cup not two inches from his hand."

Marlowe's chin lazily went up and then down, like a bird coming home to roost. John, he knew from their past, always had a point. Often interesting. Sometimes random and confusing. Once or twice, crucial.

"And lastly, I –"

"Detective Marlowe, you're here." A man's voice cut cleanly through John's sentence and the parking lot's aural clutter. "Come—"

"—knew the dead man."

"—this way."

Detective Jamie Nelson was, as usual, sprinting. The youngest and newest full-time member of Marlowe's team traveled full speed 90% of the time, even when wearing a tailored two-button navy suit. Racing through the parking lot sardined with officers, cars, and ambulance, suit coat flapping behind, he spun slightly over the front edge of a police car, did a full pivot around another, a sharp stop, turn and twist to avoid a minivan, then speeded up for the final ten feet to where Marlowe was standing, mouth open, looking at John thinking: *not again.*

"Detective Marlowe, sir." Nelson wasn't even breathing hard. "Detective Morven sent me to ensure you found Mr. Arthur, here." He pointed. "And Ainsley."

The dog strained her leash to reach the young detective, who noticed and stretched out his hand so she could sniff it. He had also worked the past case John was involved in, so knew both the man and dog.

Marlowe took a breath. Nelson may not have been worn out, but watching him cross the parking lot while John's revelation sank in had momentarily taken Marlowe's breath away. "Morning, Detective Nelson," he said. "I see you made it."

"Of course, sir. I was at Luther's London gym getting in an early HIIT workout. That's high intensity interval training. Good when you don't have a lot of time. Kettlebells, squats, revenge rows. Now that I'm a detective, I keep an extra suit at the gym." The words came out at a sprint too.

John cut in before Marlowe. "Revenge rows?"

"I meant renegade rows. My mind must have been halfway between policing and exercising. They're a great way to work the arms and core at the same—"

"Both are straying. Slow down." Marlowe let the silence sit a moment. "Nelson, Mr. Arthur was revealing that he knew our victim. Again."

"Again?" Nelson's shocked appearance could have stopped traffic.

The gold accents in John's glasses caught the sun and sparkled, as Ainsley stretched and lay down, her head reaching under the police tape to use Marlowe's shoe as a pillow. Both officers seemed to be waiting for him to speak.

"I do. Or I did. Not well, though, like the victim in the Case of the Nine Neighbors."

"The what?" Marlowe and Nelson replied simultaneously.

"That's how I refer to it in my head. A mingling of classic Erle Stanley Gardner's Perry Mason, Dame Agatha, and, if I'm not dredging too deep into the mystery firmament, Sherlock."

"Ohhhhhkay," Marlowe replied, drawing out the O slowly, as if wading on a rocky riverbed. "Today's victim?"

"I didn't know him well, but know his name is Pat Brown. Pastor at the Chapter Creek Church. Father of four."

"Do you attend that church?" Nelson jumped in. He hadn't pictured the older man as an organized religion follower, thinking his devotion to British television mysteries and books wouldn't give him the time.

"Nope. Weirdly, considering the circumstances, I knew him through baseball." John watched a stray cloud above as he mused.

"Baseball?" Marlowe asked.

"The one-time national pastime. My nephew Coen, the Ultimate player I mentioned earlier, played on a team for a while that Pat Brown helped coach. I went to a fair number of games, met him once through my sister, briefly."

"For a while?"

"What?" John snapped back from sky watching.

"You said your nephew only played for a while."

"Yes, that's true. Stopped midway through the season. Because of Pat Brown, I think, though he said he wanted to focus on Ultimate. *De mortuis nil nisi bonum*, but from what I saw and heard, Mr. Brown wasn't the friendliest or most supportive of youth sports coaches."

Nelson pulled a small notebook from his suit pocket. "De what what?"

"Latin for *of the dead speak only good*. To skip over that sentiment, I believe there were rumors about him running into trouble with coaches, parents, parishioners, too. I don't want to ramble," he said with a brief grin in Marlowe's direction, "but Pat Brown was a bit of a flash Harry as well."

"A what?" Nelson stopped note-taking.

"A flash Harry. A phrase I first heard from DS Dodds."

"DS who?" Nelson asked.

Marlowe started to speak, but John was off before he could.

"DS Dodds. *McDonald and Dodds?*" Noticing their blank stares, John quickly continued. "Amazing show. Mismatched team genre combined with the quirky detective genre. With a dash of death in lovely surrounding. Ambitious and hard-charging DCI, or Detective Chief Inspector—your level, Marlowe, in the British police universe—DCI McDonald is sent to beautiful Bath from London and paired with the sheepish, older, long-looked-over, quirky DS Dodds. They're very chalk and cheese, but soon she realizes Dodds has incredible insights in the crimes they're investigating. So a perfect pair. Even if he eats butter on his chips—what we'd call fries. Played by the outstanding Jason Watkins, who I'm sure you know?"

Marlowe and Nelson looked like pins just hit by a bowling ball, John was talking so fast.

"No? Top-notch. I've seen him play cops, a shopkeeper, *and* a werewolf."

"John." Marlowe recovered enough to raise his palm, stopping the waterfallesque flow of words. "Why was Pat Brown this flash Harry type?"

"A show-off, as far as clothes and accompaniments. Pat Brown always wore a very snazzy gold watch, a gold cross on an exuberant gold chain, and there was no missing that his clothes and shoes were of the expensive variety. Designer sunglasses even."

"Got it. We should go. You know, victim, crime."

"Definitely. I can get—"

"I know. Don't worry about it."

"It's helpful, Mr. Arthur," Nelson piped up. "You did solve the, what was it, Nine Neighbors murder."

"That was you and the other officers. I just meandered through some favorite mystery shows, which gave me some ideas."

"Very humble of you, John." Marlowe knew the man had done more.

"Like Dodds himself, 'I left my ego at home. It weighs me down.'"

Before another sidetrack back into television land, Marlowe said, "We've got to get to it. Thanks for the briefing. Nelson, let's go."

"Happy to help," John said as they walked off. "I'll be over by the school walking with Ainsley if you need anything. I've got one or two points to mull."

Marlowe gave a thumbs-up as he left.

"Wait!" John loudly said, causing the two detectives to stop. "One question. Did I hear correctly, it's now *Detective* Nelson, not Sergeant?"

Nelson beamed, brushing invisible fluff off of one sleeve. "It is."

"Congratulations, Detective Nelson. And your backup suit looks better than any suit has a right to. Way more the stylish, poetic Inspector Dalglish than the rumpled and sleepless Broadchurchian Detective Inspector Alec Hardy. That's the new version of Inspector Dalglish, I'm referring—"

"Come on, Nelson," Marlowe growled, before John soared back into flights of British TV mystery fancy. "Work to do." They waved over their shoulders as John and Ainsley went the other direction.

"Strange, Mr. Arthur being here," Nelson said as they walked. "After that past murder. I'd forgotten how odd he can be."

"He's an individual, that's for certain." Marlowe slowed, forcing Nelson into a less brisk pace.

"You don't consider him any sort of suspect, right? More, wrong place, wrong time? Or, right place, right time, considering his fascination with mysteries and crime shows."

"We can probably keep him off the list."

Nelson leapt one-legged off a curb they were walking over. "Agreed. But maybe worth keeping him in the loop? He did help a lot in the past."

"You trying to get someone to do your job, Nelson?" Marlowe kidded.

"No sir, not at all, sir. Oh, you're joking. I didn't talk to Mr. Arthur much during the last case, but what he said today seems logical, in a Mr. Arthur way. Him being a widower without kids of his own who spends a fair amount of time alone, probably fun for him to come watch a game. Until the IOR. Incident of record, I mean." Nelson loved initialisms and acronyms.

"Makes sense. Nelson, no need for the sir or saluting. Detective Marlowe is fine."

"Got it. Did you know, *Detective* Marlowe, that Ultimate Frisbee is one of the fastest growing sports in the world in popularity? An increase of 168% in team memberships since 2004. Seven million players in eighty countries."

Marlowe didn't reply, continuing to the scurry of people in white protective bodysuits.

2

Before they got much farther, another strand of yellow police tape stopped them. It was in a half circle—cut by the fence separating field from spectators—around one of the two sets of bleachers on this side of the field. Tall screens stood in the middle, shielding the victim from view beyond the further fence, at the other fields, and in the parking lot.

From the screens' edge, a woman dressed in a full white bodysuit gave them a wave and walked over. They could see her face—light-brown skin, pretty features—and a single stand of dark hair curling out from the protective gear like a slow S, the rest in crown plait on top of her head, pushing up the hood of the suit slightly.

"Detective Marlowe, I see Detective Nelson discovered you on his ramble." Her serious look shifted into a small smile as she spoke.

"I wasn't rambling," Nelson replied. "I was specifically expanding the scene according to SOP and looking for Detective Marlowe."

"Good morning, Detective Morven," Marlowe said. Tessa Morven, the officer inside the suit, had worked as a detective alongside Marlowe for a few years, providing a steadiness and reliability he didn't believe he could now do without, though he knew she would have a team of her own before long. "Thanks for donning the white suit. Should we?"

"Solely booties should be good now. Luckily, I have them ready for you." She held out two sets of protective slips to go over their shoes, Marlowe's scuffed penny loafers the shade of peanut butter, dull alongside Nelson's shining camel-colored Oxfords.

"Any early reports?" Marlowe asked.

"Definitely a suspicious death, though nothing specific yet. I have officers gathering names from those nearest when it happened. Forensics is here bagging and tagging."

"Happily?"

"Somewhat. I did overhear one talking about how a scene this overrun by families and their detritus would involve many overtime hours."

"That it will. It's like a gully after a cattle drive's gone past, all muddled and muddied."

Morven let that lie, then continued. Nelson seemed to be doing standing crunches while she spoke. "We do have the name of the—"

"Pat Brown?"

"That's it. How?" Morven was surprised, though the older detective tended to pick things up quickly.

"Ran into Mr. Arthur."

"I talked to him briefly too. I'll never forget his backyard monologue, as he called it, from that case with him. Learn anything?"

"He was in those bleachers when it happened." He pointed at the far set. "And he knew the victim."

"Again?" she said, shocked. "He didn't mention that to me." She pushed the helmet of the suit off her head and tucked the strand of hair in front of her face behind an ear.

"He's already worked a British mystery series I'd never heard of into the case," Nelson said.

While wondering again how such a blue-skied summer day could be the setting for a suspicious death, Marlowe refrained from going down the Arthur rabbit hole, then remembered the man had indeed dropped a rabbit quote earlier. From the Belgian—wait, French—detective. He kept it to himself. "Is the doc attending?"

"Doctor Peterson is behind the screens, yes, making initial findings. He asked if you were attending and said you could come in when you arrived. He also said something about the blast of war blowing in his ear? In reference to it being overly crowded around him, I surmised, as he followed it by saying, 'Just Marlowe.'"

"Smart to divide and conquer," Marlowe said. "Nelson, you reconnoitrer with uniform, get that list of witnesses first thing. I'll hit up the doc. Morven, could you check with the other scientists, see if anything's blossomed?" He ducked under the tape, heading toward the screen.

Morven said, "Sure. Meet up back here?"

"Good plan," Marlowe replied over a shoulder.

Morven strode off to the nearest grouping of CSIs, as Nelson bent down to remove the booties he'd just put on and retie his shoes.

After wandering the parking lot, Ainsley stopping to smell tires, a Butterfingers wrapper, and numerous bird droppings, John headed to the school's north end, which merged into a park. A trickling stream ran past a slide, a few plastic saddled animals on giant springs—turtle, rabbit, duck, dog—and four battered metal tables cemented into the ground with attached bench seating. The space was empty currently, any weekend traffic driven away by sirens and police.

John perched on one bench, staring across the lot at the constant activity, as Ainsley flopped down at his feet, instantly asleep. Her ability to transition within a second from full-on smell-play-jump mode into completely sleeping amazed him. He mulled the morning, going from slight shock at seeing another dead body to curiosity at how it might have happened. It could have been a heart attack, or other physical issue. Pat Brown seemed healthy, but you never know what's going on inside. But that didn't feel right. He'd seen far too many murder mysteries, and it colored his viewpoint. Those shows had, he believed, developed some instincts inside him.

"If one can *develop* instincts? Not sure about that, Ains. Wouldn't anyone who watched enough mysteries begin to, let's say, sense when a crime had been committed?" *I keep talking to the dog, and I'll be committed*, he thought. He knew he wouldn't stop talking to her, though. Living alone with just Ainsley since his wife died, he tended to talk to the dog a lot, filling the emptiness. He didn't worry about it. It's when she started talking back that he'd worry.

"What is the logical next step?" he said aloud again, causing Ainsley to momentarily raise her head in case treats were approaching. "What might Poirot do? 'Order and method.' Review what you know, hoping to connect something you didn't connect before. Can we make any connections?" He stopped talking, noticing a small squirrel staring from a Louisville-Slugger-sized oak tree branch ten feet above him. "What do you think?" he said to the animal, which chittered at him before scurrying away.

"I'm sorry, were you talking to me?"

John brought his view back earthward and saw a mid-thirties blonde woman in a bellflower blue skirt and white tank top. She was holding the hand of a young girl, maybe eight, wearing a matching skirt and tank and carrying a yellow-and-black striped, bee-shaped backpack. The woman gave him a *should we be worried about this old man* examining gaze.

Ainsley popped up, straining their direction, adding a further line to the women's concerned forehead wrinkling.

"Ains, sit," John said, replying after she did. "My apologies. I wasn't talking to you. It might sound strange, but I was talking to a squirrel. Knowing it wouldn't talk back. So really, talking to myself."

"Oh, got it. But everything's good? For you, I mean, obviously not over there." She motioned to the police activity.

"Everything is fine, thank you. Taking Ainsley here for a walk and stopped to rest." John felt it wasn't the time to sidetrack into his knowledge of the police activity or any crime-related tangents.

"Just checking." She made to walk off, but the girl didn't budge, instead speaking up.

"Hey, mister? Is your dog named Ainsley?"

"Yes, she is."

"I have a friend named Ashley. That's like Ainsley. And a friend named Fisher. He's a boy. My name is Dorothy."

"It's a good name." John laughed.

"Come on Dot," the woman said, slightly pulling.

Dot ignored her. "Is she, Ainsley the dog, friendly?"

"Very friendly." He caught the mom's eye. "Is it okay to meet her?" Ainsley by this time was once again straining toward the girl. "She likes children."

"I suppose. If she's friendly. Just for a moment, Dot. *One* moment."

John stood up and walked over, keeping Ainsley on a short leash. Reaching the girl, Ainsley started licking her hand as Dot scratched between the dog's ears.

"She's neat," Dot said. "I want a dog, Mom. Remember?"

Exasperated, her mom replied, "Yes, Dot, I remember. I remember the twenty other times you've said it. But we have to go. Thank you," this to John, "for letting us pet your dog."

"Thank you, Dot, for petting her." Before they got a foot away, a lightbulb seemed to go off over John's head. "Sorry, one question?"

The mom stopped slowly, and cautiously replied. "Yes?"

"Is there any chance you have some paper and a pencil in that bee backpack I could borrow?"

Marlowe, booties donned, followed a path of plastic squares on the ground to the area where the victim lay behind the tall screens. They were rigged up directly on the edge of the bleachers, shoehorned in between them and the twenty-foot protective chain-link fencing that ensured–or tried to–no errant foul balls caused injury. *They didn't protect Pat Brown*, Marlowe thought, pausing, taking it in. He noticed a squat wooden shed about ten feet directly behind home plate, a metal sign reading what appeared to be Concessions, but so faded it could have been concussions or confessions. Pushing aside plastic acting as a doorway to the scene, he edged in slowly.

The body's slightly clenched posture distorted, but he felt Pat Brown was probably 5' 10"-ish, with short hair the color of an acorn's cap, grayer at the temples, and a muscular build slightly thickening at the waist. Radiant white T-shirt, newish blue jeans, and matching bright-white high-tops. Only one other person was in attendance, a short man in a white bodysuit bending over the body, tut-tutting to himself, not noticing Marlowe. Bright spotlights gave a strangely elongated shadow.

"Doctor Peterson," Marlowe broke in on the man's muttering, causing a start.

"What potions have I drunk of Siren tears," he replied, "causing Marlowe to appear?"

The pathologist had a wonderfully oval face and round, wire-rimmed glasses, which he took off repeatedly while talking. He pulled down the facemask he'd been wearing over nose and mouth when turning to face the detective.

Doctor Jones Peterson aka the doc aka Doc Scientist. His Shakespeare—Marlowe thought it was Shakespeare, though honestly not completely sure—quoting confused, but the head pathologist knew his stuff. "Body equals my appearance, Doc, and I'd wager a newborn calf you were expecting me."

"Indeed, I was waiting with bated breath in hopes you'd arrive like an angel with a decent cappuccino. But your hands are empty as the wind."

"Apologies. Could have an officer round one up."

"They are busier than the laboring spider. I will survive. You probably have queries?"

"I do, at that. Cause of death possible? Or too early?" Marlowe's reply was cautious, as one couldn't know what the doc would reveal at the scene.

Doctor Peterson smiled. "The wise pathologist knows themselves a fool if they pronounce causes before autopsies." The corner of Marlowe's smile drooped. "However. As our paths have crossed many times, I will unearth a few ideas within the confines of this room we're within." He made a circling gesture with his hand. "First: he is dead. Second: don't take this for truth, yet, but I would say it was respiratory failure that caused him to drop mortality's strong hand." He pointed at Marlowe. "Caused, at an early guess given in good faith between two gentlemen, by poison."

"Poison?"

"Your brain rebels at the thought?"

"It's not something you see every day. Even by accident. Could it be . . ." Marlowe trailed off, thinking.

"Accidental? Me doubts the veracity of that voyage. But perhaps."

"Suicide? Or murder? First feels off. Accident? Quite a misstep." Marlowe's musing continued.

"Those questions are for you. As you move forward do contend."

"Sure, Doc." He snapped back to focus. "Time of death yet?"

"Within a few scant hours I am willing to say, as we are here quickly as if on blackbird wing."

"Thanks. Other early points?"

"He died, no matter the method, in pain." He stooped to point at some wetness on the ground near the victim. "There is this alcohol and fruit juice scented stain, which we will analyze, and which came I would hazard from a cup removeth from here, along with a bag of chips and a napkin, plus his phone. He also had a wallet, gold watch on a braided leather band with gold beading, gold chain necklace, wedding ring, and another ring, expensive it appears, emerald shining."

"All helpful. We'll wait for more details, photos, the lot. Remove the body when you want." As Marlowe left, he heard Doctor Peterson say to his retreating form, "Dream on, dream on, of bloody deeds and death, Detective."

The first person to catch Marlowe's eye was Morven, over the shoulder of another white-suited CSI person, undistinguishable with their back turned his way. Angling her direction, he passed the concession stand. Closer, he could see clearly how rickety it was, once sapphire-blue paint peeling, faded gray here and there, faded to nothing in some spots. Through the front window he saw a boxed assortment of candy and granola bars, gun-metal colored register that wouldn't have been out of place in a 1920s diner, soda fountain, a small cooler packed with water bottles, and a bowl of weedy apples.

"You found Doctor Peterson?" she asked. They walked the outer perimeter as they talked.

Nodding, he replied, "Not much information. Seems suspicious. There's Nelson," he said, pointing to where the junior detective was talking to a uniformed African American officer towering over him. "Let's wrangle."

"I'll get him." She jogged off, white hood trailing behind her, leaving Marlowe momentarily alone, quiet in the buzz of activity.

Murder at a baseball diamond. A kid's baseball diamond. Might be better if it was suicide. Still tough to chew for family and friends. Accidental, same as. What did his grandfather say? "If you climb in the saddle, be ready for the ride." No matter which, and Marlowe had a hard time believing it was suicide—the place, the manner felt wrong—or accidental, it was going to be a hard ride, the specter of the kids and families affected looming. Death at a baseball game. Hard to believe, no matter how many shows John Arthur's watched where murders revolved around sporting events.

The arrival of the two other detectives interrupted his thoughts. They stood on a small island in the parking lot where, strangely, a triangle of grass survived, a decent-sized curly willow growing out of it. He huddled them under the tree.

"Quick roundup?" The other two's affirmative looks led him on. "Victim: Pat Brown. Nothing set in stone, but Doc did say he thought death due to respiratory failure."

"Could that be strangling somehow?" Nelson asked.

"Doubtful. Hard to be strangled in front of people without anyone noticing."

"So?"

"Doc thinks poison."

"Poison," Morven said. "That's super surprising. Not something you see as much as the public would believe."

Nelson raised his hand.

"No need for formalities, Nelson." She motioned him to speak.

"Did you know," he asked, "that poisoning covers only one half of a percent of all homicides?"

"I did not know that. Also, I'm not sure we know if this is a homicide yet. Let's call it a suspicious death."

"Agreed." Marlowe nodded.

"Got it," Nelson replied. "But we do *think* it's a murder, correct? It has to be, I'd guess."

"Suspicious death at the moment," Marlowe replied. "Morven, further details from the white coats? Doc mentioned a cup, straw, napkin, chip bag, phone, and personal items recovered?"

"That's the list of items found near the victim." Morven wiped her hands together while talking. "Plus a few candy wrappers, probably older. They've loaded those items up and are bagging, I quote, 'A garbage truck load of DNA' from the area nearest the victim, plus the general field area and bleachers. I've asked for a rush on fingerprinting the food and drink containers and the phone, which we'll need to return to the family unless we want to request a court order to break into it. Plus, victim toxicology and cup, bag, and napkin tox. In addition, the liquid residue near the victim. Testing that too. Not sure on results timing, but they know our goal is beyond ASAP."

"Nice work." Marlowe appreciated Morven's thoroughness.

"Liquid residue? Like blood? Spinal fluid?"

"Hard to say Nelson. Not blood. A spill is my take. Weirdly, John—Mr. Arthur—brought it up to me first."

"He doesn't miss much, for a noncom." Nelson had a little awe for the older man after their last case.

"Not sure he's an officer. Of any kind. That needed." Marlowe motioned at the tree, which Nelson had started doing standing pushups against.

"Sorry, sir, was getting too stationary. And Mr. Arthur is not an officer, I know. He seems to have insights like he could be. He doesn't have an accent, but are we sure he's wasn't an officer in an English or French, or was it Belgian, detective bureau? What did he say? Arrangement and strategy? Structure and system? I can hear him in my head. We're sure he's not involved?"

"Only in the witness sense. Distant witness. Nelson, what did you pick up?"

"I talked to the uniformed officer in charge, Officer Troy, who has been doing tons of work and coordinating uniform's efforts. They have names and addresses for every parent and child on the two bleachers, including Mr. Arthur, as well as a few folks found milling about during the game or working. It's very thorough from what I can tell, and starts with the immediate family of the victim—wife and four children."

All three stood silent for a second. Marlowe sighed. "Four. Sorry for them. What's her name?"

"Officer Troy is working on providing a full list, but yes, we have her name: Bridgette Brown."

"Nelson, quick question," Morven said. "Do we know if she and the kids were sitting near the victim?"

"I believe that information should be coming via the FRIs. We can follow up with–"

"Nelson," she stopped him. "FRI? Should we know that one?"

"I don't." Marlowe managed to beat Nelson to the reply for once.

"FRI?" Nelson acted as if he hadn't made up the initialism. "First responder interviews?"

"Ah." Marlowe pulled his cap down as if it had slipped off. "Family still here?"

"I believe so. They'd like to be let go, so would the other suspects. And witnesses. Both. Did you want to talk to her first?"

Marlowe considered, then gave a short wave with his hand. "No. Let the family go. And witnesses. But triple check that names and addresses are finalized against photo ID before the herd hits the trail. One more for you, Nelson. Ask Troy to have some uniforms sort and collect the trash from any surrounding receptacles. Coordinate with CSI to get it checked by them."

"Already did it," Nelson said, smiling. "On Detective Morven's advice."

"Excellent work. You two skedaddle back to the office. Set up the board."

"You following us down soon?" Morven asked.

"Going to. First, sending myself to the bleachers." He caught a question in her eyes. "Soak in atmosphere. I'll be downtown quicker than a rattler's rattle."

Perched on the top corner of the rickety metal southern-most bleachers, one away from where the victim—now removed—had been, Marlowe felt like a massive mustachioed turkey vulture lurking over the scene. Leaning back gently, he caught the sun on his face. What a day. Faultless sky, temperature warming, and he could hear kids on a playground, no worries in the world. He wondered if this was where John Arthur sat as he watched the game.

Closing his eyes, he tried to picture it, the moments before the death: thwap of ball on bat, lighter smack of ball into glove, the calls—safe, out, strike three, foul—cheers, good-natured groans, scuffle of feet on basepaths, oohs and aahs as a ball was hit high into the sky, a can of corn, before dropping to land in gloved hand or on grassy earth. Baseball. He'd played when younger, and thinner, up until high school. Third base, mostly. A little right field or left field when needed, with one disastrous try at pitching. "Respectable glove work," his coach used to say after a successful inning. Not a bad hitter, either. Not such a sweet swing as to portend professional ambitions, but not bad.

"Detective." A deep bass voice interrupted his reverie. "You awake?"

Opening his eye with a jolt that caused him to sway precariously before steading himself with a wide palm, Marlowe saw Officer Troy. Nearly 6'3" in height, Troy boasted stocky, muscled shoulders and a plentiful mustache that might have rivaled Marlowe's own if it wasn't well-trimmed.

"Officer Troy, morning. Soaking it in."

Troy removed his hat, fanning his face. "Starting to heat up. Sad place for, well, whatever happened here."

"That it is. Baseball fan?" Marlowe began to carefully make his way down the bleachers.

"Somewhat. Never played. Rugby for me. I do enjoy a summer day at the ballpark, though. You?"

"Guilty as charged. Was going to ask—you seem off your patch. Usually south a smidge and a ways west?"

"Keen eye, Marlowe. Never stop detecting." A smile widened on Troy's face. "Came up to lead some training, not knowing it'd be on-the-scene. Speaking of the scene, we have a witness, or bystander, wanting to know if you have a moment. I've kept him past the tape, but thought it was worth checking in with you. I believe you know him."

Marlowe looked up at the man. "Know him?" It clicked. "John Arthur?"

"The very one." Troy had met John during the past case he'd been involved with. "He's getting a crime scene habit."

"Let's hope not." Marlowe brushed an imaginary crumb from his mustache.

"Feel up to chatting? Or should I direct him homeward?"

"Probably time for me to move 'em out. I'll catch him on the way. Thanks, Troy, for this and"—he gave a sweep of the arm—"everything else."

"Sure thing, Marlowe. And good luck."

Marlowe ambled off as Troy stayed in place, resting a muscled arm on one of the bleachers, gazing at the baseball field.

Nearly through the parking lot, still awash in police cars and vans, Marlowe saw John sitting at a picnic table, bent over and focused, as if taking a test.

"John?" As Marlowe starting speaking, Ainsley bounced up like a jack out of a jack-in-the-box, pulling John off the bench, tail wagging, whirling up leaves as she strained toward the detective. "And Ainsley," Marlowe added. "Who could forget you." He reached down, scratching the space between her ears while she angled to lick his hand, license tags on her collar catching sunshine, sparkling.

"Detective Marlowe. I'm glad Officer Troy found you. Please, have a seat." He scooted over, Ainsley in tow.

"Busy day, John."

"I can only imagine. But even Detective Marlowe must sit a moment, let the little gray cells, to be Poirotian, work."

"For a short spell." He sat.

"Certainly. I might be able to assist in the gray cell charging."

"You don't say?" Marlowe figured John was going to offer some TV-driven case theory or quotable words of British mystery wisdom and couldn't help kidding him.

"I do say. I won't keep you long. However, as the brusquely wonderful Detective Kristin Sims said about Detective Senior Sergeant Mike Shepherd, 'He gets a little hunch and off he goes.' I had a little hunch and here we go." John held up a piece of paper in the hand not curled around the leash.

"Almost don't want to ask. These detectives that have sent you off?"

"You don't know *The Brokenwood Mysteries*? I mentioned them earlier. They seem very Marlowe-y."

"Marlowe-y?"

"Just allow me a short sidetrack."

"How could I not. But short."

"Brokenwood is a small New Zealand town, which bearded and suit coated DSS Mike Shepherd is assigned to in episode one to help on a case, working with Detective Sims and jolly ginger DC Breen. He, the DSS, talks to the dead—"

"Supernatural show?"

"—who don't talk back. It helps him feel closer to the victims. He solves that first case and decides to stick around. It is a lovely town, which has a fair amount of murders—one per episode. Now in its tenth season. He's not like the two Inspector Barnabys from *Midsomer* I've mentioned."

Marlowe nodded. How could he forget. Once John said he could be the third—Marlowe Barnaby.

John went on. "But DSS Mike Shepherd and the show do fit the *Midsomer* aesthetic, meaning he's fairly even-keeled, tends to question in a friendly manner, and no one talks about the many murders happening in a rural locale over ten seasons. Ten non-US seasons, so four to six episodes per. No one gets thrown by the often odd and even bizarre assortment of murders, from hunting 'accidents,' to a human hand found in a crayfish pot, to a local cookbook writer pitchforked at a farmer's market, to a murdered nun. There's lots of —"

Marlowe's hand had gone up in the stop gesture.

"Too much information?"

"Mostly. And a question."

"Ask away. I'm all answers."

"As I know. But, New Zealand? I though British mysteries were your métier, as you put it."

"Marlowe, your memory is quite keen. British mysteries, yes, but my range travels farther afield. Australia and New Zealand, especially. I've learned a lot from them."

"Ah-ha," Marlowe deadpanned. "Why is *Brokenwood* Marlowe-y?"

"The interrogation continues," John said, as a grin escaped Marlowe's mustache. "Well…" He drawled out the Ls. "DSS Mike Shepherd does have a fondness for brown suit coats and drives a sweet 1971 Holden Kingswood, a car you might roll up in. More wine than your Italian cocktails, but the love of a wee tipple matches. Has many ex-wives, one point in the different-than-Marlowe column. Listens to an array of toe-tapping country cassettes in that car, lots of local New Zealand artists that Marlene—my wife, you remember?—and I then tracked down and listened to. Tami Neilson is especially swell, and even appeared in an episode. Amazing. I remember you have an ear for country tunes?"

Marlowe could feel John ramping up for even more of a tangent, so felt he'd better put the train back on track. John's theories on police procedure tunneled through a host of tv shows could fill a book. "John, what's on the paper? You mentioned helping the little gray cells?" He tapped his hat.

"That counts as a question-question, the time-honored police tactic of always answering a question with a question."

"Suppose it does, but?"

"I decided to map out the bleachers—the one Pat Brown sat on before his murder, with who else was sitting near him and where. I figure one of them has to be the murderer."

3

Marlowe gave the other man a sideways glance, both being on the same side of the picnic table. The orange brick of the school highlighted a few trees behind them. "Murder? Not sure that horse has been broke, yet."

"I should have said suspicious death. I ruled out accident, health issue, and suicide. None fit. I could elaborate?" John seemed ready go on, but Marlowe knew time was ticking.

"How about we head back to the paper."

"You need to build a murder board. I mean a suspicious death board. I recalled that from my particular spot high on the southern of the two bleachers, I had a view onto the other bleachers. No near neighbors obstructed sight lines. Thinking that if another party was involved in the suspicious death they'd been there, or passing, I felt I could map out who was sitting where and it would help with inquiries. I'm no artist, but I roughed out lines for the six bleacher seating slates, with circles for people, numbers inside, each number then given a name and short physical description in the key." He held up the paper, pointing as he spoke.

"Makes sense," Marlowe agreed. "Helpful, maybe. But." He rapped the table. "How did you know who was who? You haven't been interviewing folks in the crowd?"

"Not at all. I have no official standing, I know that. It seems a mystery within our mystery, doesn't it?"

"A bit, but why do I feel you're going to pull a rabbit out of the hat. Or the TV?"

"No TV this time," John replied. "Much more mundane. I mentioned my nephew played on Pat Brown's baseball team. My sister never missed a game, and so I called her, described the people I saw, and she supplied names when she could. She's the type of family fan who knows everyone at her kids' games. Like most parents, she spent half the time viewing my nephew's sporting exploits, half chatting. Most parents are like this. The bleachers become —"

"A Marlple-esque village."

"Detective Marlowe, excellent. That's it. 'One must take things as they are,' as she mentioned."

"John," Marlowe broke in before he could ramp up again, "you didn't tell your sister this was a murder?"

"What? No. She does know about my taste in TV mysteries." *How could she not*, Marlowe joked to himself as John talked. "I wouldn't give the goose away before it was cooked. I merely said I was at the game and thought she'd be interested in who was attending. Nostalgia's sake and all that. Now, to the list?"

"Quickly." Marlowe knew he needed to head out, but the drawing and list did seem helpful if accurate. And John tended to be accurate, if you could sift the wheat from the chaff. Or the TV plot through the commercials.

"Let's start with position one, our victim, Pastor Pat Brown." He gave a glance upward. "He was in the far north corner of the lowest row. He sat in the same spot every game, sis said. She also said she once attended a service at the Chapter Creek Church. He invited the whole team. According to her, 'He preached hell so hot that you could feel the heat.' Not her line —"

"Dolly's."

"—but Dolly's. Detective Sims once asked DSS Shepherd in a tense

Brokenwood moment, 'Is this really the time for country lyrics?' His one-word reply? 'Always.'"

"John?"

"Yes," he asked distractedly.

"Onward."

"Pat Brown, position one. He never let anyone sit near him during a game. Kept two seats on his row and the one above free. People could come up to talk for a moment or two, but everyone knew he wanted those seats empty. I'll just walk us up the numbers from there.

• Position 2: Two rows above him, same seat. His wife, Bridgette Brown. Tallish woman, 5'10" I'd estimate. Black hair, a few streaks of gray. Forties.

• Positions 3 and 4: Next row up, two seats to the north. Daniel Brown– who my sister said kids called Burton– and Sidney Brown. Two of the Browns' four kids. Oldest boy and girl, sixteen and fifteen. Brown and blonde hair. Neither moved, heads down, sketch pad and Gameboy respectively.

• Position 5: Next to Mrs. Brown, Nancy Brown, youngest child. Probably eight? Black hair like mother, who she sat very close to. Oh, their other child, Gerry, I gathered was playing. We'll call him position 6. Which leads to…

• Position 7: Row two, third seat in. Mike Ray, Deacon Mike, pastor the second at the church. I mentioned him. First to Pat Brown when he collapsed. Balding dyed black hair, 6'1", 160 pounds, black shirt. I did catch him talking to the victim once during the game.

• Position 8: One seat over, row two. I believe Kristin Ray, Mike's wife. My sister wasn't 100% here. Blonde, curly hair, 5'6".

• Position 9: Row three, nearer the bleacher's south side. Call it seat six. Nev Maloney. Older, not than me, but probably mid-50s. Blond, beginning to bald, 5'6". Jeans, T-shirt. Was the listed team coach when my nephew played. Not sure what went wrong, but bleacher-bound today. Has a young son, Dougie, plays on the team. Call Dougie Position 10. I saw Nev talking to him once through the fence in front of Pat. And saw him stop to talk to Pat, too.

• Position 11: Row 3, seat north of Nev. Gilly Maloney, his wife. Younger, mid-thirties? Brunette. Flowery dress. About his height.

• Position 12: Fifth row up, three seats in. Nikola Cassian. Church secretary. Asian-American woman, 5'4", long straight dark hair. Sis said it was once streaked blond. She stopped by to chat with Pat Brown at one point during the innings I was there. And was also the person who called 911.

• Position 13: Back down to the second row. Not very orderly of me! Poirot is cursing. Next to Kristin Ray. This one I knew myself–Tom Toomey. African-American, six foot, low 50s, close-cut hair, emerald-green sports shirt, jeans. You might know him? Ran unsuccessfully for City Council twice, as well as both state and national representative. Made a packet in construction and as a landlord. Not sure why he was there. Seemed to talk a lot over Kristin to Mike.

• Position 14: Directly above Kristin, so row three. Lean, bicyclist's body, 5'11", thin hair, maple-colored. This is my one gap. Stood up to cheer. Talked to Pat Brown at least once, when going to the bathroom I believe.

• Position 15: Back up to row five, next to Nikola to the south. Ash Willums. Long, curly strawberry-blonde hair, 5'10". Mother of a kid on team. My sister remembered her well–a gossiper, she said. And makes a Sangria well-loved by parents. Most I've mentioned consumed it during games. Lots of visitors to her spot. Also talked to Pat Brown when she went to the concession stand.

• Which leads to what we'll call Position 16. Off bleachers so not completely the same. Longtime concession stand worker Drogo Oates."

"Drogo? You sure?" It seemed a name John would have picked up from TV.

"It must be a nickname, but yes, Drogo Oates. Long ponytail, skinny as a rail, jean shorts, red and yellow tie-died shirt. Endless summer vibe."

"Why's Drogo rate the list? Thought you were bleacher focused."

"I saw him amble over to Pat Brown. Short talk, but then to me he felt part of the village. There's one more not from the bleachers too. Worth a mention?"

"Why not?" Marlowe was trying to hold back his slight exasperation.

"Probably not as important as the bleachers, but he's the groundskeeper. Not sure of the name. Older man. Pushes a cart. Saw him talking, not to Pat but to Drogo."

"You watch any of the game?"

"Nearly every at-bat for the innings there. Between innings, Arthur 'sees everything and he forgets nothing.'" The last was delivered in a horrific Belgian accent.

John passed Marlowe the paper as the latter said, "Saw a fair bit, for sure." John patted Ainsley while Marlowe checked the list again. Neither spoke, the slightly fading bustle and a few faint happy kid shrieks from the nearby playground the only sounds. Marlowe shifted his bulk up and off the bench.

"We're burning daylight. Better be off." He shook the paper, folded it, and slipped it into one of the sports coat's roomy side pockets. "This is helpful. Things are predictably muddy at this stage."

"'I'm sure it's all as clear as this beautifully opaque Merlot,'" John said, pretending to swirl a wine glass in his hand.

"Merlot?" There were times John himself was pretty opaque.

"One last nod to wine-loving DSS Shepherd. Here's to gin-clear clarity soon." He tipped the imaginary glass Marlowe's direction.

Marlowe reached his car without further interruption, the laurel tree grove empty of teenagers, no other civilians or officers hailing from distant sidewalks. Ditching his sports jacket and hat, he sat down behind the wheel. The clear-sky, sunny day inched the temperature up, and so while descending car windows with one hand, he mopped sweat traces off his bald head with a handkerchief with the other. *Heating up from every horizon*, he decided, starting the car.

Driving from the northeast neighborhood dominated by the Hettie

Patty school and grounds to the central station downtown, his pace rotated from a crawl to a stop, with intermittent moments of speed. Typical summertime Saturday afternoon, the City's residents joyfully catching sunshine, then deciding perhaps it's too hot and heading back in, over and over. He'd put the radio on for background, and by one of those quirks of coincidence that nearly made him believe in fate, the first song was Dolly Parton. Not "Daddy Was An Old Time Preacher Man," quoted by John earlier, but her delicious cover of Dusty Springfield's "Son of a Preacher Man." He sung along, so low he could barely hear himself. Once it ended, he switched the radio off, not wanting to drive the tune from his head by hearing another.

John Arthur—such a curious old man. Country lyrics, crime scene sketches, TV mysteries. That sketch would undoubtedly prove very helpful. Marlowe'd decided, even without final forensic reports, that Pat Brown's death had to be murder. And John was probably right, those sitting nearest were in the center of the frame of suspects. Knowing the type of poison would be a big key. *Here's to the unveiling of that fact rapidly*, he thought, giving an imaginary toast to the world outside his window in imitation of John's imaginary glass.

A feral minivan cut across three lanes without hesitating, screeching into a shop parking lot – The Queens of Ice Cream –, causing Marlowe and two other cars to slam brakes hard, an action leading to multiple break slammings behind them, reverberating horns, and he'd guess a wheatfield's worth of curse words. But not the air-rendering sound of metal on metal. Even the City's mildish heat, compared to other parts of the country and world, birthed chaos and demanding children.

Making it to the station's five-story, concrete bunker of a parking garage, Marlowe navigated to floor three before noticing a block of three empty space not far from the elevator. Weekends had pluses. He pulled into the middle one, noticing the wall in front of the space had been tagged *Good On You, Copper*, in scrawled ruby-hued spray paint. Walking away from his car, he said to no one, "I'm taking you as a positive omen, friend."

The room his desk resided within was vast, lacking in personality like an abandoned warehouse. Generic gray walls, tiled floor, a swarm of desks, tables, and doors to side offices. Fairly empty, twinning the parking garage. Marlowe casually said a few hellos, trekking a path to the desk he'd commandeered long ago in a far corner near a window. Morven and Nelson stood in front of a six-foot moveable corkboard on a stand—the incident board—currently only containing a couple of photos and notes. Morven had on a fawn-colored skirt and white shirt, sleeves rolled up to elbows, matching suit coat draped across one chair at the desk she currently allowed Nelson to share, his cornflower-colored coat on the other chair.

"Team," Marlowe said "how goes the frenzy?"

Nelson jumped back, smacking the board's lower edge with his hand, nearly sending it sprawling before Morven balanced it into place.

"Detective," Nelson blurted out, embarrassed, rubbing one hand with the other. "How did you sneak up on us?" Though he respected Marlowe immensely, the younger detective saw him as shambling more than soft-footed.

"Practice," Marlowe replied. "Board is boarded."

"A start. Not a lot to populate it so far," Morven said. She turned back to the board. Near the top edge was a picture of Pat Brown, a publicity photo from the church showing a stocky man with a round face, fierce hazel eyes, thin lips stretched to a small smile, short curly hair, a trace of stubble, wearing a black suit coat and a white shirt, the top few buttons unbuttoned.

"Pat Brown." Marlowe moved to the board, pointing at the picture. "Our victim."

"Victim?" Nelson asked. "Are we positive it's victim, not suicide or accident? I suppose victim could be accident victim. Victim to me implies murder, and I wasn't sure we were going past suspicious death yet."

"Could be suicide or accident, Detective, but I don't buy it."

"Forensics and the scientists will tell us more, as will interviews," Morven said, "but I would agree. Suicide by poison is very unlikely, and without a note, more so. Accident? If in a different location, you might sway me. So, murder? Though the scene makes it nearly as improbable."

"Did you know nearly 250 people per day die from poisoning?" Nelson spoke up, looking at his phone. "Could lend weight to accidental, except 95% or more of that number is drug-related. Any history for Mr. Brown in that direction?"

Morven shook her head. "Not from what we've discovered yet."

"Salient facts. Agree on victim, mostly likely murder?" Marlowe asked to answering head nods. "Check. Topline on victim?"

Morven glanced at a sheet tacked to the board. "Forty-eight years old. Pastor and founder of the Chapter Creek church in 2008, after heading up smaller churches. It's what's called a mega-church. Highly profitable. Thousands of members. Plus, a paid public speaker at conventions, etcetera. Charismatic and energetic with a dash of domineering is what one article said. Another used bullying to describe him. Some past church goers and volunteers don't speak well of him, others speak reverently. Address: 101 Tower Road SW. Church address: 6565 Waterworth Ave SW. Go into his family?"

"Wait." Marlowe reached into his pocket. "That reminds me. Ran into Mr. Arthur once more. He made a sketch of the bleachers the victim sat on, numbering those nearby. Got most of their names, short descriptions. Felt the murderer might be in the group." He tacked it to the middle of the board, then backed up to allow Nelson and Morven a closer view.

"Mr. Arthur did this?" Nelson's voice carried a touch of awe. "Is he in the center of this crowd too?"

"Nope. Nephew used to play on a team Pat Brown was associated with. Sister still remembered most folks."

"Is she also a British television mystery buff?"

"Not as far as I've found out, Nelson. Just a friendly mom in the bleachers."

"This," Morven said, still checking the paper, "is helpful. Very helpful."

Nelson did a couple of deep knee bends before saying, "Mr. Arthur. Very curious. Crime-obsessed citizen, wannabe PI, lonely old man?"

"The full lot?" Marlowe himself wasn't sure.

"Sir," Nelson continued. "Thinking OTB, outside-the-box, should we consider hiring Mr. Arthur as a consultant?"

Morven's reply had a hint of sarcasm rolling under it, like a current in a pond on a windy day. "A consultant? Like consulting detective? Like Sherlock Holmes?"

Nelson arched his back. "Yeah, like Sherlock Holmes I guess. But without the fancy hat and magnifying glass. Not that *we* can't solve any case." He straightened out. "But Mr. Arthur was helpful in the past, right? A ton. He's got an interesting way of seeing a case, even if his TV tangents, quotes, and acting are confusing. Once you get used to deciphering what's around them, he's got solid ideas. Speaking of, sir, did he make it through showing you this sketch without quotes or British TV?"

"Detective is fine, Nelson. And quotes, yes, British TV, no."

"Really?" Both spoke in unified disbelief.

"Not British. It was a New Zealand television mystery today. Broken Arrow? Broke River? No, *Brokenwood*."

In an accent half Cockney, quarter Australian, and quarter unknown, Nelson said, "Give us a couple of snags off the barbie, will ya?"

"What in the world?" Morven mocked.

"I have an ex from New Zealand. Learned the lingo. Could pass as a native she told me."

"*Brokenwood* might be for you, Nelson," Marlowe said. "From what I gathered, the lead detective boasts a host of ex-wives. Many as you have exes? Possible. Back to the corral. Not sure the City Police hires consultants. Upper management wouldn't want that escaping into the wilds of local news, for one. Don't tarnish the badge. This one is up to us." He couldn't help wondering to himself if it was true. The feeling remained, like a burr under his saddle, that they hadn't seen the last of John Arthur in relation to the case.

"Our next move seems obvious," Marlowe said.

"Start contacting this list for interviewing, and background check on victim and this list." Morven moved to her desk.

"Smart, Morven. I'd call those second and third moves. First move?" He held up one finger. "Coffee. Java. Brown gargle. Lots. Grab you some?"

"No, good here."

"I had too much earlier." Nelson followed her negative.

"Your loss, team. Be back." He walked off as Nelson turned to the board and Morven opened her laptop. The station coffee was renowned for tasting like a cross between motor oil, burnt toast, and tree bark. Marlowe consumed gallons. They avoided it like a plague.

"Let's get on it. I'll break down the list and assign names." Morven was about to start typing when Nelson spoke up again.

"Wait, one question."

"Shoot."

"Mr. Arthur is out as consulting detective. But if we're equating to the Sherlock universe, Marlowe equals Sherlock?"

She smiled. "I suppose so. Conan Doyle might be turning in his grave, as I don't believe Sherlock wore brown sports coats, but agreed."

"With that agreed upon," he said with a smile, "who is Watson?"

"I guess…" She drew out a long pause. "I don't know enough about the stories or shows. Maybe it depends on which version."

"Which version?"

"Which TV or movie version."

"Do you know about multiple Sherlocks and Watsons?"

"Ah, not me. My mami. Big fan." Morven's Puerto Rican mother, currently living in New York, had nearly a John Arthur level obsession with certain TV shows. "You may need to do some research."

"Could be. Might help with the case. I suppose in general you would be Watson." He seemed a little down thinking about it. "Is there a third detective?"

Morven sighed. "I believe there probably is a plucky third detective somewhere in Sherlock. One who's excited to dig into the case at hand."

They began preliminary backgrounds for the next few hours, building out the incident board with photos and information about the victim and people on John's list, alongside Post-it notes stuck in odd places with ideas and hopefully salient points, though currently appearing more as the beginning color splotches of a Pollock painting. They'd made multiple runs, or in Marlowe's case, ambles, to the station commissary for sandwiches, day-old doughnuts, bags of Doritos (Marlowe), honey-mustard pretzels (Morven), and mixed nuts (Nelson), plus multiple bottles of sparkling water, juice, energy drinks, and cups of coffee.

Marlowe currently reclined, size eleven feet propped up on the desk, chair leaned back far enough that most would think it as a safety hazard. He held an empty softball-sized, olive-wood bowl in his right hand. Wavy, swirling pattens of lighter and darker wood curled from the bowl's base to sides, as if cradling an array of blooms. His nose was pressed near the bowl breathing deeply, eyes closed. Picked up on a trip to Assisi, Italy, with his now long in the past ex-wife, Marlowe still smelled the olive groves in the bowl, memory of scents and scenes transporting him out of the dull station to the sun-speckled Umbrian hills. *The most beautiful garden in the world, Henry James said*, he thought. Breathe in, breathe out.

Morven, used to this quirk of Marlowe's from many years and cases, didn't look his way as he breathed. Nelson looked up once or twice, glanced at Morven, then glanced back glassy-eyed in to the board, holding a wireless keyboard in his right hand while eating an apple held in his left. At the desk they currently shared, two laptops were in a delicate détente until he could commandeer another desk. She stared at the screen, clicking occasionally. All three had coats shucked over chairs, Marlowe's currently trailing on the ground behind him. With one last deep breath in the bowl, he opened his eyes, removed his feet from the desk with a surprising gently grace, as if a bear had studied ballet, the chair giving a loud creak as two legs found the floor.

"The score," he said. "Marlowe four. Morven zero. Nelson a scant half."

"Score?" she replied. Nelson had a quarter's worth of apple in his mouth and said nothing.

"Fours cups of coffee means the win is mine."

Morven laughed. Nelson swallowed heavily before disagreeing. "If we want to tell the truth, Detective, and I did just eat an apple, so to follow along George Washington's example I *should* tell the truth, I may have faked drinking that half cup."

"Nelson, it was a cherry tree and George Washington," Morven managed to get out through continued laughter.

"You sure, Detective? Detective Marlowe?"

"Believe it was a cherry tree at that. Sorry, Nelson."

Nelson took another bite as Marlowe continued.

"But I can't see less coffee as a win. However, we can call a draw. Maybe call it a night workwise, too?"

Grateful looks flashed across faces.

"It's eight. We're getting weary. Tomorrow's gonna be a twister. Better to tuck in what we've learned, approach it bright-eyed and bushy-tailed."

Morven nodded slowly. "Agreed. This screen is starting to blur."

"The board, too," Nelson said.

"Smart, then." Marlowe stood up. "Start fresh. Don't knock about the night owls."

"As your grandfather used to say?" Morven knew where many of Marlowe's sayings originated.

"As my grandfather did indeed say."

"No worries on my part, detectives," Nelson said, tossing the apple core into a trash can. "I canceled my date hours ago. Might be time for a run. If I start soon, I could get five in."

Marlowe felt tired just hearing him talk about a run.

"If you want to skip the solitary running," Morven said, "there's a late Muay Thai class at Luther's London gym." Her advanced capability in the Thai boxing art was well known at the station.

"Not sure my skills are at the right level," Nelson nervously replied. "I've only done a couple of classes."

"Multiple skill levels welcome at this one," she reassured him. "I promise not to let anyone work you over. Too much."

"Let's go." The slightly tentative Nelson picked up his jacket, with Morven following suit, sliding into hers smoothly as a professional dancer. "Marlowe, don't stay too long." She pointed at him in a friendly way as they began walking out, Nelson darting this way and that around desks and chairs.

"Have fun," Marlowe said toward the retreating backs. "If Saturday night exercise can be fun," the latter said to himself. Grabbing his coat, he took a step, stopped, picked up the wooden bowl once more. Closing his eyes, he took another deep breath, dreaming of olive groves in roving hills under an Umbrian sky.

Leaving the station into the cooling, but still warm and sunny, evening, Marlowe considered heading straight home. Maybe get some Indian takeout from Parminder's Pakoras and More-as, have a sit-down in front of the TV, watch a few episodes of *Gunsmoke*, dream about time-traveling to buy Kitty a whiskey, try not to dwell too much, yet, on the case. Instead, he walked west, like the pioneers, headed down a nonchalantly sloping hill to the neighborhood known as Settler's Square.

Exhaustive with a quilted array of restaurants, bars, the occasional hot-dog or falafel cart, shops open and closed and opening and closing, second story high-ceilinged lofts with brick walls and astronomical prices alongside shadowed garbage-stuffed alleys that screamed "anyone in here is up to no good," Settler's on a Saturday in July ranged from mildly packed to bursting like an opened sluice, with locals and tourists alike. Wading into the outlying blocks, he slipped off sidewalk into street to avoid a gaggle of giggling mid-twenties men in blinking crowns, four pushing one in a shopping cart with a sign on it saying "here comes the groom," then circumvented a hushed crowd encircling a teenager juggling bowling pins, nearly running into a massive—over 100 pounds, he guessed—rottweiler being walked by a petite woman wearing a Seafarers jersey and reading a copy of *Vanity Fair*. The dog surreptitiously licked Marlowe's hand as they neared, passed, separated again.

He kept walking, passing couples cooing and cuddling, groups small and large flowing in and out of bars like fish following a scientifically impossible variety of currents, tourists toting bags featuring the City's iconic Infinity Arrow tower or the museum's famous Riveting Woman sculpture, taking pictures of historic signs, faded, nearly indecipherable—*Dunbar's Laundry (Cleaner Than Yours), Ridley's Real Ales*—on the neighborhood's old pockmarked red brick buildings. The City's omnipresent downtown homeless huddled in corners. One persevering pickpocket skipped up a block every time Marlowe got within ten feet.

Then Gary's doorway appeared. His favorite bar in the City and the reason Marlowe braved Settler's Square even on a summer's weekend evening. Easing his bulk through the door, he slid past three women in jean shorts and T-shirts, one red, one green, one white, animatedly chatting. He heard "Campari," "gin," "sweet vermouth," but realized in the crowd noise he may have just been trying to manifest the words into existence. Inside it buzzed, but Marlowe wrangled his favorite stool, one at the short-end of the bar proper's L-shape. It was a hearty-sized oak bar, fifteen-feet long, taking up a chunk of Gary's available space, with a few wooden-topped tables in the room's center and wooden booths along the paralleling brick wall, mostly unadorned outside of framed antique European liqueur ads: Fernet Branca, Chartreuse, Strega, Underberg. An anomaly in the neighborhood due to the reasonable stereo volume (currently playing "Beyond Belief" by Elvis Costello) combined with lack of garage-door-sized screens (a single fifteen-inch tube TV perched pictureless behind the bar) and well-made, decently priced drinks, Gary's was utterly its own animal.

Gary himself, the owner well-known to Marlowe, was too. At the far end of the bar, wearing his customary black jeans and clean white shirt buttoned to the neck, thin as a whippet, russet-colored hair and a mild goatee streaked with gray, just past fifty and just nearing 5' 5", he required a stool to reach the highest bottle-filled shelves behind the bar. *Giotto's St. Francis reborn as a bartender*, Marlowe had mentioned to Gary numerous times, after a couple of cocktails.

Having finished pulling three drafts of Wedding Bells blond ale from local Suburban Caroline brewery, Gary scanned the bar for empty glasses, seeing none until his eyes alighted on Marlowe draping his sports coat on the red vinyl barstool before sitting down. A wide smile crossed the short bartender's face as he strode toward the other man with an open-handed, take-a-seat gesture.

"Kit," he said above the rumble. He'd bestowed Marlowe with the nickname of the 16th-Century English playwright, a nickname no one else was allowed to use. "Alright?"

"Hanging in. Busy?"

"Half hectic for a Saturday. No faffing around, mind." Even living in the states off-and-on for nearing thirty years, fifteen of those working at the bar that now carried his name, Gary was from England, in Faversham, and the accent never faded. "Your day the same, if I had to guess?"

"Trail dust obvious?" Marlowe leaned back, as if retreating from a mirror.

"Nothing so apparent, my lad. Not always my cup of tea, but news was on for a customer. Martini drinker. Quiet at the time, so tele up. Saw a report of a murder, local vicar. Felt you and your team probably got the call."

"Fair enough."

"Enough is right. Enough gabbing. What'll you have?"

"No idea. Yet. Big days ahead, so nothing too heavy. Gotta keep my wits about me."

"Set an example for the troops when under the cosh."

"Something like that."

"How about a Garibaldi?"

"Remind me?"

"Simple but delicious. And nutritious. Old compadre Campari with fresh OJ over ice. Campari taking the edge off and stimulating the brain, orange juice for vitamins and sweet citrus, ice to chill it out. Named for Giuseppe Garibaldi, the general who was one of those behind the wheel unifying your beloved Italy. National hero. Led his Redshirt army, shirts as red as Campari. Ideal for leaders and for the vitamin C deficient. Horses for courses and all, but you'll enjoy."

"I will. Hit me."

Gary grabbed a glass and a bottle of Campari and started making the drink, saying, "Interestingly, the redshirts kicked off when Garibaldi was helping the Uruguayan civil war. A military leader with national independence and republican ideals, our Giuseppe." He placed the drink in front of Marlowe with a flourish. "Must dash. Duty calls bartenders too."

Marlowe raised the glass slowly to take the first sip, as if wanting to memorialize the moment.

4

In the station the next morning, Marlowe was glad he'd only enlisted in the Garibaldi army for three tours the night before. The drink was delicious (and restorative, he'd decided), with the tang from the citrus mingling around Campari's brightly bitter notes. But Gary's had soon been engulfed in a Saturday rush, reducing the ability to chat with the genial English-born bartender. Plus, heading into that third round, he'd felt the enticing pull of the fourth and fifth, and the busy day ahead wouldn't be as navigable if he hadn't resisted.

On the way home, he'd scored two pizza slices the size of bigfoot feet—one with roasted broccoli and gorgonzola, one quattro formaggi—from Hugh D's Heavenly Hot Slices, savoring them once home while watching *Gunsmoke*. Randomly picking a DVD from his complete set, the episode coincidentally featured a preacher, a temperance one at that, named Amos attempting to shut down Kitty's Long Branch Saloon. Tension and tippling-in-danger ensued, alongside cowboys, a bullet, a Bible, and, most important in Marlowe's eyes, more screen time for Kitty. He'd tucked into bed believing he'd snooze the night away in the show's western world, sipping dreamland beer at her bar.

Instead, he'd been an officer in an Italian army unit, fighting on an upward sloping hill covered in grape vines slowly decimated by the struggle.

Not wielding sword or gun but a Louisville Slugger baseball bat and a shield constructed of rainbow plastic drink straws, the figures his redshirted pals and he fought against became faceless the instant he woke. *Better shake that off like dust at trail's end*, he thought, leaving the police station elevator.

He removed his sports coat, a brown the color of muddy dirt after a long rainstorm, a color matched by his slacks, set off by red suspenders tacked with tiny white stars, stark against mildly wrinkled white button-down. Sitting with his first cup of station coffee–oily muck even in the morning–in one hand, second backup cup cooling on the desk, he saw Nelson across the cavernous room. As opposed to most mornings, the younger detective wasn't traversing the space at speed. He inchwormed nearer slowly, Marlowe noticing a slight limp.

Once two desks away, Marlowe gave a light shout. "Morning. Busted hoof?"

Nelson leaned on an unoccupied desk. "Morning, sir. Bruised calf. Not too bad. I'll be all right." Limping the rest of the way to Morven's desk, he sat down gingerly, as if the chair were hot.

"Some workout?" Marlowe asked kindly.

"It was going awesomely. First time I felt I was getting it, the Muay Thai. You know when you're doing a sport or workout routine, a new one, and at first it doesn't click?"

Marlowe gave a slow, negative head movement.

"It was like that, but clicking. Then–"

"Good morning, Detective Marlowe." Morven walked up. "And good morning, Detective Nelson. Calf?"

Marlowe gave a wave as Nelson spoke. "I was telling Marlowe the Muay Thai tale. How it was clicking, you know?"

"You were starting to pick it up, I felt." She looked down at him sadly.

"I was." Some of his energetic nature was waking up. "It felt good, like getting in a zone, you know? Then we went to sparring. Morven and I decided to be sparring partners, though she is levels above me in skill, and she caught me with a shot right as all my weight was on that one leg and down I went." Nelson managed to raise himself halfway off the chair, then flopped back down as he finished.

Morven looked genuinely worried for the younger man. "You sure you don't need to see a doctor? And, Nelson, apologies again."

"No worries, Detective Morven. It's just a bruise. Barely bothering me. If we were in some sort of competition, I'd still compete. And we are, in a way. A competition with whoever is responsible for yesterday's suspicious death, as we decided to call it."

"Maybe a cup of joe?" With a twinge of nearly submerged regret, Marlowe held out his second cup in Nelson's direction.

"Thanks, but no." Nelson's hands stayed close to his side. "Not sure coffee is best for a calf bruise."

"Okey dokey." Marlowe pulled the coffee back as Morven sat and both she and Nelson clicked computers on. "Glad you aren't a horse, or we might have to shoot you. Crying shame. Because, to switch my moving metaphors, it's all hands on deck. First: scientific updates?"

Morven got into her inbox. "Yes. An email from Doctor Peterson with some preliminary findings. Work still in its infancy, but he is true as truth's simplicity, simpler than the infancy of truth. Sorry, you know the Doc—always attempting the Elizabethan. He gives particulars of the victim, which we knew, plus no tattoos. Here we are. Death by poisoning."

Nelson had raised his hand.

"Yes, Nelson?"

"Did you two know Somalia has the most poison deaths per year per capita?" He checked both of the other's blank faces. "No?"

"Back to the Doc," Morven continued. "He says brain death caused by respiratory failure induced by strychnine. That's a first for me."

Nelson gave a tiny gasp. "That seems very unusual. Sir? Detective Marlowe, have you worked a strychnine suspicious death before?"

"Can't say I have. Odd one. Not readily available. Used to be used, I believe, in rat poison. Not unsurprising, now that it's on the table, given the initial scene reports mentioned what appeared to be muscle spasming and pain in the victim pre-death. Anything more?"

"Doc believes it was ingested, possibly via a wine-brandy-fruit-juice drink, which along with some potato chips and a hot dog made up the contents of the victim's stomach. The instruments of darkness tell us truth–not sure where he's going there–he surmises, but wouldn't swear, the victim would have tasted it in the food, but the drink combination might have camouflaged the poison's sting. Then something about more things in heaven and earth. You know."

"I do know. Any forensics? Feels like that recovered cup has risen to the top of the stream."

"Nothing I see," Morven replied, with a, "Me neither," tossed in from Nelson.

Marlowe parsed his own inbox, taking a deep gulp of coffee. "Nope." He stood up, rubbed his bald head, walked to the board. "Poison in the drink. Let's take that as gospel. Murder of Pastor Pat Brown. Who might want to kill him? That's the ride we're climbing in the saddle for."

Nelson cleared his throat. "Not to be genderist, or cliché, but you hear poison is a women's weapon historically, and it's mentioned as such in *Game of Thrones* even. But recent numbers say it's 60% male usage to 40% female."

"In-ter-esting," Marlowe drawled it out. Nelson raised his hand once more. "This isn't study hall, Nelson, what is it?"

"Following along Mr. Arthur's diagram, should we start by focusing on those sitting near the victim and those Mr. Arthur saw talking to the victim, thinking only they could have managed to slip him the poison in his drink?"

As Nelson spoke, Marlowe couldn't help but wonder how Nelson had changed in regard to the British-mystery-loving older man. Nelson had considered John a suspect in the earlier case, but today was completely in thrall.

"Even Mr. Arthur may not have seen every suspect. Eyes and ears open. You can disagree, but I feel our lariats should aim to rope a couple cows to begin." He held up fingers as he spoke. "One: did anyone else feel any strychnine-like effects? Two: has DNA or fingerprints been found on that cup, and have the remaining contents—if any—or spillage been tested? Three: when did those closest to the victim, his wife and"—He looked at the board—"Deacon Mike Ray, notice the victim suffering?" He stopped a moment, considering. "Plus, let's moniker this three A, since those two were close both physically and emotionally, do they have ideas on who might want to harm him. Four: if not already done, request voluntary fingerprints and DNA samples. Which leads to five: who was the man Mr. Arthur didn't have a name for?"

"Makes sense," Morven replied. She'd been typing and looked up. "I would posit one more addition to the list. Financial checks on the victim and bleacher group, I guess we'll call them. While we can't dig too deep without a judge's okay, doing what when can around that group will help."

"Just don't call it a village," Marlowe muttered.

"Actually, I have one more," Morven said. "Seven: put together a list of others at the game. South bleachers, opposing bleachers, coaches, umpires, staff. It might not be one from the north bleachers. Office Troy I'm sure has this information."

"Fair points. Seems our day is crammed as a Dodge City saloon on a cattle drive's final day. Divide and conquer. Nelson, I know you're pulling up lame. I'm gonna keep you desk bound." Nelson appeared more pained than he had before, but gave an assenting nod. "Morven," Marlowe said, "can you start by interviewing Deacon Mike? I'll interview Mrs. Brown. It being Sunday, he might be hard to herd."

Morven nodded rapidly, face back to her computer as she typed. "We've had harder to herd, I'll wager. Nelson, can you assist me with the I-POA beforehand?"

"Sure," Nelson replied glumly. Even Morven's usage of one of his own acronym creations, I-POA for Interview Plan of Action, couldn't shake off enforced sticking to the station.

"Dandy. Let's get to work. Nelson, need a coffee?"

A groan was his only reply.

At his desk, Nelson squeezed stress balls colored like stop signs in each hand, peering at his laptop screen. Marlowe and Morven left for their interviews after some preliminary research. Morven had picked him up a cranberry, feta, spinach salad with lime vinaigrette before leaving; she may have felt a little bad about his injury. He forked at the salad abstractedly. It wasn't a *bad* salad, probably the healthiest item available on the commissary menu. But it wasn't a *good* one, either, wilted and worn in appearance.

For the tenth time that morning, he gave his sore leg a stretch, pulling toes to calf. Then he jumped up, grimaced, and sat tentatively back down. "Stupid leg," he said to himself, as if leg was a curse word. The old-school, square, beige phone on his desk rang, cracking open the quiet Sunday station atmosphere like a shot, causing Nelson to jump up again, grimace again, and sit again, less tentatively this time. He picked the phone up as the second ring began its jangle.

"Detective Nelson." He could answer with his usual briskness even if he couldn't walk that way.

The strident officer's voice on the other end of the line reverberated. "No," Nelson said, his responses audible at the other side of the room, if anyone were there to hear, echoing his one-sided conversation. "Marlowe's not here atm. At the moment. Who is it? Wait, *he's* actually here, in the station? About yesterday's murder? No, keep him there, I can talk to him. I'll be down in a sec. Actually, give me a couple minutes. Can you book me an interview room? Sure. Thanks."

He hung up. John Arthur was in the station lobby. He'd asked for Marlowe, saying he had information about the murder. *John Arthur, back again*, Nelson thought, limping across the room. Then he reversed course, taking a hop to the murder board, as he liked to call it when by himself, unpinning John's bleacher sketch and list of names. *Doesn't hurt to bring this*, he decided. *Maybe he wants to follow up on it.*

He had the elevator to himself, straightening his tie in the mirrored surface surrounding the floor buttons. Today's suit was olive-green linen, single-breasted, two-button closure, patch pockets, over a bright-white collared shirt and jaune-colored tie with faint checks. *Not bad for a junior detective,* he thought. Switching to the elderly man with the mystery TV obsession, he wondered what drove someone to want to be involved with a murder case. Mentally instability? Loneliness? Obsession? He knew Morven and Marlowe leaned into the second choice, with maybe a dash of the latter, as John was a widower, living alone with his dog and memories of his deceased wife. The man had been helpful, and Marlowe, usually not the most *avant-garde* of police, had opened to his help in the past. *Avant-garde* policing. The last thing he'd use as a descriptor for Marlowe.

Opening the door on the back side of the station's sweeping lobby, he saw Mr. Arthur conversing with 6'5", 300-pound Officer Coleman, currently staffing the main lobby behind a sheet of bulletproof glass. Nelson headed their way, then stopped abruptly. They weren't conversing, they were singing. The huge officer's handlebar mustache, which nearly matched Marlowe's in scale, bounced along with the tune.

"When constabulary duty's to be done, to be done,

A policeman's lot is not a happy one, happy one."

They faded laughingly to piccolo, and John noticed Nelson. "DS Nelson, so nice of you to meet me down here. Just in time for the end of the song. My guess is you're busy as a hive of bees, so"—he faced back to the larger man behind the glass barrier—"Officer Coleman, I'll bid you adieu."

"See you later, Mr. Arthur," Office Coleman's baritone rumbled. "Thanks for the song."

"My voice isn't a patch on yours. Detective, shall we head to the grilling room?"

Nelson's face carried a curious combination of shock and awe, as if hit with a cartoon hammer, an expression John instilled in the younger detective. Maybe it was John's outfit as well as the singing. He boasted blue shorts, knee-high brown socks with squirrels and red-capped mushrooms, a black T-shirt with a cartoon drawing of a pouty Rottweiler in a unicorn hat, and blue baseball cap.

"Yes. Please follow me. Officer Coleman booked a room. This way."

Retracing his path, John close behind, Nelson opened the door to interview room four, gesturing John in. It was another of the station's collection of nondescript interview rooms—white plastic-topped square table, metal-legged chairs with uncomfortable plastic seats and backs, two blank walls the color of geriatric wet concrete, and one mirrored wall. The black ceiling hosted six recessed canned lights, bright enough to blind but few enough that parts of the room were left in shadows.

John sat without invitation, seemingly at ease. Nelson slowly edged into the seat opposite as John began speaking, looking at his reflection in the mirrored wall. "Tell me truthfully, is Detective Marlowe behind the glass? Feverishly turning knobs and flipping switches adjusting the levels on recording devices and arranging his notepad?"

"Mr. Arthur." Nelson's voice took a serious tone, trying to project an authoritative air. "You came to us, remember? We didn't call you in for an interview this time. I'm not sure we called you in last time, during the, what did you call it?"

"Case of the Nine Neighbors."

"That's the one. Do you have pertinent information about yesterday's incident? It is busy here, even on Sunday." He'd carried the bleacher sketch in a manilla folder, opening it up to bring the paper out. "This sketch and list, we can admit, has been helpful as we begin our CAP investigation."

"Cap?" John pulled his hat down.

"Crime against person." An acronym always perked Nelson up.

"Makes sense, DS Nelson, so –"

"Wait." Nelson gave him the palms up gesture he'd seen Marlowe use before, quieting John momentarily. "DS? It is Detective Nelson." He was proud of his recent promotion and wanted to be sure John knew his status.

"My profound apologies *Detective* Nelson. I was watching *Midsomer Murders* before coming down and have DSes on the brain. And you remind me somewhat of the Midsomer DSes."

Nelson couldn't help himself. "Remind me what DS means. And *Midsomer*. That's one of the British mysteries you're ob—interested in?"

"One of the all-time classics. Murder of the week in a small town, or different small towns, in an imaginary British county, that being Midsomer. You're not a watcher?"

"No, not at this juncture." Nelson got caught up in the man's enthusiasm. "After the Case of the Nine Neighbors, I did feel maybe I should *start* watching some of the shows you mentioned, get a list of the top ones you've learned from."

"Happy to provide and expand British mystery fandom further. Back to DS. It's short for Detective *Sergeant*. There are many in *Midsomer Murders*, working with first Detective Chief Inspector Tom and then John, Barnaby, like you with Detective Morven and Detective Marlowe. The DS is also called the DCI's bagman. You hear that in older shows or shows set in the past, like *Endeavor*."

"Bagman? That's cool. But, to be clear, there are two senior detectives with the same name in one show?" Nelson knew he needed to get back on track, but couldn't help himself, the words tumbling out as if water from a leaky hose. "With many DSes?"

"It is confusing. DCI *Tom* Barnaby was first, then the actor, the brilliant John Nettles, retired. But the show is so popular, they popped in a replacement, his cousin"—John air-quoted the last word—"DCI *John* Barnaby. Played by the also-swell Neil Dudgeon. There have been a bunch of DSes supporting, some helpful, some less helpful. The current one, DS Winter, played by Nick Hendrix, is a wee bit Detective Nelson-y—an athletic, go get 'em type in a sharp suit. No suspect's going to outrun him. Speaking of, I noticed you hobbling?"

It took Nelson a moment, still glowing from the "athletic" and "sharp suit" descriptions John allocated him. "Calf issue. Workout injury." He pulled his mind back. "But you didn't come to educate me on British mysteries today, did you Mr. Arthur."

"No, yesterday's murder brought me. Even if, as I believe John Barnaby once said, 'I'm not in the habit of using murder as an excuse.'"

"Suspicious death."

"Of course. Nothing announced yet."

"Why would you think murder?"

"Wrong place and person for a suicide. Poisoning accidently at a ballgame could happen, but I doubt it. Which leaves murder."

"How did you know it was poisoning?"

"For one, I overheard someone talking about his clenching beforehand, and then the stain, which I felt at first might be blood but didn't smell right. The cup nearby plus the agonized appearance points to poison. I've seen lots of poisonings. On TV, I mean. Devil's Snare here, perhaps?"

"The magical plant from Harry Potter?"

"I meant jimsonweed. Poisonous plant, also called Devil's Snare, long before Daniel Radcliffe played Harry. The name an ironic fit for the death of a pastor. Are you a Potterverse fan?"

"An ex of mine was huge into the movies. We watched them multiple times. Between you and me, Mr. Arthur, we are currently considering poisoning as a method, so very alert of you. And this list, as said, is helpful. But what else do you know about the suspicious death that brings you here?"

"Stay on track. Detective Marlowe has taught you well." John reached into his pocket, pulling out another piece of paper. "I was thinking on the crime while watching *Midsomer*, hard not to. It's a tragedy—for the victim, for his family and friends, coworkers, acquaintances, all those people suffering. I know in one part of my mind that's true, and that I shouldn't be equating a real murder with a TV one. But my mind just wandered back to it, how it relates to all the murders I've seen, the TV ones. This dilemma bouncing around my mind like so many balls, and it hit me–the baseball game was important."

"The game? How?"

"First, the setting itself. I'm still mulling that aspect, but it feels important. Even more importantly, I believe this *particular* game of baseball matters. How it played out, the hits, runs, outs. I wasn't there the whole time, so I have no complete scorecard. I mentioned the game briefly to Detective Marlowe, but in reflection, I told it jumbled, like clothes fresh out of the dryer. Warm but unfolded. We—I mean you detectives—need to get the earlier innings from another spectator. Poirot?" He paused to make sure Nelson was still following along.

"The Belgian detective with the mustache, order and method?"

"Exactly, Detective. Poirot would want to know exactly what happened in the game." He put the paper down between them. It had a series of bullet points, each aligned to a different inning of the game. "Beginning in the bottom of the third, Reign the home team, Torrent the visitors."

• Third Inning, 6 to 1 Torrent. Bottom, Reign up. Missed the first two outs, but bases were loaded. Three-RBI triple. Wild slide at third, cloud of dust and foul line chalk. I believe the triple was hit by the victim's son, Gerry Brown. Followed by a strikeout.

• Fourth Inning, 6 to 4 Torrent, top. Single, two fly outs, two walks, one strikeout.

• Fourth Inning, bottom. Ground out to first. Single. Double play—Tinker to Evers to Chance. Or, short to second to first.

• Fifth Inning, 6 to 4 Torrent, top. Two strikeouts, but long pitch counts, one ground out to first.

• Fifth Inning, bottom (pitching change for Torrent). Single, single, infield fly out, sacrifice fly to right, run scored. Long pitch count ending suddenly and anticlimactically in a foul ball fly out.

• Sixth inning, 6 to 5 Torrent, top (pitching change for Reign). Bunt single. Ground out, third to first, runner advanced. Strikeout. Fly out.

• Sixth inning, bottom. Three pitch strikeout. Walk. Full count single into right. Two on, one out. Big kid up, hits first pitch. I'd say it was going way over the right fielder.

John looked up. "After that hit, as the cheers started, the first scream broke through, followed by a second, and then you know what happened next."

"You feel the baseball played is important?" Nelson screwed up his face as if imagining how it could be.

John smiled ruefully. "Detective, you might think old Mr. Arthur has tipped off his rocker face-first into the television. But it's the setting of the murder, part of the scene, what was happening as the murder took place. It's an awful thing, a murder, any time. But at a kid's baseball game? I decided all hands on deck, that I should bring this to you." He held up the paper and passed it to Nelson.

Nelson took both pieces of paper, the game overview and bleacher map, and slid them in the folder. "Thank you," he said, staring at the folder. "I'm not sure how the second piece helps, but you never know." Sitting quietly for some seconds, he continued. "Thank you, again, Mr. Arthur, for your help with our inquires. I'm sure Marlowe will be sad he wasn't here himself."

"Maybe sad." John stretched the A in maybe out as if string needing straightening, then chuckled. "Happy to assist the police." He rose out of the chair, as did Nelson.

Then the latter stopped, asking, "Why did you believe it was someone on the south bleacher?"

"Proximity seemed important for opportunity and means. Motive, no idea. But when you find the motive, my guess it will be someone who 'wanted to see the agony on his face' as one *Midsomer* murderer said."

"Back to *Midsomer*, Mr. Arthur?" Nelson asked as they left the room.

"The classics can always teach us something."

Nelson opened the door to the lobby, saying, "Oh, Mr. Arthur, one last thing."

"Yes?" John paused.

"Detective Marlowe doesn't do anything feverishly."

Marlowe tucked his car delicately against the curb in front of the Browns' house, 101 Tower Road SW, which loomed over a cul-de-sac containing only one other house. He'd parked directly behind a marked police car and, before walking up to the house, gave a succinct knock on the passenger door, leaning down like a tired walrus. Two officers occupied the car, an Indian American woman with long, raven-black hair pulled back in a thick plait scanning her phone, and a thin Caucasian man with short, wheat-colored hair behind the wheel, coffee in one hand, protein bar in the other. The well-worn cliché of cops and doughnuts had faded somewhat as health concerns rose, but Marlowe maintained a fondness for apple fritters when on a stakeout.

"Morning, Officer Sohota, Office Lomax. How goes the day?"

"Detective Marlowe," Officer Sohota said. "Good morning. We took bets on when you'd arrive. Lomax, next coffee's on you."

"Yeah, yeah. Detective, top of the morning to you. You're here sooner than expected."

"Early bird catches the cuckoo stealing his nest, and all that." Both looked askance at Marlowe's reply, but said nothing. "Anything worth reporting?"

"A few reporters stopped," Sohota said, as Lomax sipped coffee. "But we softly dissuaded them from bothering the family. No movement from inside."

"Another officer inside?"

"The family requested being alone from what we were told."

"Check." He stood. "Suppose I'd better mosey up. Thanks."

The two officers gave short waves as he walked up the driveway toward the house, a substantial block of colonial architecture that wouldn't have seemed out of place in the antebellum south. Two looming stories, ample garage add-on, white with pewter-shaded trim around tall windows, black accents, pillars, and a door he decided was the color of aged parmesan. He raised the ornate, angel-shaped knocker and rapped it twice against the door.

After five seconds, the door opened slowly halfway, a woman peering around it with a strained, questioning look, but no words. She seemed frightened, like a mouse before the cat pounces.

"Mrs. Bridgette Brown?" He tried to add a kind note to his tone.

She gave a faint nod, then gazed over his shoulder as if expecting more people behind him.

Bringing out wallet with badge and photo from his pocket, opening it slowly, he said, "I'm Detective Marlowe. Hate to be a bother, but is there any chance I could come in, ask a few questions?"

A quick flutter passed across Bridgette's face. "Detective, yes, please, come in." Her voice pitched very low and had an airy quality about it. "I thought you might be another reporter and couldn't stand it." Backing up, she pointing to a living area sunken down a step from the doorway. "Is here on the couch fine?"

"Dandy, Mrs. Brown." Marlowe eased down the step. Two white leather couches dominated the room like sittable cows. A sort of hall led from the door on one side, the other stepping up into an open kitchen sparkling with white cabinets and countertops. On one sat a big bouquet of flowers in a wicker basket, powder-blue hydrangeas pale against white roses.

The living room's floor was black tile, accented by a red rug. *Very dramatic*, Marlowe thought, sitting carefully onto the couch against the front window, directly across from the other couch. An ebony fireplace with fake fire set into the wall to his right, adding to the stark theatricality, above which hung a five-by-six foot picture of Pat Brown, taken from the side as he appeared to be fervently preaching, forehead dappled with sweat, on a stage to a crowd made featureless by bright lights. Looming over them, Marlowe couldn't help glancing up at it as they talked, as if it might start taking part in the conversation. The fireplace mantle itself was barren, none of the usual family pictures or small flowers in vases.

Bridgette sat across, pulling long legs up under her protectively. She had shoulder-length black hair, pitch-black outside of a rustle of occasional gray streaks when moving her head, the slightest wave at the ends curling around her chin. She had well-worn jeans on and a white sweater–the house must have a powerful air conditioner, as it felt nearer 60 than the 73 outside—no shoes, a broad gold wedding ring her only jewelry. Her face was nearly paper white against the dark hair, from the experience or naturally Marlowe wasn't sure, and while starkly pretty, somewhat worn.

"I apologize for the hesitation at the door," she said once they sat. "We've been mostly unbothered, but a few persistent reporters have knocked."

"We apologize. The police, I mean. Hopefully the officers out front spook off the rest of the reporter pack."

She gave a dismissive gesture with one hand. A hint of regalness underpinned her bearing, as if she were displaced royalty long since in power remembering past glories.

Pulling a small notebook and pen out, Marlowe said, "I know you have been through a traumatic experience. Sure the questions are okay?"

"I would like to say no, but would like to help if possible."

"We can keep it short. We're beginning inquires and every answer helps."

Her hand fluttered up like a wounded bird, hovering in the air momentarily, then brushed back a strand of hair that slipped onto her cheek. "Inquiries? So, you are treating this . . ." She faded off.

"We are currently looking at your husband's death as suspicious, I am sorry to have to tell you."

"It feels impossible, but I felt it had to be."

"Mind if I ask why?"

"My husband was vigorously healthy, Detective. A health-related accident would have been unbelievable."

"Again, sorry to dredge up the traumatic, but do you remember anything from the moments before your husband collapsed?" Something about the woman had Marlowe treading extra softly, though he knew she had to be considered a suspect. She hadn't cried since he'd arrived but appeared wrung out. He didn't want to wring her more.

"I do. The game was exciting. My son, Gerry, had played well. It had gotten very close, and Pat becomes, became very tense in close games. He took them seriously, as most things. We—the family and most of the flock—

knew to give him space. I saw him tensing up, sensed from past history it was mental, but also noticed him—" She stopped for a moment, the hand rising, brushing back another strand of hair, before she continued. "Clenching his body. I thought it was the game. Then there was a big hit, cheering, and I noticed him falling to the ground, almost as if his body was being pulled into itself. I couldn't do anything for a moment. The sky seemed so perfectly blue. By the time I got to him, he was insensible, and then passed."

Marlowe didn't say a word for a moment. Then, in a tone most who knew him rarely heard, not a whisper but near, said, "Thank you, ma'am. Sorry. Did you see what he might have eaten or drank during the game?"

She brought her legs out from under one at a time, pulling both knees tight to her chest, breathed in, then out. "I know he had a hotdog and chips from the concession stand. And at least one, maybe two cups of sangria."

"Made by Mrs. Ash Willums?"

"Miss, I believe. She's divorced. And yes, she makes the sangria."

"Any good?"

"I'm sorry?"

"The sangria."

"I wouldn't know. Pat didn't like me drinking. He liked it, however. Do you think? No, it's too horrible."

"Ma'am?"

"He was killed by the sangria? Or something he ate? Was anyone else sick?"

"We are looking at all lines of inquiry at the moment. We do think his death was suspicious."

"You can't say anything now." She relaxed her posture slightly. "But you will let us know?"

"Yes, we will. Just a few more questions. One about the game. We believe no one was sitting directly by your husband?"

"Correct. He demanded his space at times. Most times. This was one of them."

"Can you think of any person who might have wanted to harm your husband?"

"Harm my husband?"

"I'm sure it sounds impossible, but did he have arguments or incidents with anyone recently?"

A hint of a smile crept upon her face, like a shy dog peeking around a corner, reminding him for a moment of a glance Audrey Hepburn might give. Then it retreated. "Not impossible. My husband could be a confrontational man. And is—was—emotional, fiery. He was right in his mind, full stop. Every time. In arguments continually. But he didn't hold his anger. You know the saying 'beware the anger of a patient man?' He was the opposite. Rubbed many the wrong way and some the right, but never hung on to an argument. I brought it to his attention once, as he never noticed. He just said that he had the Lord's work to do and was going to do it how he felt was best, and as a champion of righteousness had to hold himself to a different standard. So, yes, probably many arguments recently. *I* can't think of specific ones. Deacon Mike Ray might. They were thick as thiev—" She paused. "They were very close. Or Nikola Cassien. They were closer yet. They saw my husband more than I."

"Thank you." Marlowe wrote in his notebook. "A couple more?"

"Ask away."

"Any financial issues causing your husband worry?"

"Hah." Her momentary laugh contained no humor, flat and hard as the floor tiles. "None that he told me about. I doubt it. The camel passing through the eye of the needle proverb wasn't one Pat adhered to."

"Did he leave a will?"

"Pat told me he made one, splitting everything between family and church. You'd need to go through our lawyer for specifics. Shane Buchanan."

"Work problems? I mean the church."

"I believe that's fine. But problems there, yes." She paused. "Again, Deacon Mike will help. I will say, it is a big organization, and Pat was king, if that doesn't sound heretical, ruling with an iron fist. People got ruffled. But came back, most of the time."

"Why, do you think?"

"Pat's charisma and innate self-belief was, cliché as it sounds, a force of nature. People wanted to be a part of it."

"He must have been very busy. But still managed to make it to all the games?"

"I wish I could say it was familial devotion." She leaned her head back, and he noticed a small scar on her cheek, like an abandoned boat on a wide open ocean. "Don't get me wrong. He was devoted in a way, but in this case to baseball. He said if not called by God, he would have been called by the diamond."

"Ah." Marlowe had met many who lived out their childhood dreams via their children's sporting activities. It often didn't end well. He saw her head dip, guessed she was tired. "Did you feel ill in any way at the game?"

She shook her head.

"The children felt okay too?"

"They did."

"Did you all have food from the concession stand?"

"Yes. Burton and Sidney had chips. Lucky–sorry, Nancy, we call her Lucky–also, plus a candy bar, a Twix. I didn't have anything."

"Can you think of anything else that might help us as we move forward?"

"No. Nothing now."

"How are your kids?" Marlowe asked.

"Shocked, Detective. Pat was a blazing sun and we the small planets orbiting. Having the sun go out? An impossibility you can't prepare for. Will you need to talk to them? They are resting."

"Not currently. If so, I'll be sure to reach out to you. We will have an officer come by for DNA samples from the family, if you are open to it. As we try to sort through the scene, it could be helpful."

She breathed out, nodded.

He stood up, and she followed suit. Making a move towards the door., he said, "We'll also return personal effects as soon as possible. Jewelry, his phone, that kind of thing."

She'd managed to get in front of him, opening the door, saying, "Thank you, Detective. Marlowe, was it?"

"Yes, ma'am. Here's a card."

She took the card, the diminutive smile once more creeping on and off her face like a murmur in a quiet room. "Must be difficult; a police detective named Marlowe, like Philip Marlowe."

Marlowe's mustache rose wistfully as he grinned. "Some days, Mrs. Brown, it is. Thank you for your time. We will keep you posted."

Walking back to his car, John Arthur popped up in Marlowe's mind like a weed in a flower patch. Sure as shooting, the TV mystery buff would show up again during their investigation with quotes from fictional detectives and theories about what had and what was happening, blurring the lines between fiction and fact, scripts and reality, in a way that, while helpful, caused Marlowe to overthink a case. It felt a little weird not to be driving in the direction of the man's north Seattle neighborhood after the case where he'd run into John and Ainsley often. *Wonder if there's ever a chapter in a book or series of scenes where the detective doesn't appear?* He'd have to ask.

Saluting the parked officers a mock tilt of an invisible hat, he gave the Browns' house another once-over while leaning on his car's hood, snapping his suspenders abstractedly, like a banjo player flicking strings between songs. The front lawn's immaculate bright green evidence of repeated summertime waterings, not a blade of grass out of place, pristine. But what lies beneath? *No lawn is ever that placidly perfect*, he thought, sliding his sports coat off and sliding into the car. A mole or two's always waiting to dig a hole, deposit the dirt on top. It's just a matter of finding them.

5

The Chapter Creek Church was a considerable corner building, brick painted gray with the name high on each of the corner's street-facing sides in ten-foot white letters. A smaller building attached to one side via a glass walkway, stark against the windowless main building. A wide, manicured lawn grew in front, L-ing around the side where it shared space with a good-sized parking lot. All in all, the complex took up nearly half of a suburban block, assured in its domain by fences blocking the few houses on the block's other side. It appeared quiet for a Sunday, morning services done, and Morven felt pulling up that a subdued atmosphere clouded over the complex. Not surprising, given the tragic circumstances. She gave herself a quick glance in the mirror—hair pulled up in her traditional style, blue eyes sharp as steel. Buttoning her coat, she took a last lukewarm sip of the cappuccino picked up on the way before heading up the sidewalk toward the smaller building, the church offices.

Two police cars were parked in front, and Morven waved their way as she walked. She'd done more than her fair share of solo witness interviews in her policing career, and with Marlowe. So she wasn't nervous—you don't make it to detective being overly nervous—but excitement bubbled up like Champagne in a flute. Every time she went into an interview, she relished the anticipatory moments, much like she relished interviewing itself. The feeling of going to talk to someone who may either be involved with or have a pertinent fact about a case? A case they could then solve? She cherished these moments like some people cherished diamonds.

When they'd called to set up the interview, Deacon Mike Ray had tried to sidestep, saying he didn't have time; it was a Sunday, he was booked. Her calm persistence eventually paid off, and he'd relented. She wondered what kind of reception there would be. Walking in the open office door, she found herself in a completely empty routine space—cherry-wood desk topped with computer and stack of binders, red leather couch at one paneled wall, a hefty framed picture of an iridescent sunrise above it, window opposite. The same as any unfilled business office on a Sunday afternoon, quiet as midnight. Besides the glass door she'd come through, there stood a plain, almond-brown wooden door behind the desk and another in the far wall opposite.

"Hello?" she said to the emptiness, the word echoing faintly. "Is anyone here?"

The door opposite opened and out walked a man probably six inches taller than her 5'8", spare in build, slick glossy strands of black hair plastered down over a balding, oval-shaped head highlighted by a mustache a shade thicker than a pencil. He wore jeans and a jet-black clerical shirt, looking somewhat like a goth praying mantis, bent slightly, eyes open wide, reaching out a hand to her. A fat gold watch on a black braided leather band with three chunky gold beads glimmered garishly, caught by a stray sunbeam filtering through the window.

"You must be Detective Morven. Glad you could make it." His hand was awkwardly damp.

"Mike Ray?"

"Yes, I am blessed to be Deacon Mike Ray, a shepherd here at the glorious Chapter Creek Church. You can call me Deacon. Would you like to step into my office?" He walked back through the door, momentarily stopping halfway. "My wife, Kristin, is here if that's okay?"

"That's good. We were going to want to talk to her too."

In the office were an identical desk and couch, as well as a chair to the side of the desk, a thick oak number with a red flat cushion and arms as wide as a large man's hands. On the couch reclining into one corner was a short, slender woman with mousy platinum-blonde hair teased up and candy-apple red lipstick, wearing a crimson pencil skirt, tight white button-front shirt, and gold hoop earrings. A picture of someone heading to one of the City's downtown dance clubs, not one who conceivably recently went to church. Both, Morven estimated, were late forties in age. The woman fondled an old-fashioned style glass in one hand, out of which the juniper scent of gin floated. She gave Morven a half-smile, half-wave combo as the detective entered.

"Please, officer, take this chair." Mike motioned, moving behind the desk. "We are shocked and saddened by the death of our great pastor. As the Bible says, 'live every day as if you might die tomorrow.' He did, but it is hard to believe his tomorrow has come."

Morven wasn't sure on his quoting but didn't want to get diverted. "Thank you for assisting us in our inquiries. I just have a few questions. First, you sat, not directly beside but nearest Mr. Brown at the game. Did you talk to him much before or during?"

"Certainly. We often consulted about church business, and before the game, we talked about today's services. Which he sadly did not get to attend." He bowed his head for a moment, before starting again. "During the game? I don't believe so."

"Are you sure about that, sir?" She remembered John Arthur's list, and note about Mike talking to the victim.

"Let me think." He rubbed his chin with one hand, long arm angled, making him appear more insect-like. Morven caught Kristin rolling her eyes as she took a sip. "I *did* stop to chat for a moment. About the game. Yes, that's it. Pastor Mike's team, the Reign, were behind. But I knew if they kept positive and believed, they would win in the end, so stopped to give some words of support. As the good book says, 'the journey of a thousand miles begins with one step.'"

"Does it?" Morven couldn't help herself.

He smiled patronizingly. "I'm sure of it."

"Did Mr. Brown appear out of sorts to you at the game, or before?"

"He was a man who gave his all, to the church, to family—"

"To his secretary," Kristin stage-whispered, which Mike ignored.

"—to the team. With that kind of devotion, Detective, comes an intensity of spirit. He carried that, a blessing and a curse. And while it did seem the game was making him tense, I took it as part of his glowing soul. If only I would have done something" He shook his head solemnly. "But there is no room for regret."

"You were the first to reach him after he collapsed. Did he say anything? Did you notice anything?"

"I was in shock, Detective, but the pastor, my brother shepherd of the flock, was in agony. I had to act. Sadly, he was beyond my help, beyond the ability to speak, and before I knew it, beyond our mortal veil. I couldn't help him." He held up one finger. "But while every day isn't good, there is good in every day. I believe the pastor enjoyed his last moments of sun before transitioning."

"Did you notice anything suspicious or anyone interacting oddly with Mr. Brown?"

"Suspicious? At a child's baseball game?" Mike seemed skeptical. "Nothing until the accident. Wait. You are considering this an accident? Tragic, yes, but an accident."

"We are keeping all lines of inquiry open."

Kirsten raised her glass, tinkling the ice. "Excuse me, it's Detective?" Morven nodded. "When you say *inquiries*, that makes me think suspicious death. I've watched *Law and Order*, you know. Are you saying Pastor Pat, um, met with foul play?"

"Could you think of anyone who might wish him harm?"

"Could I—" Kristin said, as Mike said simultaneously, "Not the pastor—" before he held up a hand at his wife, then continued. "Pastor Pat believed in himself, allowing him to believe in every one else in our church.

'Nothing can dim the light which shines from within' as the Bible says. His light was very strong."

Kristin took another sip, then spoke up, smiling to show sizeable perfectly aligned, bright-white teeth stained slightly red by lipstick. "Very strong. Listen, Detective, you're going to hear it anyway, but Pat could be a hard-ass, excuse my language. In the service of the church, naturally." Another sip. "And that rubbed a few wrong."

"Any in particular?"

"No–" Mike started to speak, but Kristin interrupted. "I can think of two. Three. Not saying they're suspects, as I'm sure his end will be signed off as accidental, but you should talk to Nikola Cassien, the, we'll say, secretary." She dug the word out as if she'd bitten a bitter orange. "And Nev Maloney, who *used* to be the team coach. Not to gossip, but I saw our Pastor Pat arguing with Tom Toomey, too."

"Darling, you know those members of our flock would never harm the pastor." He gave her a playful finger wag, causing his wife to lean her head way back on the couch. "You must forgive my wife, Detective, she has taken the pastor's passing very deeply. Forgiveness is one of the cardinal virtues. Now, are we done with questions?"

"Nikola Cassien, how long has she been the secretary here?"

"Five years last Monday, Detective. A ray of light in our offices," Mike replied.

Morven took notes while talking. "How was her working relationship with Mr. Brown?"

The two spoke simultaneously again, with Kristin saying, "Very close," and Mike saying, "Very professional."

"Why were they having issues?"

Before Kristin could speak, Mike shushed her, then spoke. "They worked wonderfully together in the service of the Chapter Creek Church, but it was decided between them, mutually, that dear Nikola's time here should come to a close. As secretary. I'm sure she'll remain in the flock."

"Why a close?"

"Sometimes you have to get lost before you can find yourself. He believed Nikola needed a fresh challenge. Even officers within the *calmness* of the police station leave on occasion, I'm guessing?"

"Stopping as secretary caused friction between her and Mr. Brown?"

"It was nothing. Pat felt she needed a reverent push to continue on her path in life." He mimicked a pushing gesture over the desk.

"And what about Mr. Maloney?"

Kristin's eyes were closed, but Mike suggested, "Nev has been part of our extended family for years, and the coach of Pastor Pat's baseball team in the past. He gave 110%, but even in sunshine, there is rain."

"He's not the coach currently?"

"Sadly, no," Mike wistfully replied. "Decisions, tough decisions, have to be made. Perhaps this one fluffed his hat a tiny bit, if you'll excuse a cliché, but it was momentary. He and the pastor remained as two candles on the altar."

"Do you know what the argument with"—Morven checked her notes—"Mr. Toomey was about?"

Kristin raised her head, then shook it negative.

"Minor differences arise," Mike said, staring out the window with a sigh. "As I'm sure you understand from your own work with troubled people within our vast community. But here, with Pastor Pat? Nothing serious. Scripture dialogue between two reverent men. Are we almost through? We have the church's business, it being a Sunday."

"A few more questions," Morven said. "Did either of you feel any ill effect while attending the game?"

"Ill?" Mike looked shocked. "Perish the thought. Healthy mind, healthy body, right, my dear?"

His wife's smile could have soured milk. "Right dear. We both felt fine at the game and after."

"Did either of you have any of the sangria made by Ash Willums?"

Kristin chimed in first. "It's the only way to make it through a game."

Mike gave her another playful finger wag. "Don't give the detective the wrong idea. I did not partake, not that I'm teetotal. All things in moderation and moderating all things."

"How long had you known Mr. Brown?"

"We'd been shepherds together fifteen years. Beginning at our smaller location north of the City, then in the City center, and finally here, walking the path through many mountains and some deep valleys. We all have our share of tragedies. Now, I will walk alone." He considered, then continued. "With my wife, of course."

Kristin tipped her glass high, as if to coax a few last sips out, ice clanking against her teeth like miniature icebergs hitting a porcelain ship's hull.

Morven stood, then asked, "Would you consider them successful years?"

"We brought light into many people's lives. More people each day want to support and be a part of our—I guess I should now say *my*—flock. If that answers your question?"

"Somewhat. What about financially?"

"We serve our flock, not mammon. Our flock supports us in return. I could count a thousand tears in today's service when word of Pastor Mike's passing spread. Now, we really must be going, Detective."

"Thank you for your help. We may reach out with more questions later as our investigation continues."

"Any time. A shepherd's work is never done."

Nelson walked slow figure eights around the desk he and Morven shared and Marlowe's desk. The leg caused mild twinges of pain nearly every time he put full weight on it, but he'd found if he walked every fifteen minutes instead of solely sitting in front of his computer, it helped the aches. Turned them less like an ice pick pushing in and more like a finger poking. And anyway, he liked to keep moving in the healthiest of times, and squeezing stress balls as he clicked through available financial and background info wasn't enough.

He'd chatted with forensics, and while many tests were being done, and would continue to be done over the next few days, the only specific fact given was that no other fingerprints had been found on the cup the victim had been drinking from or the straw he'd been drinking with. Nelson wasn't sure whether that was helpful or not. He'd also compiled addresses and numbers for those sitting on the same bleacher as the victim, as well as Drogo Oates, the concession worker, and Ford David, the maintenance and grounds keeper, and reached out to uniform to double-check on potential fingerprinting and DNA samples—an activity that should be done by the next day if everyone was willing.

There'd been one mystery baseball fan to be identified, sitting in Position 14 according to Mr. Arthur's list. Staring at John's paper sketch, Nelson tried to decide what Morven might do if in the same situation. He shook his head, put the paper down. Instantly, he realized what he should do—call Ash Willums. The woman hadn't been sitting next to the mystery man, instead in Position 15, which was, un-methodically, in Row 5. But aAs a known gossiper, and the sangria maker, Nelson decided she probably knew everyone, probably the type to small talk during the middle of an inning. Not his type of fan, but one who knew names.

She picked up on the first ring, exclaiming loudly, "Ash here," as if she believed the caller was not on a telephone line but across the street. He replied with who he was, and she was off, talking with the speed and ferocity of a horse starting the Kentucky Derby.

"Detective from the City police? I knew you'd call, was waiting for your call. Not that I'm a hearse chaser or morbid, and not that I'm involved in what happen to Pat Brown, either, if you're going to try to use this call to lull me into a trap."

He managed to break the flow. "Excuse me, Mrs. Willums, we at the City police don't trap. I only have a quick question we were hoping you could answer."

"Just one? I can't believe *that*, Detective Nelson. You should be talking to me, because I have things to tell you, believe me you. It's *Miss*

Willums, by the way. Where should we start?"

"Are you saying you have information that might be of material importance as we investigate the incident that happened yesterday?"

"That was quite a procedural mouthful, Detective, but you bet your booties. Do you have a pen? Or are you recording this?"

"Not recording, no. If you have pertinent information, it would be best if we could conduct a more formal interview." Nelson knew that in person interviews were better. And besides, getting an I-POA ready was key. "Could you come to the station later today?"

"Not today, Detective. But the police station? Really? I've never been, if you can believe that, and what a story that might be. I have a bridge appointment tonight, Detective, and I'm not going to miss for hell or high water."

Nelson made a snap decision, weighing out how important her information actually was versus how important she thought it was. "Tomorrow, ten a.m.?"

"I'll have to duck out of work, so keep it between us that I'm coming down. Hush-hush, you know? I'm not one to gossip, and I certainly don't want my office humming with coworkers chatting about me and the fuzz, dear."

"Certainly. We will expect you tomorrow then." He almost hung up before remembering his original reason for calling. "Wait, Miss Willums, one question today. We are rounding up the names of people in the bleachers at the game where the incident occurred, and one person is proving difficult. We thought you might know—"

"Why would you think I would know? I'm not a people directory."

Nelson responded as tactfully and friendly as possible. "Well, Miss Willums, you did make the sangria. We've heard it's quite a treat, the MVB, most valuable beverage, of the bleachers, so felt everyone would have stopped by to see you at some point."

"MVB? That's a hoot, Detective. You're quite a joker, my friend. Nice voice too. I *certainly* look forward to meeting you in person. Shoot. Who do you need to put the screws on?"

"We are compiling a list, no screws." She laughed as he talked, an unbridled cawing that had him pulling the phone an inch away from his ear. "The one person whose contact details we don't have was sitting two rows down from you. A man, lean in build, approximately 5'11", light-brown hair, perhaps a hint of red in it."

"A hint of red. *Oo-la-la*. Name is Jack Page. Energetic guy, Jack. Nice enough. Want me to scoop up some dirt?"

"The name is very helpful. Do you have any contact details by chance?"

She gave him Jack Page's number, laughing, saying she couldn't wait to "really get going" at the next day's interview, then hung up.

It's been a full-court press kind of Sunday, he thought. Rubbing his ear, he walked his circuit, wondering how Marlowe and Morven's interviews were going, glad he'd snuck in an interview of his own. Wait, *two* interviews, as he'd had one with Mr. Arthur as well. An interview in a manner of speaking. He considered the older man nearly a member of the team, a sixth man kind of. "Which reminds me," he spoke out loud. He stopped walking, reaching into his suit coat to draw out his notebook and a small pencil. Restarting the figure eights, he began writing a list in the notebook.

"*Midsomer Murders*, with two Barnabys, small towns, murder every week. Then the Belgian detective, Hercules, last name Poirot, by Agatha Christie. As is the elderly lady detective, Mrs., I want to say marbles. No, *Mrs. Marple*. Then next is the one Mr. Arthur mentioned when he solved the last case and nearly fell off his porch. Death something or other. *Death in Paradise*. Nelson scores. Now, other shows? One with a priest, seems apropos. Father… *Father Brown*. Last name like the victim. Marlowe mentioned one, not British, New Zealand—*Brokenwood*. I know there are more. I'll ask next time I see him, but that's a strong watchlist."

"Detective Nelson?" A voice behind him broke into his musing. Startled, he bumped into Marlowe's chair, causing his leg to flare up, then slid into the same chair, almost falling. Trying to make it appear natural and planned, he ran his fingers through his hair with Officer Coleman's bulk looming over him.

"Yes, Office Coleman?" Nelson replied cooly.

"Everything okay up here in Detective HQ?" He swept a thick arm toward the cavernous room.

Nelson tried and failed to put on a nonchalantly Cary Grant-esque voice. "Fine. Case is sprinting along."

"Great. I was heading to the cantina, remembered your gammy leg, thought I'd ask if you need anything."

"Thanks a bunch. I'm all set."

Officer Coleman said, "Check," and turned to leave.

Before a second of his hefty steps found the floor, Nelson hobbled up. "Maybe I'll limp along with you. Might be healthy to stretch the leg. And to leave this solitary room for a bit."

John Arthur sat in one of the shellacked wooden booths at Gary's bar, directly under an antique framed print advertising the bitter Italian digestif Fernet-Branca, their eagle-on-the-world graphic over the phrase *Aperitivo Digestivo Il Re Degli Amari*. Ainsley napped under the booth, head on his feet, popping up on the rare occasions the door opened into the bar's dimly lit Sunday late-afternoon quiet and every time Gary stopped by. It wasn't specifically a doggy bar, one of those watering holes designed to make the City's many dog owners extra welcome with outdoor seating and stacks of plastic water dishes, but John began making more regular stops after the last case, and Gary agreed that if not too busy, Ains could come along. He'd brought her by a few times, and it had worked out. Especially for Ainsley, as Gary was fond of locally made Causton Chews, a savory sausage snack stick that wasn't *too* spicey, and shared the odd nibble with her.

The bar was currently bereft of customers outside of John, his dog, and two twentysomething women in bike shorts and T-shirts on stools near the front window, full arm and leg sleeve tattoos visible like moveable artworks. The gray Retrospec road bikes they arrived on were tattooed themselves with a thick covering of stickers and locked to a bike rack outside. Both drank, John guessed by the color and glass, margaritas. *Not a bad choice on a sunny day mid-ride*, he thought, as Gary set another round in front of them before strolling the other direction, humming along to Bowie's "Life on Mars?" that was coming out at reasonable volume from speakers suspended in ceiling corners. The slender barman wiped the bar's top absentmindedly before hanging his towel at bar's end, heading out to the booths. As he approached, John felt Ains' tail wag wildly, knocking his ankles like he'd slipped off a boat into the propellers. Gripping a hand around her collar the moment she moved to vacate the booth's radius, he said quietly, "Not too far, Ains, he'll come this way."

"How pours the Sunday, John? Hunky-dory?" Gary squatted down to pet the dog and sneak her a bite of sausage, his head hovering near the table edge for a moment like a magician's assistant mid-trick.

"Not bad, Gary, thanks. You?"

"Perfect Sunday in my view. Not too frantic. Not too forlorn. What's your poison?"

"How's the Suburban Caroline Noisy Neighbors?"

"Proper German-style pilsner that one. Crisp finish. Bit of backbone. Clear as summer itself, or as it should be."

"Sounds great. Pint'll be perfect."

"Out in a jiffy. H20 for Ains?" Hearing her name, the dog popped up for a quick pet, and Gary happily obliged.

"If it's not a pain?"

"Not t'all." Gary made his way back to the L-shaped wooden bar. Waiting for his beer, John tapped his ancient phone with one finger, a modern mimicking of poor mechanical typists. The single-digit scrolling stopped as he began to read a Pat Brown bio piece in local rag *The New Order*, whose '40s-radio serial-esque tagline *Because The City Never Sleeps* made him grin no matter how many times he saw it. Only a paragraph in, Ainsley's moving and stretching alerted him that Gary had arrived.

"Jar of pils for you, John, enjoy." Gary set a coaster down, then the beer, its pale yellow color tempting and mirroring the golden in John's glasses. Then he set a down a white ceramic bowl of water in front of Ainsley, remaining as John took a first refreshing sip.

"Delicious," John praised. "Just what I needed. A beer that tastes of beer."

Gary noticed the article on John's phone, face up on the table, picture of Pat Brown front and center, his intense gaze like a hawk perched on a telephone pole near a rustling field. "Death of a vicar. And it a Sunday."

"'Never a dull moment in Broughton, it seems,'" John replied vaguely.

"Broughton? What's that, old sod?" Gary knew from personal recent acquaintance and Marlowe's stories about the John's tendency to tangent into a world of TV mysteries and detectives, most from the country of the barman's birth. Gary himself had a nostalgic fondness for many of the series floating into cocktail conversation, though not at John's level.

"Sorry. Mind was wandering. Right into *Midsomer*."

"As it's been known to."

"As I've been known to." John laughed, taking another deep drink "You'll know this, but if memory serves, didn't a vicar end up burned to death inside a straw man in one old episode?"

"Straw woman I believe. Let me think." He took another sip. "Yes, an episode actually called *The Straw Woman*. A second reverend also murdered. Three murders by burning? Thought to be spontaneous combustion, but Barnaby, John at this point, never goes for that. I may need to rewatch."

"Nasty way to go, burning. Give me drowning in a vat of this fine pils. Fair amount of TV vicars involved in mysteries, both sides."

"Definitely. There are the crime-solving vicars, like good-hearted Father Brown."

"Acted by the legendary Mark Williams."

"Indeed. And the Grantchester trio—first, chestnut-maned Sidney Chambers, then black-locked Will Davenport, followed by also black-locked Rishi Nair. All three hunky vicars *and* action-oriented crime solvers. Plus, a whole heavenly host of supporting vicars, naturally highlighted as if from above by the first appearance of the immortal Jane in *Murder at the Vicarage*, she being neighbor to the St. Mary Mead vicar Reverend Leonard Clement. And *then* the murdered and murderous walk-on clergy, like so many black-shirted penguins following each other into the afterlife. In each of the Morse-verse shows, a person of the cloth comes to a bad end—one American bishop I remember, one Catholic priest, one warden. To circle back to dear old Midsomer, that county has a handful or two, including one murdered in 1870 whose death resonates."

"As they do. Don't forget to take a breath there, Johnny, or a drink. That speech was stout as a sermon. Don't forget *Brother Cadfael*, either. A favorite of my mum's."

John toasted the air. "Derek Jacobi. One of the greats. Here's to him. My dad was a vicar. Not a murderous one."

"Was he now. Didn't realize."

"I suppose reverend would be correct, terminology-wise. Not COE but as close as you can get over here."

"Episcopalian?" Gary guessed.

"Got it in one. Dean of a cathedral for a spell, as well as a traveling reverend serving congregations across a few small Kansas counties. Passed away fifteen years ago. Never took notes up to give his sermons, went off the cuff. Probably influenced my tendency to ramble. Still, kept the parishioners on their toes."

"Fire and brimstone?"

"Not so much. Friendly, storytelling, supportive type. Used to use my high school sports teams as examples from the pulpit for whatever scripture he was extolling. Overcoming fourth and ten, virtues of prior practice when the clock ticks down, whatever sport, he'd work a story in."

Gary laughed. "Did he now?"

John laughed, taking another sip.

"Not to run a dodgy shift back round the wickets." Gary pointed at the phone. "Yesterday's incident occurred at a sporting event too. Baseball game. Kids. Gutted to hear it."

"I was there at the game," John admitted. "Randomly. Talked to our pal Marlowe."

"Another one? Arthur arrives, someone dies. Be back in a jiff. Duty and margaritas call." Gary headed bar-wards, giving a thumbs-up to the woman catching his eye as she tipped back her glass.

John wondered, was the genial bartender right? Did he have some murderous magnetic attraction? It was only two, had to be coincidence. He *had* been thinking about the recent death, how could he not? Repelled recognizing the reality, a man had died, John understood dwelling on it probably made him appear morbid. But he kept rewinding what he knew, what he saw, in his head, going over the list of suspects and the game, the innings watched. He felt he was missing something, like the detective in a show's first third before the braincells go from dim to brightness in the final act. Even if he wasn't a card-carrying detective, if he could align the picture in his mind, help Marlowe and team, that might help the family come to some sort of grips with the murder.

What happened in the earlier innings? Before deciding to come to the bar, he'd nearly dialed the station to see if Marlowe had returned and would ask one of the people at the game for him. But picturing himself telling the burly detective about how he'd seen enough shows to know those innings and those people were important, he heard Marlowe's voice growling in his head like some kind of mustached Greek oracle. "It's not TV John, it's real life." *To mangle Marple*, he thought, *I never mean to speak lightly of murder, hating to tempt fate*. Sometimes the words, references, and quotes just filled the air before he could stop them, like blood fills an open wound.

Gary arrived with a second pint as he finished the beer's heeltap.

"This might be a two-pint problem, Sherlock mate." Gary expertly set down the glass, not a drop creeping over the rim.

"He'd make short work of it. 'There is nothing in which deduction is so necessary as in religion.' I'd better leave deduction and solving of crimes to Marlowe and team." He sipped the new beer. "There *were* a few things about the scene, the moments before, bouncing around in my head like ice in a shaker."

"You'd find something suspicious in a saint's sock drawer."

"The case of the missing sock. An eternal problem. Unsolvable even by Sherlock."

"Then it's in the bin. Speaking of unsolvable, and baseball, the Seafarers game comes apace." Gary liked the other man, but didn't want to go too deeply in the case. It *was* a mellow Sunday. "Management seems a sandwich short of a picnic, though this year perhaps?"

"Perhaps. Better to watch a game on the field, win or lose, then sit talking tragedies. Sorry if I've gone on a bit. I had an overactive imagination as a kid, as one of the detective vicars said, and it never moved to underactive."

"Good bars serve all kinds. Even detectives who can't leave it at the door." Gary paused, squatted a third time to reach down and scratch Ainsley behind the right ear, then stood, fishing a retro remote the size of a hoagie out of his pocket. Pointing it at the twenty-four-inch television above the bar, he walked toward it pressing buttons. "Time for tele, then, and say goodbye to the singular Mr. David Bowie on the stereo. *He took it all too far, but boy could he play guitar.*"

6

Leaving the Browns' mansion looming over green grass, Marlow swung by the Chapter Creek Church, curving suburban streets turning into busier Golden West Drive for four blocks, then angling off onto another side street. And there it was, popping into view as if newly made. A big corner building dominating its neighbors. He didn't know if Detective Moven would still be conducting her Mike Ray interview, and certainly wouldn't interrupt. Stopping an interview midway was like pulling bread out of the proofing drawer too soon. But as he was close to the church, and as the victim was the titular head of it, taking it in felt smart.

Snailing his car to the street in front of the church, he saw Morven's shining black Honda Fit, a Bison logo Atoll Board Co. sticker in the window, and two marked police cars. Parking on a stretch of curb behind the former, he thought, *interesting space*, drawing out the first word like taffy. Once out of his car, propped against the hood, he took a long look at the building. The sun blazing down in a cloudless summer sky brought a level of heat most in the City would find a way to complain about, even fully knowing the rest of the country's temperatures soared higher. But it still felt warm, perceptions established by locality. He'd left his sports coat in the car and rolled the cuffs on his white shirt.

Not what pops into my mind when I think church, he realized, the Romanesque rose window in the Basilica of St. Francis in Assisi, which he had seen long ago and never forgotten, having arisen in his memories. Two churches, really, that Basilica, the upper and lower. He gave his head a shake like a distracted dog trying to forget a rabbit. There's a certain solidity here that probably provides comfort to those coming in. Takes all kinds. Didn't resonate with the picture they'd been given of the charismatic preaching pastor Pat, more subdued. Maybe that made it work, his personality providing dramatic touches? He certainly seemed to touch a lot of people; this wasn't a small space. Probably fit hundreds depending on layout. Should gander insider too. Starting to head in the direction of the church door, he slowed. *Now wait a minute, Marlowe,* he chided himself, *you just said you didn't want to bother Morven, and here you are bumbling in like a blind bear. Let her get on with it and get out of her way.* He paused in the middle of the sidewalk.

As if the slowing and his arms decreasing their swing worked an incantation, the church door swung open and Morven walked through it, noticing Marlowe.

"Detective Marlowe," she said, smiling. "This is a surprise."

"Sorry 'bout that, Detective. Was passing." He motioned his hand at the church as if introducing it. "Wanted to take the pulse of the place."

"I forgot how close the Browns' house is. What do you think of it?"

"Subdued. Quiet as—" He caught himself before saying *as the grave.* "As the high desert at night."

"I believe they cut normal Sunday activities short due to circumstances."

"Makes sense. Mike Ray in?"

"Yes, and his wife, Kristin."

"Helpful?" Realizing they remained in the middle of the sidewalk halfway to the church, he spoke before she could answer. "Hold that. Let's amble over to the car."

Marlowe propped on the side panel in front of the passenger door, and Morven leaned on the car beside him. For a moment, he expected to see John Arthur and Ainsley loping up, even as he knew the man's house was many miles north, as they once did in the past when the detectives were leaning nearly the same way on a car. It felt a moment the two would curiously show up for, asking questions, dropping British quotes, befuddling and enlightening the investigation.

"Kristin Ray." Morven shook him back to the actual scene.

He gave both directions a glance. "As we're alone, let's do a quick debrief."

"Great. I'm thinking, if okay, of trying to dial Nelson in. He looked pretty distraught about being bound to his desk."

Marlowe gave an affirmative head tilt and she fished her phone out of her pocket, ringing Nelson's desk phone, with no answer, then the younger detective's cell, with the same result. Both phones sat on the currently empty desk side by side, Nelson away on his snack search.

"No Nelson. He'll be sad to miss, but we can catch him up."

"Hope that busted leg didn't take him out to pasture." Marlowe grinned. "On to it."

Leaning on the car, sunshine illuminating the scene, they went over their respective interviews. Morven stepped off and paced while detailing salient points, arms swaying describing the interactions between the deacon and his wife, checking off imaginary numbers in the air as she went over the list of other potential suspects. Marlowe inclined against the car throughout like a bald, paunchy, mustached James Dean, continuing to do so even for his own retelling, which he kept short, not sidetracking into lawn theories. After finishing, they stood in silence before he spoke up.

"Heaps to take in, and no mistake, going be many gullies to ride down."

"Agreed. Time to head back to the station, check in with forensics, and Nelson."

"Yep." He stretched his arms. A ruby-red Miata zoomed into the church parking lot, squeaking brakes in need of a tune-up. Out popped a short woman, who began walking the sidewalk from lot to church door, first briskly, as if in a hurry, then pausing and gazing around before adopting a more leisurely stroll.

"Who might that be?" he wondered aloud.

"I think that's Nikola Cassian. Surprising to see her here after Mike Ray implying she no longer held church employment. Maybe a service soon?"

"Surprising indeed. Fortuitous, too. Up for an impromptu interview?"

"Always." She grinned with a hint of ferociousness, a leopard about to pounce on an unsuspecting antelope.

Leaving the car at a pace Marlowe might call too rapid, they soon came to the attention of Nikola, who gave them a toes-to-head curious glance, stopping before the building's door.

"Nikola Cassian?" Marlowe asked.

"Can I help you? The church isn't currently open to the public. And no reporters." She was firm, one hand on a hip sheathed in a form-fitting black skirt. The five silver buttons accenting each thigh reflected the bright pink of the silk blouse she wore, along with patent black ankle boots boasting stiletto heels, delicate gold watch on one arm, black plastic bangles and a beaded leather bracelet with gold beads on the other, and pearl earrings. Her long brown hair was cut straight across except for two blonde streaks framing a round face, full lips pursed in a don't-even-start attitude.

"City Police, ma'am." Something about her reminded Marlowe of a stern third-grade teacher, Mrs. Lu, who haunted his rare dreams of being late or unprepared in class, and who once told him his best outcome was probably cowboy, a prediction taken as high praise. "Investigating yesterday's incident. Time for a few questions? I'm Detective Marlowe, this is Detective Morven."

It was as if a director yelled *Action*. Nikola's face altered from stern to welcoming wide smile, eyes with a wink went from defensive cloudiness to almost glowing warmth. She moved closer to the police pair, at the same time reaching out, clasping one of Marlowe's plate-sized hands in one of her elegant and recently manicured ones, nails matching shirt pink for pink, slipping the other under his arm. Her hand, he noticed, was cool and dry.

"Detective, I apologize. Forgive me. If I'd known you were police, I wouldn't have been so rude. While I am devastated, dev-a-stat-ed"—she drew out the word, licking lips at the end—"by what happened yesterday, I am not so injured to not talk to you. Let's go inside, we can sit in the church and talk by ourselves." Somehow, she maneuvered Marlowe's hefty size around and had him walking toward the door before he even knew what had happened, as if she were a tugboat sneaking a ship out of port without the captain's knowledge.

Morven had a hard time resisting a visible eye roll, fighting the urge off. Nikola hadn't even given a nod in her direction while talking and then moving over and through the door, which might have shut in Morven's face if she hadn't been quick to catch it. Nikola, she decided, following in their wake, was definitely a man-talker. It was a phenomenon she'd run into many times in the past from both sides—man-talkers and woman-talkers. If a man-talker was chatting to two people of the opposite sex, whether coworkers or a couple or during a police interview, it was as if the female part of the duo didn't exist. Conversation, gestures, the entire focus solely on the male. Exactly opposite phenomenon with male woman-talkers, more prevalent perhaps, with a man meeting a mixed-gender pair and focusing like a laser on the female. But Morven wasn't shy, speeding up to ensure she was a part of the interview whether Nikola liked it or not.

Nikola breezily talked to Marlowe. "*Detective.* Classy ring to it. Let's skip the office, too stuffy. The church itself, that feels the wrong place for a cozy chat. There's a library, with couches, right up here."

Passing the office door on the right, Nikola choose instead a second door, also on the right. On the left, they'd passed multiple doors leading into the church proper. Opening the door, shooing Marlowe through, she followed close behind, nearly shutting a door in Morven's face for a second time. Nikola still had Marlowe by the elbow, moving him to a deep gingerbread-shaded leather loveseat. A matching one sat against a second wall, a round wooden table with metal chairs taking up the middle of the room, bookshelves containing mostly magazines and a few books on the third wall, and a small refrigerator in one corner. Marlowe lowered into a couch corner, Nikola smoothly sitting beside him, flattening skirt over legs as she sat, leaving just enough space between them to ensure Morven couldn't sit on the couch. Morven grabbed a chair from the table, pulling it close to the couch and pulling out her notebook.

"Detective." Even dwarfed by the man, Nikola patted his knee as if he was a child. "Not to dredge up a painful moment, but how I can help?"

"We're following up all lines of inquiry." Marlowe was dazed somewhat, like a bird who's flown into a window unexpectedly. "As you knew Pat Brown, you might be able to aid us."

She folded her hands together. "Ask me anything."

Morven spoke up. "Did you notice anything out of the ordinary at yesterday's game?"

Not looking at her, Nikola responded, "You mean besides my pastor dying?"

"Yes, before that," Morven dryly replied.

"Nope. Just a kid's baseball game. Not overly exciting. Very dull, actually." She blew on her nails.

Morven looked directly at Nikola, who was staring up at Marlowe. "Why did you go to the games, spend part of your weekend there, if they weren't exciting?"

"Why go?" The other woman seemed caught off guard. She was silent for a moment. "Support my employer, my friend and pastor, and his family, I suppose. They were sometimes fun. Sitting outside when the weather was nice. Miss Willums' sangria. Catching up with Drogo."

"We were told Pat Brown was no longer your employer, that he'd fired you and argued with you about it."

"What?" Nikola shot a venomous voice-raiser at Morven, the cloudy appearance descending over her eyes. "Who told you that?"

"Mike Ray, who we interviewed earlier," Marlowe replied.

Nikola's face changed into a calmness cool as an evening ocean breeze. "Mike's a kidder. I'm still church secretary. That's why I'm here. We can go ask him." She rose, noticed neither of the others moving, and sat back down.

"We'll do that in a minute." Marlowe was so settled into the couch, he wasn't sure he could move. "Double check. In the main, how was your relationship with Pat Brown?"

"Solid," she replied. "Energetic. Mutually agreeable. I've been here under him for many years, and working closely with him, I learned a lot."

"Can you think of anyone who might want to harm him?"

Nikola closed her eyes before speaking. "Not, not really. Was he murdered?"

"We are following multiple lines of inquiry, but treating his death as suspicious." Morven trotted out the line. "He got along with everyone, no issues?"

"Nothing violent." Nikola rapped the manicured nails of one hand on the couch, pink flittering against the leather. "He was a passionate man, and passion runs the blood hot." She gazed at Marlowe, who was studying the ceiling. "That passion drove the church but could rub parishioners and people the wrong way."

"Specific people?" Marlowe asked.

"No one I can think of, but if you give me your card, I can call you if anything pops up." Nikola smiled warmly.

"What do you mean," Morven cut in, "specifically when you say rub people the wrong way?"

Nikola angled her head at Morven while looking at Marlowe, as if saying telepathically, *what's she going on for?*, then replied, "Pat demanded a lot out of people, that they be an active part of the church, support it, and support the causes he and Mike supported."

"Support?"

"With their time, their energy, you know."

"Financially?" Morven wasn't letting her off easily, which Marlowe admired as he felt the deep seat of the couch pulling him in.

"That too. It's not cheap having a church this size; some people wanted in only partially, weren't a complete part of the family, and ended up leaving or not understanding the commitment. There's a small staff, but it's a big building. Everything costs."

"Are you and Mike the only other staff?" Marlowe asked.

She smiled carelessly. "Hard to believe, isn't it? But we are the only other paid staff. Certain followers help with the upkeep or this and that." For a moment the smiled rescinded. "We have had staff additions in the past. None now."

"Names?"

"Really, there was only one. Dan Jesse. Nice kid."

"He's not here currently?"

"Sadly, he passed away." Nikola stared down as she talked.

Morven tacked back to yesterday. "At any time yesterday did you feel ill?"

"Nope. I'm healthy." Nikola's voice purred.

"Notice anyone else attending showing ill effects?"

Nikola didn't look at Morven, but shook her head negative.

"You stopped by to talk to Pat Brown during the game, what did you talk about?"

"What?" Her temper flared momentarily. "Was someone spying on me?"

"No." Marlowe's hands made a calming-the-waves gesture. "Someone attending the game noticed, that's all."

"Who? You probably can't tell me. That's okay, sugar, I get it. Policing." She pouted her lips. "Yes, I stopped to talk to Pat. He didn't like his baseball watching interrupted, but he tended to be happy to see me."

"What did you talk about?"

"Nothing serious. I asked him if he needed more sangria, or a snack. That's it."

"Did he?"

"Did he what? Oh, I see." Nikola hmm'd her lips. "Did he need more sangria? Yes. Now, much as I'd like to chat, I do need to work." She put a hand on Marlowe's shoulder, pushing herself off the couch.

Marlowe didn't move, both because getting off the couch was going to take some wrangling and because he wasn't finished asking questions. "You mentioned Drogo. Concession worker?"

Propping herself on the couch's arm, she stretched her legs, pointing her toes. "He's my second cousin. Third cousin. Nephew. It's complicated."

"How so?"

"His mom married my uncle, divorced, then married my cousin. Then, after another divorce, married my much older brother. We're related. Drogo is silly but enjoyable. Not a bright star, but a reliable one. Slow to start but there in a pinch." She reached out as if to pinch Marlowe, but Morven spoke, causing her to stop part way.

"Does Drogo attend the church?"

"Not his wave to surf, as he'd say. Or not his precious. He's hilarious. He liked to call Pat Sauron, from the movie with the hibbits. Hibbits? Hobbits."

"He didn't like Pat Brown?" Morven knew enough about *Lord of the Rings* to know who Sauron was.

"Drogo likes everyone. It was a joke, Detective." Nikola covered the last word with syrupy scorn. "Pat could be prickly with people like Drogo, non-driven people. Can we be off? Let me give you a hand." She reached out to Marlowe, grasping his hand and giving a playful pull. He didn't budge for a moment, then pushing while she pulled, escaped the couch. Morven had already walked out of the door. Nikola held his hand for a long moment before he, as gracefully as possible, pulled his to his side.

In the hallway, Morven looked in one of the doors to the church, the size of one the City's bigger school auditoriums. "Quite a space."

Nikola sidestepped her, shutting the door. "It suits our needs. Many people attend, three services a week. Plus charity events, talks, fundraisers, concerts, weddings—"

"Funerals?" Marlowe asked.

Nikola paused. "Not too many. Let's not dwell, you two are busy, I'm busy."

"Wait," Morven said. "Mind if we double-check with Mike on your current employment status?"

Nikola huffed, sighed, caught Marlowe's eye, patted his arm. "Sure.

I'm still employed. I wouldn't lie to you, Detective Marlowe." She gave the office door a loud knock. "Better let them know we're coming in." She gave another booming knock, opened the door a sliver. "Mike, it's Nikola. The detectives are here."

The first room was empty, but the door to Mike's office opened as they entered. Mike walked through, buttoning his top button. "Nikola, how nice. A ray of sunshine. Detective Morven, had we not finished? And you are?"

"Detective Marlowe. One quick follow-up question. Is Miss Cassian still employed as secretary?"

"She is indeed. As Moses said, it's the courage to continue that counts, and we couldn't continue without our little rock of courage."

Did Moses say that, Marlowe thought, as Morven jumped in.

"Earlier, Mr. Ray, you said it was decided that Miss Cassian's time here had come to a close."

Mike folded his hands. "I believe I said *Pat* and Nikola decided that. But Pat is no longer with us, to our eternal sadness. And Nikola is remaining, where she belongs."

Nikola's smile neared smirk.

"Detectives," Mike continued, "we have used enough of your time, which waits for no one." He gestured to the door, which the detectives used to exit. Nikola closed it quickly, but not before sneaking a wink at a retreating Marlowe.

Back at Marlowe's car, he thought out loud. "That was curious. Helpful? Miss Cassian was nice enough, but could be prickly as a cactus I'll bet."

Morven nodded absently. "The duck-feather pillows. It feels as if the ducks are still in them." She noticed Marlowe's confusion. "Sorry, Detective. My mother used to say that. An item that appears soft but isn't. I'd put her on the suspect list."

"Can't rule out any calf in the herd. Let's get back, start the machines, hash it out."

Marlowe and Morven arrived back at the station simultaneously, even managing parking spots on the same floor. He'd nearly detoured to hunt for a croissant and coffee combo, but realized this late any day, much less Sunday, the City's bakeries were closed. And while he might discover a lingering pastry in the deep reaches of a baked-goods shelf, it wouldn't be worth the hunt. It was a shame bakeries closed early, but probably best for his waistline.

Strolling into the mostly quiet room housing the detective's desks, they saw Nelson pacing figure eights, head down, notebook in hand, whispering to himself. The board had more documents, Post-its, photos, a collage emanating out from a Pat Brown photo in the middle like the eye in the middle of an investigative hurricane.

"Very focused," Marlowe rumbled low to Morven as they walked closer.

"Nelson doesn't do anything halfway," she replied with a grin. "He's barely limping. He'll have solved the case before we even make it to him."

Nelson's eye caught them as a flicker of movement, like a bee flying around your head, causing him to jump back, wince, wave, and bellow at a volume that could have been heard back in the parking garage, "Detective Marlowe, Detective Morven, barely saw you come in."

"Nelson." Morven seemed pushed back by Nelson's amplification. "Volume?"

"What? Volume?" He pulled earbud headphones from his ears. "Sorry, forgot I had in these in. Was focusing while stretching the leg. Which is nearly better. You know, light exercise can be very helpful in a tight muscle. Not overdoing it. A little walking, loosen it up."

"Check." Marlowe moved over to the board, while Morven shucked her coat onto a desk chair, noticing Nelson's screen.

"Nelson," she said curiously, "are you watching Miss Marple?"

"Listening, actually." He set the headphones down, moving to view where the show had paused on his screen, listing the title.

Marlowe gave a questioning glance over his shoulder, eyebrows raised.

"It's good, sir. I felt it might help round out the investigation, keep me focused while I was taking my stretching walk. Mr. Arthur was here earlier and—"

"Was he?" Marlowe's eyebrows went up again.

"I'll give you the full report, but first, when he was here, I had a brainstorm. You know, he has some helpful insights, and learned his investigative technique from watching British mysteries. I decided to make a list of the shows he's mentioned and watch, or listen as the situation allows, to them. See if they provide a few different angles. I felt I'd start with the Belgian, Poirot, but wasn't sure if there'd be too much foreign language usage, so went to his detective sibling, as they were both written by Agatha Christie, you know?"

Marlowe nodded slowly as the younger man raced on.

"Miss Marple. Dove right in. Don't worry, it's not taking me out of my lane workwise, but great background."

Marlowe took a deep breath, as if he were a parent whose child had announced they were trying out for an unheard of sports team. "Uh-huh. Not sure two British mystery buffs are needed, but okey dokey." He turned back to the board.

Morven switched on her own computer and sat, as Nelson sat beside her. "Learn anything during your Marple marathon?"

"Not a marathon, Morven, so far. And yes. She's quite elderly for one. And they drink a lot of tea."

"About the case?"

"'It's very dangerous to believe people. I never have for years.'" Nelson's English accent sounded more 18th-century urchin than small-town spinster. "She said that. I knew that, and that people are only like 50% likely to tell the truth, less to police, but it was nice to have her underline the point."

Before Morven answered, Marlowe broke in. "Right," he said firmly. "Lots to chew on. You've had a day, Nelson, as have we. Conference time."

"Yes, sir." Nelson jumped up, sat back down. "Still twinges." Back up more slowly, he and Morven came to the board.

She took it in, saying, "Where to begin?"

"The perfect question, almost." Marlowe hesitated. "But first–"

"Coffee?" Morven groaned.

"Yep."

"I can get it," she volunteered, beginning to head out.

"Thanks Morven. Large for me." Marlowe made a drinking motion.

"Check. Nelson, bring you a cup?"

"'I shouldn't drink it if you did.'" he replied, scruffy English accent back like a cough, then dropped as he continued while Morven got farther away, not turning back. "Wait, that was Miss Marple, Detective Morven. I'd take a club soda if that's okay. Can you hear me still hear me?"

They'd spent the last hour and a half catching up, roaming between desks and board, beginning to input interview notes, stopping to stand up again to pace and make points and tell interview tales. Marlowe took many deep breaths from his olive wood bowl and draughts of coffee (currently on a third cup). He'd been surprised for a moment, then completely unsurprised, that John Arthur had stopped by and made Nelson go through the innings twice. He didn't get exactly what John was driving at, but felt the man probably had a point about knowing what happened on every level the minutes before the murder.

After the catchup, he knew they were accumulating information, lots of it. But were they getting anywhere? He felt lost, searching for the proper trail out of the brush and thicket of information. If a case could be considered a full day, once said and done, they remained only in early morning. Lots of hours ahead. Morven and Nelson's fingers tapped like ten woodpeckers on keys during the momentary lull in conversation.

Taking another deep breath, bowl held up to his nose, a glimpse of gnarled hundred-year-old olive trees on an impossibly green hillside floated through his mind.

"Enough," he said, putting the bowl down. "Back to reality. Nelson?"

Nelson paused in a rare instance saying nothing.

"You had an unexpected visitor, and call, so don't get your saddle out of joint if not, but any financial background wrangled from basic checks?"

"I did do some digging into the finances of those suspects, or witnesses, on the list. Not digging up dirt." He remembered his talk with Miss Willums. "What I could find out through internet searches. Some interesting stuff."

"Do tell."

"The church has been very successful, moving into bigger buildings but still holding on to the older locations, which is a good strategy. Did you know real estate prices have increased 82% over the last ten years in the City? The church's wealth has increased, too, as has our victim's, who makes both a six-figure salary and reported bonuses. There was a fairly in-depth piece about it in the local paper a year ago. Mr. Ray seems to be doing well too. There have been rumors of financial malfeasance, a few stories, shot down quickly as hatchet jobs by the church. Not that we want to delve into rumors *too* much, but sometimes where there's smoke, as the saying goes. Our other suspects, nothing jumps out. One note, Tom Toomey, who may have had an incident with the victim as Detective Morven found out, is quite a player in the local real estate scene, commercial side, and very wealthy, as well as politically connected. I'd say he is the most powerful person locally connected to the church, steadfast in his support, and the pastor vocally backed him in his, to this point failed, political campaigns." He stopped to breathe.

"Church business is booming." Marlowe scratched his bald head. "Important? Maybe?"

"We should have more reports from forensics tomorrow." Morven glanced at the date displayed under the institutional black metal clock on the wall. "And more interviews."

"That'll help. Glad we got what we got on a Sunday. Speaking of." Marlowe slipped into thought.

"Yes?"

"The point about the cup and the straw, and the lack of fingerprints."

"None besides the victim. Maybe that wasn't how the poison was delivered. Or the killer wore gloves, though you'd think someone would have noticed that on a summer day. It's not the 1940s; everyone knows about fingerprints, so not *too* surprising."

"True. On the other hand, you'd expect Mrs. Willums's fingerprints, perhaps, since she was dolling out the sangria. Or Drogo's, who may have supplied the cup and straw."

"Good points," Morven agreed. "Definitely questions for both. We don't have motive, but they seem suspects with means. Maybe opportunity."

"Maybe." Marlowe stood slowly. "Lots to discover. Lots to ask. Lots to . . ." he faded into silence. "Getting late. Even coffee can't fuel us all night." Walking over to the other desk, he covered the computer screens with his hands. "QT, you two. Tomorrow's gonna be quite a day. Detective Nelson, you have Mrs. Williams on for ten a.m.?"

Nelson affirmatively underlined the time. "Ten a.m. I can interview her alone, or we can duo. And it's *Miss* Willums."

"Ah. Let's see."

Morven stood, stretching arms above her head gracefully as a dancer. "I'll call Neville Maloney first thing. Drogo Oates second, set up interviews. Feels we need more from the bleacher group. Might be harder with Tom Toomey. Political."

"Thanks, Detective, and yeah, political indeed," Marlowe replied as Morven bent down making notes.

"Also, we keep backgrounding. Pushing forensics and pathology. It's murder, should be top of the list."

"Big day coming. Better knock off, rest up. You two skedaddle."

"Yes, sir." Nelson made to high-five Morven, who ignored him, grabbing her coat. Moving more gingerly, Nelson grabbed his, too, along with an athletic bag and keys.

    Marlowe waved them off. "Nelson, no gym. Rest that hoof."

    "Of course, sir," Nelson called back, heading toward the door.

    Turning back to the board, Marlowe mumbled, "Somebody saw something. We just need to burn the brush, scare out the rabbit."

7

Exiting the station, Marlowe set his compass pointing in the direction of Gary's. It neared nine thirty, the cloudless late summer sky a shade darker than indigo, streetlights and headlights cutting into night like their taller seaside relations cut into fog over rough waters. He'd stayed longer than expected staring at the board, thinking of his grandfather, who had been a police officer as well. Uniform his whole career, and who raised Marlowe with the help of numerous western-style sayings and words of campfire wisdom. What would he have made of the prosperous pastor victim and witnesses so far, not to mention the always-popping-up anglophile John Arthur? He'd probably have said an oblique phrase that younger Marlowe would have laughed at, discounted, then later come to realize had hit the nail on the proverbial. Something like: "Always have a long look at what you're about to eat. Not so as to know exactly what it is now, but so you get a better idea of what it was." A phrase his grandfather dropped on Marlowe multiple times, never while eating. He chuckled, turning back toward the station garage. If his mind was delving deep into the past, skipping Sunday night at the bar was safest. No need to add an extra layer of haze to the morning, as much as he loved a well-made drink and chatting with the English bartender.

He woke bright-eyed Monday morning, having even skipped watching *Gunsmoke* or other TV the night before, keeping his evening bare of all but a few chapters of Dickens's *Dombey and Son*, having rekindled a high school fondness for the legendary English writer during the last case where John Arthur had shown up. John had his mystery addiction, but turns out also didn't go many months without reading Dickens or contemporaries George Elliott and Anthony Trollope. Talking about them with the older man pushed Marlowe into picking up a few Dickens novels, *Dombey* his current bedside book. He loved it, with one caveat: the feisty, messy, loyal dog in it, Diogenes, with his *rough, old, loving, foolish head* made Marlowe want a dog when reading every page Dickens's fictional dog featured within. This then had him wandering to dogs he'd had, dogs he'd like to have, and dogs he knew, including John's dog, the tail-waggiest Ainsley. But a single cop's life didn't match up well with dog ownership. This morning, for example, he'd tumbled out of bed and skedaddled out without time for dog walking, or even dog petting. He even omitted stopping at Sampson's Sips for a cappuccino. No dawdling.

At the station, the detective room hummed like a hive in summer, police officers, plainclothes and uniform, walking quickly, talking quickly, typing quickly. A morning marine layer sloughed in off the sound surrounding the City, so the building—and the buildings nearby—appeared to be wearing misty peacoats. Marlowe's own sports coat, removed while navigating to his deck, was a favored sandy brown, matching slacks, shirt wrinkled but bright white, suspenders blue with tiny old-fashioned glasses in gold on them. While early as blackbirds, Morven and Nelson had beaten him, laptops up, headphones on, fingers flying on keys.

Heck, he thought, *they'd probably each already done some intense type of workout he'd never heard of, if Nelson's leg allowed him.*

"Top of the morning, team," he said, voice like a foghorn above the room's din and echo.

Both pushed back from desks, removed headphones, and replied, as if synchronized. "Detective Marlowe."

"It is I." He made a mock bow.

Nelson cheered, clapping his hands. "That sounds Shakespearean, Marlowe. To be, or not to be, solving this case today."

Morven, more subdued, backed an inch from the bubbly Nelson. "Good morning. Hope you had a good night."

"Passably fine, thanks. You two? Nicely bright and bushytailed, I see."

Nelson beat Morven to a reply. "Great night, sir, did some stretching routines, soaked, and the leg feels nearly 100%. Even after a light morning Pilates workout. You know Pilates? Sort of a whole body stretch, strengthen, balance routine, bringing western and eastern exercise philosophies together. Very popular, too, nearly ten million people in the US do it. Not completely over the leg yet, but Pilates was the ideal exercise choice. I'm ready to get back in action."

Marlowe felt listening to Nelson was often like a workout. "Detective Morven, you pie-lot-ies?"

"Somewhat. Nelson convinced me to meet him at Luther's London gym this morning for the class. It was fun."

"Was it?" Marlowe took them off the exercise mat. "Hope so. And here, Monday. What's tricks?"

"We've heard from forensics and pathology. But only that there are no specific updates." Morven watched her screen as she talked. "Doctor Peterson said 'greatest scandal waits on greatest state,' whatever that might mean, when asked. Waiting for a fuller DNA picture, though forensics did call the bleacher and surrounding area 'like a playground for sharks,' which felt rather descriptive."

"Separating the wheat from the chaff day, sounds like." Marlowe leaned back in his chair, shoes on desk, causing the chair legs to creak.

"They also said we could return the victim's jewelry, phone, and items found on his person. Nothing to report outside of the ordinary. They asked if we wanted to hang on to the phone in case we get the okay to break in to it. I felt, thinking about the family, we could return it, recalling it if needed later."

"Makes sense."

"I've managed," Morven said, "to reach Mr. Maloney and set up an interview at his house at two. Nelson, you have Mrs. Williums on for ten a.m.?"

Nelson affirmatively underlined the time. "Ten a.m. I can interview her alone, or we can duo. And it's *Miss* Willums."

"Check. I have not reached Drogo Oates directly, but left two messages to call."

"Perfect. Solid work." Marlowe rocked back dangerously. He had broken an identical chair in the past, but couldn't help himself. "Let's see. Double up, keep them guessing? Feels right as rain. Both of you interview Willums here, then head to the Maloney house. Miss Willums seems mighty fond of you, Nelson. Probably best not to leave you alone."

Nelson's blush covered his face all at once, as if the older detective had waved a wand. "Any words of advice?" he asked.

"Follow Morven's lead," Marlowe replied, then decided he should give a little more advice. "Let's see, Miss Willums is a talker, so let her talk. As for Mr. Maloney, we know he and the victim weren't simpatico, let's say. Used to be coach. Ruffled feathers. Be wary. Don't go in unless you know the way out. Walking and questioning."

"And be sure," Nelson skipped in, "to have an I-POA in order. And OBSE."

"OBSE?"

"Observational eye." Nelson eyed the room like a professor searching for students goofing off in a lecture hall's back row. "Watch for little details. Maybe have a separate page for them in your notebook ready. A strategy of my own devices."

"Okay, Nelson. Detective Morven?" Marlowe rubbed his head, leaning back again, chair wobbling. "Anything else you can think of?"

"Keep an *observational* eye on email, see how quickly we can jump on reports. I think we should try and corral Tom Toomey for an interview. He might be hard to schedule. Marlowe, that one I think is yours."

"Yep," he agreed, nodding.

"You'll get the drop on him." Nelson went into a crouch, poking his head around as if sneaking up on a suspect.

"Fingers crossed. Might as well wade in. If either of you are heading thataway." Marlowe motioned generally east.

"I'll grab you a cuppa—cuppa coffee that is—no problem." Nelson rose as Marlowe picked up his phone and began to dial, all four legs back on the ground.

"Thanks, Nelson. Maybe two?"

Nelson laughed, nodded, then trotted off with a barely noticeable limp showing every few steps. Marlowe began talking on the phone, one finger pushing the bowl on his desk an inch north, then back an inch south as his one-sided conversation filled their back corner.

"Hello. Detective Marlowe, City police. I'm trying to reach Tom Toomey. Transfer me to his PA? Um, surely. Detective Marlowe, City police. This is important. Yes, very. I gather that Mr. Toomey is busy as a saloonkeeper on payday, but still. Yes, important. Meet him where? Wear a hard hat. I don't? Oh, okay. Anytime between 10 and 10:30. Ma'am, I won't be late. Thank you, ma'am. You too."

He hung up. "Whew. She was cantankerous as Dirty Sally."

Morven stopped typing. "Dirty who?"

"*Gunsmoke*. Before your time. Mr. Toomey has quite a minder."

"Big business. Not a lot of time for us, I suppose. I feel like Nelson unveiling this random fact, but did you know Mr. Toomey was once listed as the thirteenth-richest person in the greater City area?"

"Do tell. Rhetorical. No need to tell more."

"Did you get the interview set up? Sounds like the same time as Miss Willums?"

"More or less. But no time to meet at home, office, or here. Gotta go on site."

"On site?" Morven had visions of Indiana Jones and an archeological dig.

"Apartment construction. Up north. Not far past Mr. Arthur's."

"That hard hat makes sense. An amazing amount of construction going on up there, and in the City in general."

Nelson appeared behind them, coffee cup in each hand. "Did you know that construction rates of housing and housing units is up 19% year over year?"

They shook their heads, both at the fact and that he'd managed the coffee so quickly.

"Oh yeah, it's still exploding even with the boom over the last ten years. More and more cranes and—"

"Nelson?"

"Yes, Detective Marlowe?"

"Maybe point our ponies to solving this murder today, solve the construction conundrum later down the road a bit?"

"That makes sense. We are the detectives."

"We are, at that."

As Morven and Nelson opened the door to the station's lobby, they heard an expansive braying laugh emanating from the far side of the room like the air from a human balloon. It came from a tallish, curvy woman wearing a mid-length, umber-colored skirt with a wide black belt and bronze buckle, and a ribbed, tight, dusty-orange sweater. He shoulder-length strawberry-blonde curly hair bounced as she continued laughing, saying to the slightly cowed older gentleman in a pork pie hat—they were the only two currently in the room—next to her, "And they asked me to come to the station. My first time, can you believe it?"

Before he sputtered out a response, the two detectives were there. Morven spoke up. "Miss Willums?"

Ash's laugh trailed off, though her broad face sparkled mirthfully from big blue eyes to rosy cheeks down to smiling mouth. "Ash here. You," she said rapidly, in mock sternness, to Nelson, "must be the charming Detective Nelson that I had such an interesting conversation with on the phone yesterday. I felt our little *tête-à-tête* might be us two?" She dropped him an exaggerated wink. "But for me, the more the merrier. It's a party. I *am* Ash Willums. And you, miss, are?" She reached a hand Morven's direction.

Morven, caught up in the wave of energy, reached out and shook Ash's hand vigorously, noticing it was surprisingly muscular. "I'm Detective Morven, thank you for coming down."

"Yes, Miss Willums, thank you for aiding us with our inquiries. If we could walk this way?" Nelson gestured to the door, which Ash began walking toward, the two detectives closely behind.

"Aiding with inquires," Ash said, "so formal."

Passing through the door, Morven glided in front and into the hall, Nelson and Ash in a jumble, shoulder to shoulder, behind.

Ash continued talking as they walked. "Are you putting me under the bright lights? The third degree? The *fourth* degree? I'm glad I put on extra deodorant." Her laugh bounced like unexpected sunshine off the plain gray walls.

"Just a few questions, Miss Willums, in here." Morven opened the door to interview room six, one of the smaller rooms: a table, four metal chairs, and walls the color of grass that hadn't been watered in far too long.

"Lovely." Ash's flow barely paused as they entered and sat at the table, she on one side, the two detectives on the other. "Who did the decorating, Hannibal Lecter? This room might make me confess to any number of crimes." Another broad wink, like a clown at a child's birthday party after a joke. "I kid. I'm as innocent as untouched snow. Maybe not *that* innocent. Detective Morven, you know what I mean, though for this curly haired cherub we'll keep it PG-13. Now you've booked me here, start the grilling, coppers."

"Miss Willums," Nelson said decorously. "We haven't booked you. We just have a few questions. First, would you like coffee, water, or tea—" "Or me?" She broke in, chuckling full blast. "I kid, Nellie. No beverage. Unless it's the MVB."

"MVB?" Morven asked.

"Um," Nelson said as Ash laughed again. "Most valuable beverage. A term I used when referring to Miss Willums's sangria, which appeared to be very popular at the game."

Morven tried, and was nearly successful, to not roll her eyes.

"It *is* very popular." Ash shook her curls. "Everyone tells me they love it. We should have a pitcher. Even detectives like it."

"Speaking of the game." Morven wanted to get back on track. "Did you notice anything out of the ordinary there, before or after the incident involving Pat Brown?"

"The incident. You mean murder? Pastor Pat put out of the way, on into eternity."

"We are currently treating his death as suspicious, yes. But?"

"Back to the question. Very serious, Detective. Unlike this bashful one. Let me wrack the old brainpan. Nothing out of the ordinary stands out. Sangria sipping, watching the kids—my son, Hugo, is on the team, for my sins. The pastor sitting in his almighty bubble doling out instructions and proclamations like the king of all. No, I can't recall anything different than any other baseball Saturday." She seemed, for once, quiet in thought.

Morven followed up. "You don't seem overly fond of Pat Brown."
"The pastor? Not to speak badly of the dead, but we weren't the closest bottles on the shelf. Believe he found me too boisterous, if you can imagine? Between us, I cheer loud, and maybe it's not to everyone's taste; everyone with a stick up their ass. He used to give me the shut-up stare, and finally told me to 'act with more decorum.' At a baseball game. I told him where to shove it, and then, magically, Hugo was benched. So, not overly fond. None of that kept him from the sangria, but he'd have his little Nikola or the Mrs. or stick bug Mike or whoever was around get him a cup. It *is* good sangria."

Nelson recovered from the winks enough to speak up. "So he's not your favorite person. Can you think of anyone else who might have been rubbed the wrong way by Pat Brown?"

"Rubbed the wrong way?" Ash leaned back, hair touching the far bottom of the chair back. "Rubbed the wrong way? You are a clever duck, Nellie. I never rub the wrong way, my fit young friend. From what I know, pinchy Pastor didn't either."

"Could you elaborate?" Morven asked.

"I'm not one to gossip, mind you, but preachy Pat wasn't an angel." She leaned in conspiratorially. "I caught him and Nikola *in flagrante delicious*, if you know what I mean, clutched together tighter than Cher's pants in a hidden nook near the playground bathrooms, of all places. Wasn't the first time, either. I may like sangria, but I see things."

"Were they having an affair?" Morven tried to pin her down.

Ash tapped a finger on her nose, opening eyes wide. "Pastor may have preached fidelity, but I don't believe he practiced it. That's all I'm saying. I don't want to be telling tales. If I did, I'd say that Patty boy wasn't as loved as you might believe from the teeth-gnashing and wailing I'd bet was going on in the church yesterday, as much as the last church tragedy. Heck, I heard him and the big man, Tom Toomey—who tended to turn down my sangria, jerk face—arguing that very day. And," she kept going at a rush, "he and poor Nev, the less said the better. Then there was Nelson's favorite, Jack Page, sunshine streaking out of his pores but cursing the pastor when his back was turned. And the way the pastor treated his wife, he'd shame a goose."

Finally, Ash noticed Morven had raised her hand in a stop gesture and stopped the flow as the detective spoke. "This is all very helpful, Miss Willums. What were Mr. Brown and Mr. Toomey arguing about?"

"I'm no eavesdropper." They both shook their heads as Ash looked them straight in the eyes, one after another. "To be clear. But between us chickens, I heard Tommy boy in the parking lot say something like, 'You owe me,' and Pat reply, 'There is nothing to owe—don't forget your next campaign.' Then I bounced up. Heated, darlings."

"And Jack?"

"Jack? He likes my sangria, too, and me, but who doesn't, right

Nellie?" She coyly cocked her head. "Not sure what he and Pat scrapped about. If they did. Maybe it was churchy, but daggers from Jack toward him when he thought no one was looking."

"What about Mr. Maloney?" Nelson was blushing, but pushing past it to get involved.

"You're a little pink pumpkin, Nellie. Nev used to be coach of the team. Life's ambition, I'd say. Then something—I don't know what, so no pumping me—happened between him and Pat and poof." She smacked her hands together in a ferocious clap. "Nev is coach no longer." Glancing at her watch exaggeratedly, Ash made a slight Marilyn Monroe pout. "Much as I'd like to stay and chew the fat from dawn until midnight, Ash may have to duck out soon. It's not playtime, but worktime."

"One or two more quick questions—"

"Then I'll be free to go?"

Morven, in time-honored police practice, ignored her question. "You mentioned Mike Ray. Did he and Pat get along well to your knowledge?"

"None closer. Making out like brotherly bandits. I mean, word on the street is that they've wrung every penny out of that church for themselves. Never proven. They are, or were, too sly for that. An old con like Mike and a charismatic man like Pat Brown? Smooth setup. Our Mike was an accountant before a dabbling deacon, after all." She crouched up out of her chair.

"One more moment," Morven said, as she and Nelson also stood. "You mentioned a tragedy at the church."

"Did I? I'm not a churchgoer, but there was a young man who committed suicide there. Sad case. Not the pastor's fault, I'm sure. Just a depressed kid. Stuck with me, having a kid of my own."

They walked toward the door, and as Morven began to open it, Nelson slipped up, keeping it nearly shut, saying, "Did you notice anyone else having ill effects from the—at the game?"

Ash grabbed his arm in mock distress. "Were you going to say from the sangria? For shame, my poppet. The sangria was fine. I should know."

she winked. "I not only made it, but drank my fair share of it. And no one seemed to be suffering at the game. Except the pastor."

Marlowe was well hungry by the time he reached the construction site in the City's northwestern neighborhoods where he was to meet businessman-wannabe-politician Tom Toomey. And wishing he'd upped his coffee level with at least one more cup before leaving the station. His plan had been to follow 15th Avenue NW once crossing the Corston bridge, one of three city bridges over Lake Pearl and the easiest route from downtown north, which would take him fairly rapidly where he needed to go. Rapidly enough that he could stop at lemon-yellow painted Lynley's Café. Not the snazziest café in the City, and probably not perched atop any Top Ten list on well-commented-upon websites, but it was cozy, the cappuccinos constructed via an ideal balance of foam to espresso, and croissants flakey and fresh as if in France. He'd developed an affection for it and its slightly deaf owner, Nate, when working a past case—the one John Arthur called the Case of the Nine Neighbors; a name burred into Marlowe's mind no matter how hard he tried to shake it loose. But when pulling into the snug café parking lot, a lime-green paper sign stuck to the door with black electrical tape said in thick black block lettering: "Closed for the Week. Sorry, friends." Both Marlowe and his stomach nearly cried at the sight. He hadn't time to circle around tracking down another spot, and after rifling fruitlessly in his glove box for a forgotten bag of chips or misplaced granola bar, resigned himself to failure as he left his car, donning his suit coat.

He'd parked on the street as the construction site didn't have dedicated parking outside of five already-full spaces near a corrugated metal, crocodile-colored, mobile-home style building set in the most northerly corner of the building lot. A lot that appeared to be another massive apartment complex in mid-build, concrete supports viewable like ancient dinosaur bones uncovered. The City had settled into a population explosion whose blast extended fifteen years, construction cranes and sites omnipresent. *Rare,* Marlowe thought, *to see a person of Mr. Toomey's status on an actual site as opposed to in the office. Maybe a hands-on corporate head? Maybe I don't know as much about the building business, either? I suppose I should be wearing a hard hat?* He stopped the self-questioning climbing the three steps leading to the door into the building, figuring he shouldn't just wander onto the site, hammering, sawing, and other industrial noises ringing out in the air. A sign on the door—*must be my morning for handprinted signs*—said in scrawled marker: No Admittance Except on Toomey Construction Business. *I might count,* Marlowe decided, twisting the knob and opening the door.

Inside, he saw an office that seemed to have welcomed a small whirlwind. Filing cabinets jammed in corners, scattered folders on top, maps taped to walls, metal chairs flat and in stacks, and two metal desks, on top of which were papers held down by hammers, alongside staplers and dispersed pens and pencils. At one desk sat two men in dusty, hickory-colored Carhartt pants, long-sleeved black shirts covered by orange vests, orange hard hats like half pumpkins on the table in front of them. Looming over them stood a rawboned African American man with gray flattop hair, slightly taller than Marlowe, wearing a casual tan linen suit that radiated dollar signs and a cream-colored shirt. The latter had been talking, something about "timing" Marlowe hadn't made out, when he'd walked in, causing the trio to stare his way, before one of the seated men spoke.

"Can we help you? Construction site employees only here."

Flipping out his badge, Marlowe replied, "Detective Marlowe, City police. I'm supposed to meet Mr. Tom Toomey."

The suited man cleared his throat. "I nearly forgot." He glanced at the seated men. "About that business with Pastor Pat Brown, I'm sure you read about it?" They nodded half-heartedly. It wasn't good to disagree with the boss. "One moment. I'll meet you outside." The request came as a statement not to be ignored, as Tom pointed directly at the door.

Marlowe gave a short nod. Exiting, he heard Tom talking as he left.

"Keep hitting those figures. Think outside the box. I don't need excuses."

He waited five minutes, patience beginning to expire, when Tom finally came out. "Business waits for no man, officer," he said, walking past Marlowe in the direction of a black Escalade polished mirror bright. He didn't lean completely on the SUV, but tilted slightly against the driver's door. "I can give you five. Make sure we're on the same page. I'm a big fan of our local officers, you know. More than those so-called city servants currently in office. The police chief and I have even hit the links together. She's got a fine backswing."

"Sure." Marlowe never liked hearing about the chief. Less said, the better. "I have a few questions about Pat Brown, but won't pen up too much of your time."

"Fine. ASAP might be new for some, but it's my normal pace. This City of ours won't stand still, and I can't either."

"How well did you know Pat Brown?"

"I'm a long-time supporter of his church and mission. He was a good man, good pastor. I consider myself one too. God and I, both builders."

"Can you think of anyone who might want to harm him?"

"Harm? Is his death suspicious? I try not to drink the Kool-Aid and think every death some murderous plot, that there's a murderer around every corner. Though crime is rampant."

A phrase John Arthur once said popped into Marlowe's mind, altered to fit the current situation. *Sir, a man has been murdered at a baseball game. Therefore, it follows there must be a murderer.* He didn't feel Tom would think kindly of his mind wandering. "We are treating it as suspicious, yes. Anyone?"

"Harm Pastor Pat? Hard to believe." He rubbed fingers through his hair, scratched his head, glanced at his watch, to Marlowe's eye a Rolex. "My advice? Hit the low-hanging fruit. Anti-religious zealots. In business, you use your time wisely to make money. I'd expect using your time wisely to make arrests is the same idea. Maybe spending time here isn't as profitable."

"Did you often attend little league baseball games with him?"

"I'm a big supporter of many causes, including kids' sports. Played football myself." He left it at that.

"You know Mike Ray as well?"

"Deacon Mike? Sure. Fine man. Diverse background. Knows how to break down silos, get granular. All in the name of doing good work."

"Break down silos?" The phrase appealed to Marlowe's country side, but he wasn't sure what the man meant.

Tom gave him an exasperated look. "I don't mean corn. Let's say his door was always open."

"You talked to him a lot at the game? And in general?"

Tom nodded, saying nothing.

"See anything peculiar?"

"At the game? Just baseball. Which can be a lot like business. Be a team player, drive it forward, step up to the plate. One minute more, Detective. Literally."

Marlowe fought the urge to walk away. "You were seen arguing with Pat Brown. Mind telling me what that was about?"

" Arguing?" Tom paused. "Don't recall any arguments. Discussions, sure, about church and charity. Strong leaders discuss. Disagree. Come to consensus. It's called synergy. Can I get back to beautifying our city? Should I call my lawyer? Or the chief? This interview is at an end."

Marlowe knew further questioning would only annoy him and not get anything more out of the man. He'd need to bring him in. But for someone of Tom's standing, he'd need a higher-up okay before demanding that. "That's fine, Mr. Toomey. For now." And anyway, he was hungry.

Pulling his car back onto 15th heading south, Marlowe's frustration at the interview and Toomey's dismissiveness nearly made him run a red light into heavy traffic, grumbling like Scrooge under his breath. *He'd actually brought up the chief? And synergy? What did that even mean?* Continuing to grumble, he randomly turned onto a side street to avoid traffic. Or, it seemed random at first, before he realized he was heading in the direction of John Arthur's house. *Well, it's come to that,* he thought. *I'm bringing in the consulting detective. And his dog.* Somehow, the idea made him smile, which morphed into laughing out loud, a small stream suddenly expanding into a rushing river unexpectedly. By the time he pulled up in front of the cottage-style white house with gray trim and blindingly bright-yellow front door, the laughter reached a fortissimo that John, who happened to be watering some late-summer daffodils in the front yard, heard even with the car doors closed.

Wiping his eyes, Marlowe shook off the laugh attack, opened the door, took off his sports coat (he'd forgotten when getting in earlier), and walked up the five short concrete-and-stone steps leading from sidewalk to yard.

Before getting there, John called out, "What's funny, Detective? You almost checked the curb."

Marlowe noticed the blind down on the window closest to that yellow door being pushed up by Ainsley's nose, which then alternatingly smudged against the window and backed off to allow her to bark. "Honestly, Mr. Arthur, John, the opposite of funny. Annoying job moment got to me. Realized it was silly. How goes the irrigating?"

John, noticing he still had the hose on soaking the ground between them, reached around a bush to twist off the spigot. "Oops. Better get your wellies on."

It begins. Marlowe smiled. John's usage of terms more at home in England could be maddening, but was such a part of the older man, he'd gotten used to it.

"Detective Marlowe," John continued, "back in the neighborhood. Not another murder my way?"

"Nope. Just nearby on an interview. Thought I'd check in." Ainsley's barking was higher-pitched than you'd expect from a sixty-five pounder, as if a much smaller dog was trapped inside.

"Always glad to see you. Sorry I missed you when stopping at the station. Hope Detective Nelson passed on the notes? I've been mulling the case, you know."

"Hard to imagine."

"You're joking, I see. You know, not to sound too Poirot-ish, I have my own order and methods, even when not involved in a case. Though partially involved, me being there. It was very odd to be near another murder, but then Poirot and Marple, anywhere they went it was a murder. They probably stopped being invited places for fear of it. I haven't gotten to that level. Yet."

"Looks like lawn and mud more than order and method, at the moment. But," he went on, before John could start, "Nelson did mention you stopping. And the game notes. Interesting."

John repeated the word, a dramatic pause between syllables. "In-ter-est-ing. Okay to ask who you were interviewing?"

Marlowe didn't like to talk about cases to civilians, but something about John made it seem less of a problem, or partially so. He knew John was lonely and liked nothing better than talking. He liked, and trusted, the older man, too, after the last case. And he wanted to breathe out the remaining remnants of the frustrating interview, stuck in his craw like corn in teeth. "Tom Toomey. Not the most . . . enlightening, let's say."

"Local business tycoon and aiming-to-be politician. That's a high roller to try and roll information out of. A bright star in the City firmament."

"Indeed. Surprised you didn't say he was guilty."

John's questioning glance flipped the normal state of their chats, as usually it was his tangential observations throwing Marlowe off.

"Your theory. What was it? BTO?"

John's short chortle caused Ainsley to momentarily stop barking. "BTO? No '70s bands, or no *actual* '70s bands show up in the British mystery TV canon which birthed that theory, and a few others of mine.

Strangely, there are a number of episodes with bands *made up* for the story being told, including in *Lewis*, and a *Midsommer*. I digress. You are referring to, ironically perhaps, BST."

"Got it in one. Thereabouts."

"Biggest star theory. Where the guest star in an episodic British mystery series who you recognize first when watching a *particular* episode inevitably did it. The best-known actor is the killer, to put it another way. And Tom Toomey is the best-known suspect, or person of interest as police say, which equals him being our murderer. But the BST theory is often turned on its head nowadays, to throw viewers off the track, where the main guest star *isn't* the killer, or where the show's lead is. It's a jumble in order to modernize, like post-modern architecture. I was watching a show last night, *Van de Valk*, the new version, not the old version, starring Marc Warren as the titular hero and Amsterdammer–it's in English–police detective, and remembered the first time I'd seen it, when I said *he did it* out loud the instant he arrived on the small screen. Because I recognized him from a host of other shows where usually he'd been a proper villain—*Life on Mars* to the *Musketeers* to *Jonathan Strange*. Biggest star, villainous look, and then I realized he was the police detective in charge. Topsy-turvy. BST is only one theory, as you might . . ." The tailless sentence faded, as he'd noticed Marlowe's grin. "Right. I go on and on. Back to Toomey. A suspect?"

"We are–"

"Conducting multiple lines of inquiry?"

"Again, got it in one."

"'It's my impression, sir, that senior officers are rarely so direct.'" Noticing Marlowe's eyebrows rise, he said, "Sorry, I was–"

He was interrupted by a shrill beeping nose coming from inside, as if a miniature bomb was about to explode.

8

"That's the oven going off. Have a moment to come in? Ains will be overjoyed, but you've survived her enthusiasm before. We can talk baseball and Mr. Brown." He motioned Marlowe up the stairs.

Upon opening the door, Marlowe was indeed nearly bowled over by the dog. John swerved around the canine cyclone, grabbing her collar and tugging her backward into the house, the beeping continuing, accompanying his running commentary like a drum. "Ainsley, sit. Ains-ley, give the detective some room. Come on, Ains, back, sit." She finally sat.

Marlowe made his way in, her tail on the ground pushing the living room rug into wrinkles. "Ainsley." Marlowe reached out one hand, which she delightedly began licking and sniffing. "Not much to smell today."

"She smells today, yesterday, last week, sometimes I believe even the future." The beeping was insistent from the kitchen. "Mind if I go attend to the stove?"

Waving John off, Marlowe moved to sit on a big blue couch along one wall, above which hung a massive print of all three books of Dante's *Divine Comedy*, tiny Italian words in three heavenly pillars. Ains jumped up beside him, sniffing his ear as he petted her. The room looked much as it had the last time he'd been there: a pie safe with TV on top on another wall, another couch, plants and an orange metal cabinet, lamps in needed of dusting, and bookshelves overflowing with books of all kinds—old, new, Dickens, Christie, history, cooking, cocktails—as well as ephemera ranging from a comical ceramic Hamlet to paintings of rottweilers to an array of tiny colorful houses, to pictures of John with a dark-haired woman sporting mirrored sunglasses.

A pastry-vegetal smell wafted in from the kitchen like a dream. Still hungry, Marlowe's stomach growled as John came around the corner.
"In the mood for an early lunch?" he asked. Both Marlowe and Ainsley, currently napping beside him, looked attentively up. John sat on the other couch. "No guarantees on the taste, but happy to share the provisions if you can stick around for a few."

"Why not. Meant to stop by Lynley's Café for a bite, but it was shuttered up temporarily."

"Nate, the owner, and his old band, If Wishes Were Horses, are on a mini reunion tour. Which means here, Portland, Eugene, and Olympia. About lunch. As a warning, I was watching old episodes of *Pie in the Sky* this morning. Catching Marlowe's eye, slightly expanded as if in readiness, he changed directions in his speech. "You don't know *Pie in the Sky*?"

"Nope."

"Is that possible? Late '90s somewhat police-ish show. Starred the memorable, may he rest in peace, Richard Griffiths. Rotund actor with expressively small eyes. He can say more about a case with those eyes than a speech. But you know *him*. He was in Harry Potter, boy wizard. Played the dastardly uncle."

Marlowe's slow dip of the mustache was his only reply.

"Griffiths plays Detective Inspector Henry Crabbe wonderfully in *Pie in the Sky*, a man who wants to retire from the force to be a chef. At the last moment in episode one, he ends up letting the criminal get away, an act which his boss, the delightfully slightly dishonorable Assistant Chief Constable Fisher, uses to make Henry keep working with the police. But at the same time, he chefs it up at a restaurant he owns with his wife, the marvelous Maggie Sneed, called *Pie in the Sky* serving refined, I'd guess you'd say, British classics. Amazing combination of criminals and cooking. You've really never seen it?"

"Nope."

"Put it on your list."

"Not sure I have a list. But John?" Marlowe wasn't getting less hungry.

"Yes?" John's reply was distracted as he gazed in his mind into the show's made-up town of Middleton.

"What's this have to do with lunch?"

"Here's the connection. Henry Crabbe whips up delicious English-style savory pies, most famously a steak and kidney pie with oysters and anchovies. All that pie chat made me hungry for a savory pie. I'm no chef Crabbe, but my veggie pie hopefully isn't too bad. It's probably cooled enough. I'll grab us a few slices. To drink? 'Why not live dangerously, have a glass of sweet wine?'" John's English accent, adopted for quotes, returned like a bad curtain call for the last sentence.

"Water is dandy." Marlowe wasn't sure John was kidding on the wine, but he avoided drinks during work. And avoided sweet wine in general.

"Mind grabbing the TV trays?" John pointed to two wooden contraptions topped with riotous pink, red, and blue flower wallpaper leftovers. Managing to move Ainsley without waking her, Marlowe unfolded the trays, placing one in front of each couch, easing his bulk behind one as if parking a battleship, causing Ainsley to raise an eyelid while keeping the eye closed.

John walked in, balancing plates with the skill of an ex-waiter, a still slightly steaming slice of veggie pie on each. Placing them on the trays, he announced, "Back with the water," as Marlowe and Ainsley, her head all of a sudden miraculously at shoulder level, eyed the slice in front of them. *Intriguing*, he thought, guessing the dog thought so too. Looked like a cabbage, onion, carrot combo, topped with cheese and hard-boiled egg. On a regular pie crust. He picked up his fork, gave the slice a short jab. It held together. Smelled edible. Ainsley's nose inched nearer the pie, like a pickpocket about to grab a wallet.

"Ainsley," John called, dropping off a glass of water. "Leave the pie alone." The dog moved back a half-inch, giving a pitiful look. "Poor starving dog." He laughed, grabbing a handful of dog treats out of a ceramic jar the color of old parchment. Ainsley arched off the couch to sit in front of John, a position she kept as they ate, while he periodically gave her treats from a pile made next to his plate.

"Dig in." John lifted his fork Marlowe's direction before taking a bite.

Marlowe curiously eyed the veggie pie again. *Well, I am hungry*, he decided, managing to balance a forkful that got vegetables, cheese, egg, and crust on it. Chewing that first bite, the pie's rich mingling of milky tangy mozzarella, hearty veggies cooked in copious butter, rich egg, and slightly flakey crust, set him salivating. He took deep drink of water after. Delicious.

"John," Marlowe said seriously, angling his fork for a second big bite, "not bad."

"You're a man of infinite wisdom. But, really, thanks. Glad the crust turned out. I'm no baker. That was Marlene—she was genius with flour and stand mixers. Still look over my shoulder every time I try baking to ask her unanswered questions when things like pastry start to go awry."

Marlowe glanced at the picture of John and the woman, his wife who'd passed away years back in a car accident. "She taught you well."

"It's not bad. But we can't talk pie forever. Back to the case."

Marlowe would have tried to slow down case talk, but he'd taken such a big bite what came out was a low groan and a little finger-sized piece of carrot, luckily landing on his plate.

"Glad you agree." John tossed Ainsley a treat. "You too, Ainsley. I'm taking it for granted you haven't solved Pastor Brown's murder."

Marlowe's mouth was full, again. This time, to be safe, he just nodded, figuring that wasn't giving away too much.

"Check." John tilted his head. "There are still things about that day I know I'm missing. Tragic day. I should stop mulling it over, but it should be solved too. Not that I don't have faith in the police." Another nod from Marlowe. "But as I was there…" John took a small bite, chewing distractedly. "Starts with the victim, I've learned that much. What have you learned?"

Marlowe swallowed. "John, you know—"

"This is real life not TV?"

"Was gonna say, you know I can't go into the case too deeply."

"Sure. But maybe I can ask questions?" Ceasing and desisting wasn't John's strong suit. "Answer them or not up to you?"

"Fine." Marlowe knew John would ask anyway. "Though questioning's usually the police's purview."

"'You never ask innocent questions; it has to do with being a policeman all these years.'"

"Your pie-making detective?"

"DI Crabbe it is. To Pat Brown. Any known enemies?"

"Nope," Marlowe said, maneuvering a remaining piece of egg onto his fork. "Toomey suggested anti-religious zealots."

"Did he? Makes me think he's a BST example after all. Financial trouble? Follow the money is a nearly a TV trope, as much as detective-y characters suggest it."

"Nope. Seems Pat Brown felt a rich man and a camel might have decent odds."

"Could be something there—money jealousy, financial dealings gone wrong. Maybe Mike Ray was involved. They worked together, and his eyes have a 'strange mixture of complete stupidity and naked ambition' as Crabbe says about his backyard rooster, named Fisher after his boss. Or Tom Toomey, money magnate? Two people used to making money can equal strife if combined in a manner not equally beneficial." John stared at Marlowe, who was studiously watching his plate while chewing. For all his rambling demeanor, the older man noticed every movement or facial tick as if a falcon hunting rabbits.

"Nothing? Moving on. He was a charismatic man. *Cherchez la femme?*" John's French accent was worse than his English one, as if he'd run the words through a Parisian meat grinder. "That cliché holds up in certain shows. Perhaps Kristin Ray, leading to jealous motives via Mike. Though by appearance, Mike 'couldn't knock the skin off a rice pudding,' as Thursday said."

Thursday? Marlowe wasn't even going to ask. Instead, he focused on spearing a last cabbage leaf corner as John went on.

"Not Miss Willums, she'd be chalk and cheese with Brown. Could be a screen. Gilly Maloney? Wait a minute. Hold up. Of course, alluring secretary Nikola Cassien."

Resist as he might, Marlowe's eye brow twitched upward.

'Ah-ha. Nikola you're admitting?"

"No. Well, I wouldn't be surprised. But, John, between us."

"Naturally. Motive then for the wife, and Nikola, and even a third person, perhaps in love with the latter. Or another mistress. Because if he strayed once, he probably strayed twice." He saw Marlowe trying to embed a few final crumbs between the tines of his fork. "Another slice?"

"Thanks, I would. When a kid, I was told to not worry about biting off more than you can chew; your mouth is probably a whole lot bigger than you think. Not always the best advice. Here, might be."

"Grandfather?" John asked, leaving the room with Marlowe's plate.

"Yep."

Once a second slice was in place, Marlowe and his fork didn't waste time, as John went on. "Poison, correct?"

Marlowe nodded mid-chew.

"Which means someone nearby, on the bleachers or close. No one else affected. How'd I miss seeing it? I was right there."

Ainsley hopped onto John's couch for easier access to treats, and he petted her behind her floppy brindled ears distractedly. Marlowe reached the half-slice point of his second piece, momentarily considered abandoning the rest, but like an accomplished hiker tired midway up the mountain, realized giving up would be cowardly.

John, plate empty, took a sip of water before speaking. "Did Detective Nelson, or you, ever track the on-field action in the first two innings?"

Marlowe shook his head, unlodging a piece of pastry stuck in his mustache, sending it onto the couch. John didn't notice, eyes stuck staring at the ceiling as if the players in the game were reenacting it there. Ainsley, however, tracked the crumb as it fell.

"I can probably find out if you don't. What I need," John mused while petting, "is to revisit the scene. Classic maneuver, happens nearly every show. Back to the scene, whether old mill, cheese factory, country house, or rum distillery. Reignite the little grey cells. Poirot never left his flat in *The Disappearance of Mr. Davenheim*, but I'm no Belgian. Back–" The tink of fork hitting plate interrupted him. "Detective, second slice defeated. Nicely done. More?"

"That'll do. Tasty stuff."

"Thank you. Happy to assist the police in their inquiries, so to speak. Now–"

"Now," Marlowe interrupted, "I should get back to it. Hate to eat and run."

"Not in the least. 'Someone's dead, you find out who killed them through a process of steady but gently ceaseless prodding.'"

"More *Pie in the Sky*-ing?" As Marlowe stood, Ains leapt off the couch, scooping up the pie crust crumb, then licking his hands, his shoes, the couch, then the floor like a self-propelled vacuum.

"Ains is on the case for crumbs." John chuckled. "And no, not the robustly resolute detective inspector from the fictional Westershire. Back to *Van der Valk*."

Marlowe stretched his arms above his head, hoping to feel less full. "Right. BST turned lead detective. Amsterdam. He end up villainous or valiant?"

"Valiant, if cranky. Layered, to give him his due. Weighed down by backstory, as so many detectives are. Persistent, luckily, as multiple murders in need of solving descended in that first episode. You always have to watch out."

"For?" Marlowe moved toward the door, hand on the handle.

"What kind of show." John raised his fingers, counting off. "One murder show, two murder show, three murder show . . ."

Morven parked on the street directly in front of the Maloney house in the City's southeast Bury neighborhood. Nelson perched in the passenger seat, admitting earlier that driving caused his tweaked leg pain. The moment she turned off the car, he launched out of the door, slipping slightly on recently watered grass, catching himself before falling, twisting against the door mid-slip, a splinter of sharp metal somehow ripping a miniscule patch out of the right thigh of his impeccably pressed trousers.

He gasped. "What?"

"Nelson, are you okay?" Morven bounded around the car to help.

"I tore my pants." Nelson rubbed the pant leg, as if to weld it back together by force.

"Did you cut yourself? Or reinjury your leg?"

As if in disbelief, he repeated, "I tore my pants." Then added, sadly, "They're Dudgeons brand slacks."

"Did you hit your head? Are you in shock?"

Nelson came partially out of his stupor. "What? Shock? No. But—"

"Leg okay? Not bleeding?"

He let go of the torn pant leg, gazing at it like it was an ill favorite pet. "No blood." He gave a front kick. "Leg is fine enough. Just the pants."

"Can you recover and do this interview?"

"Yes. I can. One must rise to the occasion, overcome obstacles, and find that extra reservoir of strength if you want to cross the finish line. That's what they said at the police academy. Maybe," he considered with a final soft brush of his leg, "I'll stand on your right to avoid it being that evident."

"Sounds good, Nelson. United front. Let me know if you need a break." She walked purposefully toward the Maloney house, Neville trotting until exactly in lockstep on her right, legs moving in military unison. The sidewalk up to the house was double the normal sidewalk width, leading to a pewter-colored bungalow. Bright-white trim popped on windows and wooden pillars framed a ten-foot square cement front porch, in the center of which a caramel-shaded front door stood, a wreath of multi-colored flowers hanging on it. The front yard was greener than most this time of year, well-watered as evidenced by the patch Nelson had slipped on. A tall oak tree dominated the lawn's north side, big branches reaching over the house as if protecting it. On one branch, a ball hung suspended by an attached rope.

As their feet hit the bottom of three steps leading to the porch, the door opened. A boy with curly hair that matched the front door's color walked through backward, wearing green shorts, a white tee, and carrying a baseball bat. He appeared around ten years old, the picture of youthful summer.

"Mom, Dad," he yelled into the house, not noticing the officers. "Going to go take swings." Finishing the last word, he saw them. "Oh. You're here." Turning back, he yelled once more toward the interior. "Cops are here!" Then he walked past them, saying nothing else. Stopping in the yard, he eyed the ball hanging from the tree before taking a swing at it with the bat.

Morven half-turned as he walked by, thought about questioning him, then shrugged. She could do it later if needed. Nelson stood ramrod straight the whole time. The door remained open, but she rang the bell anyway, saying, "Hello? Mr. and Mrs. Maloney? It's—"

"Detective Morven?" A man sidled around the door's edge. Wearing faded jeans and an ocean-blue T-shirt with "Feel the Reign" in faded apple, Neville Maloney was a scant 5'7". Sandy-blond hair receded from his forehead like a wave, cautious blue eyes questioning above features that seemed muted somehow, as if brushed on when wet.

"Yes," Morven replied, "I am. This is Detective Nelson. Thank you for speaking to us."

Neville gave a brief head tilt.

Morven waited a moment for more of a reply, but when none was forthcoming, continued. "We have a few questions as we move forward with our inquiries into the death of Pat Brown. Would you rather speak here on the porch or inside?"

Neville took a cautious breath. "Inside would be best." He stepped back, allowing entry into a living room boasting two well-used, deep-seated comfy couches whose coloring matched the faded parts of Neville's jeans, each holding an array of multi-colored pillows, plants and lamps on stands beside couches. A sixty-five-inch TV was mounted to one tan wall, gray cabinet underneath with remotes on top and assorted shoes beneath like it was a footwear burrow. Family portraits on either side of the TV showed Neville, the boy outside, and a woman with curly hair matching the boy's and a pretty thin face.

Entering the room, Nelson sped up and slowed down as they walked in an effort to keep his right leg aligned with Morven's left the whole time, causing their entrance to have an oddly staged effect. Neville didn't seem to notice, moving to slightly straighten one of the photos near the TV, pointing as he did at the closest couch.

The detectives sat awkwardly, Nelson circling Morven before seating to align his ripped pant leg with the right arm of the couch. When finally seated, he pushed himself close to the arm, leg against it lightly, then tighter. She gave him a decided "What the?" look, and he shrugged, saying, "Pants," in a stage whisper as Neville sat on the other couch. If he noticed how closely huddled up onto the couch's right side Nelson was, as if his leg and the couch arm were magnets, he didn't say anything about it.

Both Morven and Nelson removed small notebooks and pens from their suit coat pockets. Morven began with the basics. "To get started, Mr. Maloney, what is your occupation?"

Neville picked up a *War and Peace*-sized pillow the color of sunflower petals, gently tossing it between his hands, watching it go from one to the other. "I manage and co-own a sports equipment store, All the World's a Sport."

"Mrs. Maloney?"

"Account Manager for Charles Dean Marketing."

"How long have you known Pat Brown?"

He stopping tossing the pillow for a moment, then resumed, still looking at it. "Nearly six years. I began as a volunteer baseball coach for the Reign. It's his team, more or less. He sponsors it. Burton, his son, played on it then, his other son, Gerry, plays now."

"Are you a member of Chapter Creek Church?"

"No. That wasn't a requirement for coaching."

"Your son plays for the team currently?"

Neville took his eyes off the pillow, dropping it. While reaching down, the words came out gently. "Yes. Usually shortstop, batting second or third. Dougie loves baseball."

"You no longer coach?"

"Not since last year."

Nelson spoke up. "Because you and Pat Brown had a falling out?"

Neville stopped tossing the pillow, still looking at it as if it were a talisman. "Somebody told you that? Gossips. Not a falling out. A disagreement."

"What about?" Morven asked.

"It may seem, may be, silly in hindsight. His son, Burton, displayed what I thought was bad sportsmanship, tripping a player. I said he had to sit out a game. Pat disagreed. Vocally."

"Then asked you stop being coach of the team?"

"Mike Ray did the actual asking. 'Best for all, be a team player, inspirational quote.' Finally, after much haranguing, I gave in."

Nelson leaned in. "But you loved coaching. That had to make you angry."

Neville clenched the pillow. "Of course I was angry. Coaching my own son playing baseball was my dream. I loved it. Yes, I was angry."

Nelson continued, lowering his voice a half pitch without realizing it, hoping he could take Neville off guard and solve this case right now. That would impress the other detectives. "Angry enough to kill Pat Brown?"

Surprising both the detectives, Neville said, "Yes. I think in the moment, I might have been. But I didn't. You have to fight for what's right, and you have to fight against that line of thought. It helped that Gilly pulled me back. I cooled off and realized there would be more coaching chances, and that Pat didn't deserve my anger." He'd glanced away from the pillow during his speech in the direction of Morven, but over her shoulder, as if he were watching a baseball game happening out on the front window, a double play taking place that caught his attention and held it even as he talked.

"You still kept going to the games?" Morven's questioned caused Neville to glance at her momentarily, before switching his gaze again over her shoulder.

"I wouldn't miss Dougie playing baseball. It'd take more than Pat Brown for that." For a moment, Neville gripped the pillow so hard it appeared about to burst, but he unclenched his hands, began tossing it once more.

"Specific to last Saturday's game, the day of the incident, did you notice anything out of the ordinary?"

"It was a tense game, not the case for the Reign much this year, as they haven't been close in many."

Did an echo of a smile play around Neville's face as he said that? Morven thought so.

"Dougie asked me about his swing mid-game through the fence. I felt they were on the comeback trail, about to put one in the W column, when Pat had his attack. Awful for the kids."

"Anyone in the bleachers you were sitting on acting oddly?"

"Not that I remember. That sangria was being poured. Don't know how people can drink it and keep up on the game."

"Did you keep a close eye on the game?" Nelson asked.

"Always," Neville replied, pillow going left to right. "Even if I'm not coach anymore, watching the game, and Dougie, is why I'm there. I wouldn't want to miss a single hit, catch, out, or run crossing home plate. I keep score in the traditional way for every game, have a book going back to when I started coaching. You have to be a keen observer not to miss a moment."

Nelson's head was down, note-taking, but he nodded in agreement with the man's sports passion.

Morven waded back in, taking the talk from the field back to the victim. "Did you have more arguments with Pat?"

"Small things. Being a coach is sometimes instinctive, sometimes intuitive, and very active. I probably raised my voice with coaching opinions—"

The woman from the picture walked into the room wearing a long-sleeved white T-shirt and jeans, hands in green gloves with dirt on them, and cut him off. "As you should, since that pompous ass shouldn't have stopped you coaching to begin with."

"Mrs. Maloney?" Morven stood, Nelson a beat behind.

The woman nodded, taking off gloves, setting them on the side table, trailing dirt, before sitting, a move the detectives mirrored.

Morven continuing as she sat. "Pompous ass? You mean Pat Brown?"

"Yes, I do. I hate to talk bad about someone who's recently died, but I wasn't a fan."

"Gilly." Neville put a hand on her knee.

"Best to be straightforward. I didn't wish him harm, or, not too much, but he wasn't a nice person. Pastor that he is. Or was."

"Did you have issues with him outside of coaching?"

Gilly brushed stray dirt off her sleeve. "I avoided him. The whole flock of the church gaggling geese. They acted as if butter wouldn't melt. I didn't enjoy Pat's or their company. I was nice at the games because Dougie likes playing and the other kids on the team, and Nev liked coaching, until the coaching *coup d'état*. After that, I went to games and cheered the kids and tried to ignore the rest—the drama, the hangers-on, the mealymouthed Mike Rays, Jack Pages, and especially the playmaking Pat Brown. Ash is fun, if loud. And Mrs. Brown tried to be friendly. I felt for her. She seemed poorly used. Like a car that hauls the rubbish but then is parked in back when company arrives."

"Notice anything last Saturday?"

"Pat Brown dying in horrible pain?"

She didn't grin, but Morven caught a stray twinkle in her eyes, like a star shining a last time in the morning light.

"Nothing outside of that, but you know about that piece of lu—" She started to say luck but managed to change before finishing the click of to the ck, "news."

"What do you mean, playmaking Pat Brown?"

"Slip of the tongue. I don't want to be a carrion crow." Gilly ruffled Nev's hair as he stared out the window. "It felt like Pat, for a married minister, was somewhat on the prowl, as the saying was. Not just for women, but opportunities, if that isn't confusing as mud. My take, you understand. Tainted probably by our baseball experience." She wrapped Neville's knee with her knuckles. "I need coach here in the garden. Have you asked the questions you wanted to ask?"

"For today." Morven stood gracefully, Nelson with a half-twist so his right leg faced the wall. "We may have more questions later. If you think of anything having to do with the incident last Saturday, please let us know." She handed Gilly a card.

Outside, Dougie was still taking swings at the hanging ball, too deep in focus to notice the two.

Back in the car, Nelson thumbed out the window toward the Maloney's as if attempting to hitchhike. "Not much overly interesting in there. He does take his little league baseball very seriously, which I can understand. Did you know that baseball participation is up 14% worldwide after a few years of decline? Solid numbers."

"I did not know. She seemed perhaps more aggravated about our victim than he. But he was intense, in a quiet way, and had his moments. Admitting you wanted to kill someone? Either you're playing a devious game or very honest."

"I felt he was probably more of the empathetic, players coach than the yelling, hard-driving coach type. But saying to us he wanted to murder the victim as a devious game? That's a smart idea, Detective. He seems very into games. I guess 'there's always an explanation for everything.'"

"Agreed." She noticed a hint of an English accent at the end, surfacing as if a very Cockney fish out of American water. "Was that line you or John Arthur?"

"Miss Marple," he admitted. "Via Mr. Arthur, if I'm honest. I started watching after talking to him."

"Honesty is the best policy. And dishonesty the second best, as my trainer Sergeant Mitchell used to say when putting himself in the position of a criminal. Let's head back to the station. Get our notes in."

"Well, yes. But?"

"Yes, Nelson?" She swerved neatly around a poorly parked truck with Armstrong's Strong Painters on it.

"Could we swing by my apartment so I can pick up a fresh suit? Being honest again, this tear would be too embarrassing."

"I think we can make time for that."

Marlowe met Morven and Nelson at the office, where they caught each other up on the various interviews and began inputting notes into computers. *Policing: 25% legwork, 75% sit on your back side work*, Marlowe often thought, knowing it wasn't categorically true. The case was starting to take shape, but amorphous still in his mind, like water being poured, but not into a vessel that would give it final form. Pat Brown's background, interactions with others, demeanor, finances, painted a picture that shouted *pastor* less and less with each interview to all of the detectives. It wasn't the profession, or avocation, that made the person. The suspect list wasn't narrowing, either, nor was it coming into sharp focus, more like when you hadn't turned the f-stops on a camera lens diagram to the right spot. *I've muddled more opaque metaphors than a bad poet,* Marlowe thought, walking out of the station.

They'd worked for hours, hoping to hear more from the scientists, but no luck on that front. First thing tomorrow was the latest update. Chewing over carved in stone facts, they realized there weren't enough. Some person at the baseball game had to have seen something, something specific having to do with the poisoning of Pat Brown. But even the reliably keen-eyed and overly happy to weigh in Mr. Arthur hadn't provided that spark of specificity to help "pin down the perp," a phrase Nelson coined during their talk, which made him happy enough to repeat it multiple times, as if a police parrot. Once a fourth time using the phrase occurred, Marlowe nearly mentioned the fact he'd noticed Nelson's suit changed from the morning's blue to one the color of old Cognac to throw him off his pin down the perp track. That thought was how he knew time was getting late, because the suit story was one he felt he could skip. So, he'd ended the day's investigative travails, like a boxing referee ending a fight in which one competitor couldn't see straight. Sadly, they were that competitor tonight.

The clear evening sky waltzed blue elegantly into a black dotted by streaks of streetlights. Another beautiful late summer day. Tomorrow, the sun rises again in the east, even for us in the west. Better to call it off, come at it with clear vision. *If that's such a strong plan, why am I heading down to Gary's*, he asked himself, deciding that occasionally you needed to shake off the day before quitting it, and one of the best places to change your outlook was an inviting bar. He argued the point internally and, before he knew it, was removing his sports coat, draping it over his favorite stool. The bar was surprisingly bouncy, three-quarters full with Monday evening revelers, The Clash's "I Fought the Law and the Law Won" on the stereo. Not today, Joe, not today.

Gary whizzed through the crowd, ducking near tables for orders, picking up empties, setting down full drinks, giving Marlowe a few more minutes to weigh the case. Maybe I should revisit the scene as John suggested? Maybe talk to Miss Willums myself, dive deeper into her gossip reservoir? Maybe cajole Tom Toomey into the station for a thorough talk? Definitely need Mike Ray downtown. The deacon knew miles more than he'd yet given up. Putting him in front of one of the two-way mirrors in a depressing station interview room would dampen even his brightly reverent quotational nature, pry out secrets hidden like rattlers under rocks, secrets important to the case. *How* the murder happened had eluded; no one so far had noticed anything amiss at the game. The why, the motive behind it, was as important, and learning more from Mike could be key. Someone hated Pat Brown enough to kill him. Could be money, could be revenge, could be passion. First thing tomorrow, time to put the verbal spurs to Mike Ray, find out what the motive might be.

"Kit." Gary's voice raised him out of his introspection. "All right? Manic Monday here. Those Bangles weren't bonkers. No time for a chinwag. What's today's tipple?"

Marlowe looked guilty. "Haven't gotten that far."

"Beastly day, eh? You need brightening. Bubbles. Spritz?"

The idea of the Italian Aperol, prosecco, soda classic, and current worldwide liquid phenom, was like a light at the end of a particularly stuffy tunnel. "Perfect. Par for the course, of course."

"You're a charmer, boyo." The bartender hadn't finished the last word before beginning to put the drink together and, before many more seconds passed, placed it in front of Marlowe, saying, "I recall when one had to cozy a bottle of Aperol into the suitcase after every Italian hols as it wasn't available stateside. Not many years ago. A change for the better. Back to the battle of Trafalgar."

Gary filled a patron's pint at the wooden bar's opposite end as Marlowe took a first sip: graceful as spring sunshine, effervescent as a cloud's kiss, citrus balancing like dawn and the babiest of bitter tastes peaking beneath the surface. Took you from one place to another faster than a horse. He sighed with the second sip, remembering the introductory Aperol spritz he'd had in Florence, years ago the afternoon after seeing Botticelli's *Primavera* for the first time.

He'd had two, plus a short glass of grappa, twin to one Gary sipped standing in front of him during a calmer moment, every drinker occupied with a drink as if by beverage magic. They talked over the Seafarers' chance to continue an end of summer winning streak—"One as rare as a rooster with socks," Marlowe said—to make a September playoff push that *actually* ended up in the playoffs, then talked about the differences between baseball and cricket, the latter sport one Marlowe couldn't get a handle on even after Gary'd slow-walked him through the rules multiple times. When Marlowe began extolling the cuteness of Sally Field in the late-60s TV show *Cricket*, a cuteness driving him to cherish his thirteen-year-old's crush on her, Gary reminded him the show was *Gidget*, not Cricket, transitioning into both wishing they'd taken up surfing when younger, when boasting more hair to shake the water out of when putting the boards up. At that point, Gary realized *many* glasses needed refilling and started pulling pints with one hand, pulling bottles for drink-making off shelves with the other, as if navigating a very tipsy Enterprise. Marlowe left soon after, the case, like the evening, gliding clean out of his mind.

Until the phone woke him at six the next morning, a tired voice saying a second dead body had been found at the same Hettie Patty baseball field.

9

Marlowe rousted himself rapidly after getting the call about the body and called Morven. She picked him up by 6:45, driving a police-issue Regatta-blue Taurus, wearing a trim tailored suit that matched the car in color so closely somewhere a designer smiled in their sleep. The suit, along with her white shirt, were immaculately pressed. Was she ironing when Marlowe made the call? Shucking his sports coat onto the seat back, he slid into the car as she smoothly pulled out into morning traffic and started talking.

"Good morning. Another victim at the same baseball field?"

He nodded a reply, still shaking off yesterday's rust.

"Two bodies discovered at the same field? It has to be related. Or I suppose it could be a copycat." She seemed to Marlowe amazingly alert for the time of day. "The number of murderers who kill twice over a period of days isn't very high, or not as high as people believe." Making a number of turns in silence, passing a bakery truck painted like a loaf of bread, she accelerated onto Highway 6 North. "And early in the morning. At this time in summer, with sunrise nearing six, more people are up earlier, taking advantage of it. But still, another body at the same baseball diamond. Hard to believe."

Marlowe gazed out the window at a sky already heartbreakingly blue, accented by rays of sunshine and slashes of morning shadow from downtown apartment buildings. Ragged rooftop lines wavered up and down before skyline broke to show an expanse of reflective water as they traveled over the Jones bridge and the ship canal cutting downtown off from the northerly neighborhoods. *Like a painting of the perfect blue sky by Perugino*, he mused, remembering an Italian artist whose paintings he'd seen, mind wandering as it often did when half awake. A single small gathering of clouds visible only in the rearview, way deep in the southwest, touched a small band of dark night not yet slipped over horizon. "You, ain't been blue . . ." he hummed, leaning big bald head back on the headrest, blue baseball cap with a golden S in his lap, thumbs tucked into red suspenders dotted with emerald stars the size of pencil erasers. He really needed coffee.

"Morven?" he asked finally, minutes after the other detective's dialogue slowed and stalled.

"Yes?"

"Did you slam espresso shots? Like three?"

"None at all," she replied, puzzled.

"Hmm," was all Marlowe said, head still back against the headrest. "You seem way more alert than I feel. Do we have any facts? Specifics?"

"Facts. Here's one. My uncle, my mami's younger brother, Uncle Adrian, lives in New York. Owns an espresso stand. Four stands, as of today. All called Adrian's. He never touches alcoholic drinks, but starts each day with a triple espresso. Then has a large Americano, made with Bustelo coffee, at his side all day in a plastic mug with the Adrian's logo on it. When younger, I'd stop by the first cart he opened, where he still worked every day, after school for a quesitos, which is like a flaky pastry shaped like a big cigar full of thick seasoned cream cheese and honey. Every time, every day, that mug never seemed less than brimming with coffee. But he sipped it continually, and it was always warm. I knew he filled it up periodically through the day, but never saw him do it. I thought as a kid that he must have a tube at the bottom that connected him to a vast coffee reservoir."

Marlowe cocked his head, watching her as she talked, more alert than before.

"Once, I asked him how he drank so much coffee. He told me that coffee was a part of him, and that he could only make good coffee if he *knew* the coffee, that it connected him to his customers. He knew each regular's order, too, and seemed to know about their lives, families, jobs, when they had fresh haircuts or new shoes, a change in their countenances from happiness to sadness. The coffee made it possible, he said, helping him remember the facts about his customers and the world around him."

She paused for a moment, and he didn't reply, thinking about her uncle, the story, and coffee.

"Facts. I did make a quick station call before arrival at your place. We don't know much yet, but we do know the victim—using the word as placeholder before we have more details—was Deacon Mike Ray of Chapter Creek Church. The body hasn't been formally identified, however, a wallet with ID was discovered within the body's jeans pockets by an officer at the scene. It was Officer Troy, who in addition to the ID, recognized him from the first incident at the playing fields."

"Mike Ray." Earlier, when being told of a body found at the field, it flashed like a lightning strike into Marlowe's mind that it was going to be John Arthur, who'd said he was going to revisit the scene. Why he'd do it during such a torturous hour Marlowe hadn't a guess, but as you could never tell with the British-TV lover, his bones told him that the man was the second victim, even if it didn't make sense. He'd become friends with John, and maybe a policeman—maybe anyone—expects the worse. While he felt bad for Mike Ray and his family, he could admit relief to himself that it wasn't John.

"Why," he asked rhetorically, "would Mr. Ray show up dead so early at the ballfields? Why would anyone?"

She shook her head. "The body was discovered at approximately 6:00 a.m. by the groundskeeper, Ford David, who called the police at 6:02, specifically. He waited until arrival, and I requested the officers on the scene have him stay. The various scene of crime teams have been alerted, including Doctor Peterson. None there as yet when we left yours."

She signaled to take them off the highway into the neighborhood as Marlowe asked, "More?"

"Not much – watch it." The latter said like a teacher to a car cutting them off, causing dramatic breaking. "Lucky we're on our way to a serious incident, not part of one. Where was I? Not much else. Here's one interesting nugget. Another person was at the scene; Drogo Oates, the concession worker we've yet to talk to."

"Was he?"

"He, too, is being kept to help us with our inquiries. We should be there in five minutes."

She began a twist of rights and lefts through a neighborhood of good-sized, faux-Georgian houses whose 80s-built sheen had begun fading, but whose Douglas Firs and Western Red Cedars arched high above the road, trickling sun dappling it with light. Marlowe utilized the minutes to place a quick call to Nelson, who was staying at the station this morning to continue shoveling background checks. It was divide and conquer time with two murders. As if a conjuror removed a sheet that'd been over a suburban block, the Hettie Patty school and playfields all of a sudden dramatically dominated the view, and soon they once again pulled into the parking lot. Less crowded, only a few non-police vehicles. Entering the lot, a City-police blazoned Ford Interceptor, sirens and lights unleashed, screeched in behind them, flooring it around them, barely missing their ear bumper as Morven more casually maneuvered toward the lot's far corner.

"Hah," she said, pulling into a spot. "That officer should slow it down, way down. Speeding here is going to cause more crimes than solve them."

Police SUVs and cars and multiple white vans made parking too close an impossibility. "Gang's nearly all here," Marlowe noticed, stepping out of the car. He looked back to the parking lot's entrance, to the space where he'd parked when attending the first crime scene. The only human presence in that direction consisted of two commendable joggers, up with the thrushes, one in neon green and one in neon orange shorts, both in white tanks and vivid headbands the color of ripe lemons. Stalled joggers currently, as they'd stopped at the entrance, staring at the hustle and bustle.

"Morven?" As Marlowe mused, she'd excited out of the car and was walking closer to where she could see police tape blocking off a section directly behind home plate, but on the spectator side of the fence. She'd made it about ten feet before realizing Marlowe wasn't trailing her.

"Yes?" she replied as he jogged up to her.

"First thing, grab a few uniforms, have them set up camp at the lot entrance. Reduce public consumption. Push the tape out."

"On it, no problem."

"Maybe the two who nearly knocked our wagon off path?"

"The speedy drivers?"

"Yep."

"I'll try to find them." She smiled as they separated, he toward the tape, she toward a grouping of uniformed officers gathered around the recently racing SUV.

Marlowe stopped at the police tape, raising it gingerly before being paused by an unidentifiable person toe-to-top in a white hazmat suit. Flashing his badge and donning white booties over scuffed penny loafers the shade of muddy Bourdeaux, a white suit of his own, and gloves, he inched closer, pausing again to not step directly into an also white suited photographer's shot. Once the flash subsided, the photographer gave a white-gloved thumbs-up like an affirming ghost, then gave one to Doctor Peterson, standing opposite Marlowe. In full white gear, but with the headpiece off, the doc stared at the body lying between them, wire-framed glasses perched upon a few straggling hairs on his forehead.

Marlowe knew it was Mike Ray, even face down. Or an awfully close match. The oval-shaped balding head, tall, thin body, jeans and black clerical shirt and collar, expensive-appearing gold watch face shining in sun, a shine at dark odds with the lifeless body.

"And so he travels to the undiscovered country from whose bourn no traveler returns." The pathologist moved closer into a half-crouch by the body.

"Indeed," Marlowe quietly intoned.

"Detective," the doc said, without looking up. "We meet again at another scene of bloody deeds. Perhaps it is our lot in life? Perhaps."

"Mike Ray, unless my information is wrong?"

"Thou shall know the man by the Athenian garments he has on. Or by his driver's license. I wouldn't say for certain without positive identification. Sad for those near to him, and those touched by his deeds."

"Contacting his wife needs to happen ASAP," Marlowe said, mostly to himself. He moved a step closer. "Have you had time for examination?"

"Before the photographer's glare, some. More will need to be undertaken. Poor choice on that last word. Death's poetry comes unbidden, like the dawn, for Mr. Ray it seems."

"Any words of wisdom? I wouldn't want to wade into your pond, but that seems probable cause of death.'" He gestured toward the back of the victim's head, battered and bloody.

"Seems is a poor word. And while I think nobly of your soul, I in no way approve of your opinion." The doctor stood, green eyes twinkling as he stepped around the body toward Marlowe. "In the matter of death's cause, it is too soon to give a definitive answer. But in this case, I can admit fairly that you may see properly. Proverbial blunt instrument could be the cause of the damage."

"Any idea, not to push, what might have been used as that proverbial?"

"For you, Detective Marlowe, I would hazard an opinion that the instrument in question was more club, less hammer, rounded, and utilized with force."

"Need to be a wielder of uncommon strength?"

"Not necessarily. If enough speed combines with some strength, the force can be enough in certain cases. I have much business with the body still before appertaining specific and final details."

"Understood." Marlowe knew the pathologist wouldn't be pushed, but couldn't help asking one more question. "Sorry, any idea on time?"

"Time?" The doctor turned back to the body, replying in a quiet singsong, "Time, time, time. It's time that you love," before continuing normally. "I'd hate to put a pin in it. Not too many hours previous is a guess. A guess. Which I hate to do. Now, leave me to my work. I cannot blame thee, but I am myself attached to weariness. Too many bodies in a place where kids should be playing."

"Understood. Take ca –"

"Doctor Peterson." Morven's steady voice broke in. She'd managed to reach nearly to where they were talking, just outside of the tape, without either man noticing. Marlowe was often surprised at how she managed to be one of those people who could move both quickly and quietly. "Good morning."

"Detective Morven," the doctor replied without getting up. "You are like the lark at morning."

"Like the lark? I'll take it at this hour."

"Maybe we'll leave the doc to it." Marlowe moved toward the tape.

"Sure." Morven pulled the tape up for him.

"Thanks, Doc," he hollered, ducking under the tape. "We'll watch for reports."

"Sweet masters, be patient," the doctor mused to their walking away backs.

Marlowe removed his white over-booties and hazmat suit few feet outside the tape, scanning the lot and seeing the vehicles and officers blocking the entrance. "Thanks." He motioned to them. "Can you also ensure someone talks in person to Kristin Ray? Let her know. Gently. We'll talk to her later today. Have them let her know that too."

"Already done." She had notebook in one hand, checking off something.

"Amazing. Thanks. Could you talk to Officer Troy?" He pointed at the broad-shoulder officer, visible in the midst of a group ten feet away.

"See if he knows if any other people have been seen this morning. We need witnesses."

"Will do. Said hello to him already, but will follow up."

"Wait." He put a hand on her shoulder as she was turning to leave. "First, thanks again. Second, the man who found the body, Mr. Ford?"

Double-checking her notebook, she said, "Mr. David. First name Ford."

"Check. Groundskeeper. What do we know?"

"So far? We've only done a brief background. Seventy-three. Widower."

"He's here?"

"He should be over near the concession stand. Drogo Oates, too. Suspicious him being here at this time. Why should he be? It's not like there are loads of kids wanting Twizzlers or granola bars."

"Fair point. What do we know?"

"Nikola Cassian's cousin. Ponytail. Thirty."

"Thirty? Old for concessions work. I'll head that way. Meet me. We'll go easy. Finding a body isn't pleasant."

Morven headed toward Office Troy at a brisk jog, Marlowe ambling past the concession stand, giving the area a once-over. The stand perched between baseball fields like an old sea trawler between docks, flaked paint fluttering in a morning breeze that'd sprung up from the southwest from over the water. The fields of the complex lay out to either side of him, behind them, trees dotted with paths through the copious forest park. Bet the high school kids love that forest area, he decided, moving to where a few benches rose alongside sidewalks, two men sitting on one, multiple uniformed officers around them.

The older man he felt was Ford David, and Marlowe angled his direction, flashing his badge at the nearest officer. "Mr. David?" The man nodded. "Detective Marlowe. Could we talk?" Another nod. "Maybe away from the commotion." A third nod.

At the same time, the other man on the bench spoke up. "Hey, Detective, can I come too? I've got things to do, and if you wanna talk to me, then I could get on with doing them."

"Drogo Oates?"

"That's me, waiting to talk to someone as I've been told to do."

"Mind waiting a few more? I'll be back."

"Mind? Sure, I mind." He rose, surprised at the three uniformed officers surrounding him as if seeing them for the first time, and sat back down. "I mind. But guess I'll wait here on this bench."

"Appreciate it."

Ford stood up, following Marlowe a short way down the sidewalk, pushing a cart-type contraption with him that had been parked next to the bench.

"That needed?" Marlowe asked, pointing at the cart. It had four wheels with a garbage can on a boxed platform on them, as well as a sort of dispenser attached underneath—like a pest sprayer under an antique crop duster. Its two pushing handles were encircled by rubber bands, leather bands with bolt nuts on them, rolls of tape, bungie cords, and string, all covered in dust. A dirt rake and pint-sized shovel wearing rust like windbreakers were attached to the can's side with bungy cords, along with a bag full of bags, gloves, small tool belt, and baseball cap faded shallow gray from blue.

Ford's voice carried like a low current where bay meets ocean, quiet but felt. "Ah. No. Force of habit." He raised his hands off the cart's handles, moving slowly in Marlowe's direction. Six feet tall, 185 pounds, with a round face and short gray hair combed back over a high forehead, Ford's hearty appearance and deep suntan pointed to full days spent working outside, offset by a mild paunch pointing to beer-drinking afternoons. His long-sleeved white T-shirt birthed a rainbow of paint drops—purple, blue, green, red—and hung over his brown pants, which had a hand-sized hole in one knee and shared with his sneakers an appearance as if magnets for the dust and chalk of the basepaths.

Once making it to an area free of police or CSI, Marlowe stopped. "This good?"

"Sure." Ford's taciturnity matched the detective's.

"Great." Marlowe sensed this interview would be like pulling teeth. At which thought he remembered it'd been too long since he'd visited his dentist, Doctor Howell. "Thank you for talking with me. To start, you're a widower?"

"That's correct. My wife died seven years ago. I started here soon after."

"No children?"

"Correct, no children in our house. It's one of the reasons I enjoy working at the playfields."

Marlowe changed direction. "What time today did you find the body?"

"Six. Sixish. I arrive then. Start work on the fields."

"Got it. What did you do when you saw it?"

"Walked over. Called the police. Waited for them to arrive. Then waited for you."

Ford's words stayed soft, evenly pitched. Marlowe knew he might still be traumatized. "This is hard, I appreciate. Did you touch anything?"

He hesitated. "Well, I did. Felt I should check."

"Pulse?"

"Yes. I took first aid, years past. Checked pulse, but didn't feel anything when doing it."

"Good to know. Notice anyone else in the playfield area when you arrived?"

"No one. It's usually empty at this time. Easier to get work done."

Taking a new tack, Marlowe tried to raise his own energy in hopes of raising Ford's. "Thanks, that's very helpful. Mind if I ask what all you do here? And is it every day?"

In his same monotone, Ford replied, "Every day in summer. General maintenance. Picking up trash, lots of it. Fixing anything small that needs fixing. Cleaning the fields first thing. Both the out and infields. Map the basepaths."

"Is that what the attachment on your cart is for?"

"That's right. Made it myself. Filled with chalk for the paths. You like baseball?"

Back to the matter at hand, Marlowe skipped answering. "This morning, did you hear anything? Notice anything different?"

"Not so much. A few cars, trucks. Daily commute. No kids yet. But they'll be here soon. Lights up soquick in the morning in the summer, they arrive early. Nice to hear while I do my work."

"I'll bet." Marlowe felt he could wrap it up. "One last question. Did you recognize the victim?"

Ford rubbed his chin with a hand carrying many small scars. "I don't think so. Could have seen him at a game here I suppose. Hard to tell. Parents, fans, the crowds start to spill together, you know?"

"Thank you, that's all for now. We may need to talk to you further, so be sure the officers have your details. Here's my card if you think of anything else."

They started walking back to the benches, when Ford slowed, stopped. "Wait. One thing. I did see someone after calling the police. As the first police car showed, there was a man across the way." One of his hands fluttered out like a wounded crow. "Hard to see. An older man? Blue hat? Walking a dog. I believe he talked to an officer later."

"That's very helpful. Thank you." Marlowe motioned to a younger, medium height, slender female uniformed officer, blonde hair tucked under her hat. "This officer will take your details and escort you to where they can take your fingerprints." He gave the officer a glance, receiving a curt nod in reply. "For exclusion purposes. If that's okay with you."

"Sure," Ford replied. "Leave the cart?"

"Probably best."

The officer and Ford walked toward one of the white vans parked in the lot.

Marlowe went over to where Drogo sat, legs stretched out over sidewalk, hands interlocked behind a head tilted back into them as if they were a basket, Palomino-shaded ponytail hanging down, eyes closed.

"Mr. Oates?"

Marlowe's voice startled the man, who opened his eyes, jumped up, sat down, crossed his legs, all before replying. "My turn already, Detective?" he said, sarcasm dripping over his words like runny honey.

"Yes. Could you come with me—with us?" He'd noticed Morven heading their way and motioned.

"Whatever you say, Detective. I'm here to help. Hopefully this doesn't take too long. Busy you know." Wearing thready jean shorts cut off at the knees, a yellow T-shirt with *I'm Just Here For the Sunshine* on it in purple sparkly text, and high-top black Chucks without socks, he shambled down the sidewalk, slender 5'8" frame undulating as if lacking some important bones.

Morven caught up with them as Marlowe and Oates stopped.

"Just a few questions, Mr. Oates. First name Drogo, correct?"

"That's me. Detective Marlowe, did you say? Like in a trench coat? And you are?"

"Detective Morven. Mr. Oates, your given first name is Martin, correct?"

"Yeah, it is. But no one, I mean no one, calls me that. Not even my mother."

"Got it. You were here this morning when the incident happened?"

"No. Well, yes. Yes and no."

"Yes and no?"

"I *was* here, in one way. My physical body was here. But I *wasn't* here in another." Drogo emphasized some words like lollipops he was sucking. "I was, uh, I was sleeping in the concession stand. I wanted to get a jump on the day."

"Sleeping here. Do that often?" Morven asked.

"Lately, yes. See, I live with my cousin, Zara. My girlfriend. My cousin *and* my girlfriend. Ex-girlfriend, you know?"

Getting confused by Drogo's wanderings, Marlowe said, "Somewhat. But Zara, she is both your ex and your cousin?"

"Sort of. Not close cousin. Not second, or third cousin, anything like that, that'd be weird. Maybe eighth? I have a very big family. It's sometimes hard to tell."

"You live with her but sleep here. Can you explain?" Morven was also having a hard time following Drogo's logic.

"Sure, man. I don't *always* sleep here. Zara was upset with me. We got in a fight, and she told me to leave, and I didn't have anywhere to go, unless I involve family, which I did *not* want to do. Not one ounce of me. Then: lightbulb moment. I have a key to the stand. It's quiet here at night. The ideal place to stay. Like camping."

Marlowe felt Drogo was someone who'd go off the tracks and into the wilderness without aid, so guided him back. "You slept here. Did you see anything this morning?"

"Nah, I was sound asleep. I'm a solid sleeper. Could sleep through a bomb, my mom said. Zara says I snore. Another problem. So no, didn't see or hear a peep. Before the first sirens, then I came out and saw old Ford and the body. Creepy."

"Notice anything, person, car, when you came out?"

"Not a thing, detectives. I'm very alert, too. Perfect vision. But nothing. Until the cop avalanche. Copalanche."

"Did you," Morven went on, "recognize the victim?"

"I didn't get near that, no way. But yes."

"Yes, you recognized them?"

"Not at first. Then I couldn't help looking. But didn't touch it. Him. Ford said stay away. But I could see. And the back of his head, the priest necklace, it clicked. He came to the games, some of them. No kid, which I thought weird, you know? Friendly, give him that. Deacon, he called himself. A talker, which *sometimes* is cool, *sometimes* a pain in the rear when you've got a line longer than the entrance to a Phish show."

"Can we take a step back to the earlier incident?" Marlowe's drawl bounced against Drogo's beach bum burst.

"The pastor dying? Yes, I was here. I'll never forget that. Creepy. But I didn't have anything to do with him. Or, I did. But not much."

"Not much?"

"Exactly. Except he had been coming to see his kids play for years.

and liked his chips. Barbecue mostly, but once in a while tortilla chips, or plain. And he didn't like to miss plays on the field, so he had me bring them to him sometimes. Even when I was busy. But he could be serious. And Nikola asked, too. She's my cousin."

"Like Zara?" Morven asked.

"Eeew, not like that. Well, in a way. Nikola is my cousin, and Zara is too. But Nikola is a *closer* cousin. Not closer closer, but regular cousin stuff. Zara is my girlfriend and *very distant* cousin. Nikola is just a cousin. You know her?"

Affirmative nods kept him going. "Nikola's cool. Snazzy, dressed up, all that. Came to the pastor's games. They're close. Were close. Not that she was involved. In his death that is, involved in *that*. She can be tough, but not that tough. She's nice to me. Anyway, Pastor. I knew him. But didn't *know* know him, you know? Nothing to do with his death. I was selling Kit Kats to a couple kids when I heard the scream. Ask them if you don't believe me. Never forget that. Seeing him dying. No one could."

"You didn't see anything out of the ordinary that day?"

"Nothing. Nada. The baseball days blend like a tie-dye, smooshing into each other. Kids buying candy bars, adults buying granola bars, everybody buying water, soda, all of it."

"How long have you worked the stand?" Morven took notes while talking.

"Concessions? Whew, you wouldn't believe it, but like ten years. Twelve years. Twelve long years. Thinking about moving into coffee. Or records. They're hot. One of my aunts got me this gig way back when I was young and I said to myself, Drogo, you'll be outside, sunshine, easy work. I should have known better. Is this about done, or do I have to go downtown or what?"

"We're good," Marlowe answered. "Might be in touch. Call us if you think of anything else from either day. Check in with an officer before leaving. They will want fingerprints."

"It won't be messy? It doesn't matter. I don't have a lunch reservation or the prom or somewhere I need to be at the moment. And I'll call. I don't know *any*thing, but if I remember stuff, I'll call."

Morven laughed as Drogo slunk off, heading in the direction of a group of officers near a white van. Marlowe gazed over the sun-sprayed southern-most baseball field, noticing encroaching clouds on the horizon, more apparent than minutes ago. Sighing deeply, as if bringing breath up from his loafers, he adjusted his hat. "Back to the bleachers, where it began?"

"I agree with that. Get a little perspective." She also stared out over the field, relaxed but focused. The look in her eyes reminded Marlowe of Michealangelo's *David*, as ease with any problem that might be in the way, no matter how large.

Moving off, she said, "One more thing, I nearly forgot."

"Yes, Morven? Burr in your saddle?"

"I can't decide if this will come as a surprise or not. Can you guess who's here?"

"John Arthur."

"The great Marlowe the mentalist reads minds. That will make solving cases much simpler. How?"

"Deduction. Beat cop, not Sherlock. Ford David said he saw a man with a dog. John mentioned he wanted to revisit the scene. A + B = Arthur and Ainsley."

"Makes sense. And Mr. Arthur has a way of turning up. After chatting with Officer Troy and putting wheels in motion, I noticed them, Mr. Arthur and his dog, and had a brief talk. Then I thought we should talk to him more and, as you're here, deduced you'd want to talk with him. I told him we'd meet him nearer the south bleachers, but made him promise to stay away from our more recent scene."

"Check." Morven slightly herded Marlowe around the concession stand and behind the first set of bleachers as he asked, "What did you talk about?"

Before an answer, they both heard Ainsley's high-pitched yapping, increasing in volume with each step taking them closer to where she and John were standing. Her leash pulled taut as he held on to the bleachers with one hand.

Stretching out putty-like, Ainsley sniffed and licked Marlowe's hand as soon as he was within reach, for a second, then, giving him a cockeyed twist, headed over to smell and lick Morven's hand and then her nose as Morven crouched to pet her.

"Sorry, Ainsley," Marlowe sadly said. "No croissant this morning."

"A crime so close to daybreak that the investigators have to skip breakfast. Not the sorriest thing to happen, but I'm still sorry to hear it. Detective Marlowe, Detective Morven." John gave a mock bow from the waist.

"Mr. Arthur, surprised to see you here this morning back at the playfields." Morven stood up, Ainsley moving to lie down between the trio. "I thought Ainsley might like walking the park area and came near the crack of dawn so we'd miss most other walkers, give her some room. I never imagined–"

"A second crime scene?" Marlowe wondered as he said it if John had actually expected just that. Not that he felt John was suspicious, but the man did have a canny way of showing up.

"Yes. And yet, 'the violent event leaves a wound, which spreads and infects everything.'" The last phrase was delivered in a clipped English accent.

"More Pie?" Morven looked askance at Marlowe when he asked the question.

"No." John was wistful. "Not this time. That line was from *Professor T*, a newer show starring Ben Miller." His tone picked up. "Interesting actor. Started more in the comedic, but was the first fish-out-of-water, or should I say, British-out-of-London detective in *Death in Paradise*, which takes place on a fictional Caribbean Island, San Marie. Then he himself was murdered in episode one, season three, starting a long line of detectives. In *Professor T*, he is, as you'd deduce, a professor. Of Criminology at Cambridge. More serious. Strange family background, very smart, knows the statistics, quirky, with OCD, not sharp or comfortable in social situations in the main, ends up assisting the police on some serious crimes. You know—"

Marlowe raised his hand. "John?"

"Yes?"

"Serious crime here, real—"

"Life not TV. Apologies. I do ramble. It's not meant as any slight on the victim, or to denigrate the seriousness of the crime. Talking about those shows I love helps me focus in a way. Weirdly. And you can learn—"

"A lot from TV."

A smile crept on Morven's face as the men filled in each other's sentences. The unlikely friendship between burly police office and older mystery TV buff was fun to watch. Nice to have a moment where the tragic weight of the crime scene was removed.

"Detective Morven," John said, noticing her smile. "You look like you've made a discovery."

"Not that. I was thinking about Detective Nelson. I'll have to mention *Professor T* to him. He's been making a list of British TV shows, with notes about each. You see, Mr. Arthur, after your help last time, he feels they possibly could help further his education. That plus working with Detective Marlowe."

"Of course." Marlowe's laconism filled the words like air in balloons.

"Does he really?" John beamed.

"He does," Morven continued. "With that, I can now tell him: *Professor T*. Ben Miller. English mystery taking place in Cambridge."

"Originally, to make your entry up-to-date, a Belgian show."

"Oh, he'll like that. A Belgian like Inspector Poirot."

"Not exactly, but Poirot is the godfather of quirky fastidious detectives assisting the police with their inquiries."

Marlowe finally spoke up. "Matter at hand?"

"Yes." John looked toward the taped-off scene. Ainsley scratched her ear.

"You came here to walk Ainsley." Ainsley stopped scratching, angling Morven's way with the mention in hope that she might have a treat, before lying down with a slight huff when realizing she didn't. "Did you see anything odd? Other people, specific cars?"

"Nothing popped out at me. I feel after the other day and today, my powers of observation have waned. No people outside of one jogger, or runner as he was moving rapidly. Fairly thin, light-brown hair, wearing a long-sleeved shirt, muted evergreen, over-the-knee shorts a slightly lighter color. Cars, I did see a white van, ladders tied on top, and a few random cars drive by."

"No worries," Marlowe said. "Why here?"

"I wanted to revisit the scene to see if it would kick-start my memory. As well as walk Ainsley." The dog's head popped up. John scratched between her ears. "The walk took precedence to the scene, so I hadn't yet made it over when I first heard a siren approaching. Then I noticed Mr. David, who I'm guessing found the body?"

Nods from both detectives kept him going. "One car showed, then, Bob's your uncle, the police cavalry. With you two arriving in the time between commercial breaks, back when such things existed."

"Bob's—"

Marlowe's raised hand cut off Morven before the question could and. He'd explain the idiom later. "You stuck around?"

Mockingly aghast, John replied, "You know I wouldn't leave a crime scene. And this crime is related to our earlier crime, neither of which should go unpunished. And if I can assist the police—"

"In our inquires."

"Quite right, then I am here to help. Deacon Mike Ray is the victim, any leads?"

Marlowe slipped his baseball cap back on, tilted it low over his eyes. "John?"

Sheepishly straightening his stripped hoodie, the man replied rapidly, as he'd had too much water too quickly after a run and had to spit some back. "That's a guess, but I've been thinking about it. I didn't get too close to the body, not wanting to damage for the scene of crime folks, but did get close enough that I could see a general body shape, long and lean, with a collared black shirt, and a bright gold watch, and I was already taking it for granted that the crimes were related—they always are—so I just thought it through and it had to be Mike Ray. But what happened?"

Shaking his head, Marlowe replied. It was impossible to try and keep things from John. "Yes, it's Mr. Ray. You are correct in your reasoning. We are pursuing—"

"Multiple lines of inquiry." John finished the stock phrase with a smile.

"At the starting line, as Nelson might say." Marlowe didn't use a lot of sporting analogies.

"Why was he here, at this time. Could he have been overnight? Very odd."

"Very."

"Time or method of death yet?"

Neither detective said anything. John laughed. "Neither? Wearing that silence like flak jackets."

"Silence is sometimes the best answer," Marlowe replied.

"As your grandfather used to say?"

"Yep, that's one of his favorites."

John laughed lightly again. "Ideal for a police detective. Time of death. Going to go out on a proverbial limb, guessing he wasn't here overnight. With Pat Brown's murder, have to imagine Kristin Ray would have made that known and he'd have been discovered sooner."

"Fair enough," Marlowe replied. "We should get back to it."

"Don't let me stop you," John said. "Not a problem if I stick around here, staying away from the actual scene?"

"Sure. Why?"

"I did want to see this scene again, even if it sounds like playing TV detective. You two, and Detective Nelson, I'm sure have been investigating thoroughly, interviewing suspects, liaising with CSI, but no collar, as they say, yet. Because today's murder and Pat Brown's I feel have to be by the same person, or perhaps persons, but that's rare."

"On TV," Marlowe slipped in.

"On TV. Maybe in real life, too? We will see, *mon amis*. My theory is they are connected and somehow the murderer enticed Mike Ray here, then surprised him. 'Most criminal enterprise relies on an element of surprise.' Another *Professor T* for you. With that theory, in order to solve today's crime, we must solve the past crime. And go even farther in the past." John could, Marlowe thought as the man talked, get a little lecture-y. "That last crime, Pat Brown's murder, is personal for me. I was here. I should have seen something. Coming back here, hopefully, will shake the little grey cells into action."

"It is funny," Marlowe said, "that no one we've talked to saw anything specifically related to that crime at the time it happened. Or no one has mentioned it yet. We know witnesses and suspects aren't always truthful. Usually those witnesses, or even just one, they tend to see *something*, sometimes the wrong thing." He noticed Morven giving him an odd look and realized he was talking about the case in front of John perhaps more than he meant to.

"Did you know 73% of wrongful convictions are due to false IDs?" John said.

Marlowe removed his hat, using it to scratch his head. "John?"

"Too much information?"

"No harm. You're welcome to stay, back here."

"I wouldn't dream of getting in the way," John agreed. "I'm going to sit a spell, think it out."

"We do appreciate the help, John." Marlowe reached out to shake John's hand, causing Ainsley to jump up and lick his hand while balancing on her back feet.

"Ainsley," John called out.

10

At the station, Nelson intently scrolled, deep into background checks. He'd gotten a series of texts from Morven during his pre-work workout after being surprised he didn't run into her at Luther's London gym. His texting style could be abrupt, as if he were writing a horror movie and trying to force in multiple jump scares. Morven's was more measured, quickly filling him in on what facts they had: a second body found at the playfields, suspicious, more to come.

Marlowe had called, asking if he could continue background checks around Pat Brown's murder, following leads as he saw fit, saying they'd divide and conquer. While going to the scene of a major crime like this carried an extra excitement, he didn't mind the digging part, either. *It was all,* he told himself, *part of the detective's education, part of getting the case across the finish line.* Digging up information around suspects and the victim had an enjoyable archeological bent, if sedentary. Plus, in the big detective room, other detectives working other cases around him, it underlined how being part of the City's police force was being part of a bigger team, something making the City a better, safer place.

He'd set herself a couple of morning tasks, writing a list in his notebook with boxes beside each item that could be checked once finished, like mile markers passed on a long run. Goal-oriented, Morven had said when he asked what was her secret to success. It almost didn't seem ambitious enough to describe the older detective, but was close, and he wanted to emulate her. One goal today was an interview with Jack Page, a name surfacing multiple times but not spoken with, yet, though Nelson had wrangled his number from Ash Willums. Jack had been evasive, until Nelson used the technique Morven once suggested, saying he'd be happy to come by Jack's office. No one wanted the police to arrive at their place of work. At that, Jack's tune changed. They were to meet later that morning.

Currently shifting financial backgrounds of the crop of suspects, Nelson hadn't an *aha!* moment to date. Nothing as dramatic as a trail laid out in funds transferred from Pat to someone or vice versa in a way that'd imply blackmail, for example, or someone in such deep debt, to the victim or otherwise, under the mountain of bills that crime appeared to provide the only handhold. Normal people with normal finances, from what he could tell. Tom Toomey's finances, or financial empire, as he was a wealthy man from reports, were more public and layered at a level that might be worth diving into, utilizing the specialized Financial Crimes Unit, or FCU. Might not be bad to check with them about Pat Brown and Mike Ray, in general, as the two appeared to be doing amazingly well from the popular church. As he picked up the desk phone to call the FCU, his cell started buzzing. More texts from Morven, letting him know the victim today was Mike Ray.

"Mike Ray." His voice echoed, causing him to glance around to make sure no one else in the room had noticed his outburst, before repeating it again softly to himself. "Mike Ray." The deacon was the second baseball field victim. Murder via a blunt instrument, though her last text said: *Let's call it suspicious death, atm. Keep the blunt instrument etc. between us.* Mike Ray and Pat Brown were close, thick as thieves Marlowe reported that Mrs. Brown had said. Both dead, murdered, in the same spot. He'd better turn his metaphorical shovel into digging deeper into Mike's past. Tilting back from his computer, Nelson took a steady drink of water out of the black Yeti Rambler water bottle he had topped up, a sticker reading "Destroying Angel" in lightening-esque letters on it, the name of a band one of his exes, Suzi Bond, fronted. *This morning,* he thought, *is getting more and more interesting.*

The City, Marlowe thought, opening the door to the passenger seat, *was unpredictable.* Not because of the second murder *per se,* even if he hadn't predicted that, but the weather. Unpredictable as the seventh game in a winner takes all seven game series. The once impeccably blue late-summer sky, sunshine ruling over things with a warming iron fist, changed to clouds, which themselves had changed from white to gray to gloom as they tromped across horizon. Settled in to the seat, attaching his seat belt, a solitary viscous drop of rain splattered on the windshield. Rain. Had to arrive at some point. While facts belied his opinion, and the City had a fairly long record of days without any precipitation, at a deeper level, Marlowe felt rain lurked around every day's corner. Not necessarily a rainstorm, and rarely a thunderstorm. But rain in some form. The windshield, dotted with increasing drops, agreed.

Morven flipped on the wipers once. "This rain isn't going to help traffic. Or the scene. They're already putting up the tents. CSI gets those tents up quickly, I'll give them that." She navigated the lot, stopping to give an officer the chance to move the SUV blocking the entrance. Her phone rang. Slipping into a parking space, she answered, Marlowe getting one side of the conversation.

"Detective Morven. Yes, Nelson, it was Mike Ray. We believe it may be connected, but it's not good to go off half-cocked, remember. Slow down a moment. Mrs. Brown called wanting to stop by the station? That makes sense. Solid work Nelson. Yes, we're heading back. Keep at it."

"That, as you can guess, was Nelson." She started the car back toward the entrance. Right as it crossed the barrier between lot and sidewalk, a bike shot in front, almost scraping the front fender. "Watch out,"

Morven exclaimed. He window was partway down, allowing air in without much rain, and she'd spoke loudly enough it caused the biker to slam on the breaks, ponytail flopping like limp spaghetti as Drogo stopped beside the car.

"Hey, man," Drogo yelled, then noticed it was Nelson and Marlowe. "Hey, detectives. You gotta watch out. We bike riders have rights too."

"Drogo," Morven said, "hold on."

Marlowe didn't say a word, wondering why Morven parked on the street. He followed her out of the car when she left it, the rain still light enough he left his coat inside.

"Uh, Detective, it's raining." Drogo held a hand out as if to catch random drops in demonstration.

"I know that, Mr. Oates. I also know you aren't wearing a helmet, which is required."

"Yeah, but nobody enforces that one, come on." Drogo shook his head hard enough to cause his ponytail to swing as if knocking off flies.

"We'll let it pass this time, but in the future, helmet. It's your welfare. Also, I have a follow-up question."

"Already? I mean, here? We just talked."

"It can be quick if you cooperate." Morven talked as Marlowe stood by silent, curious. Where was his detective partner going? Morven opened her notebook. "Speaking about your cousin Nikola Cassian and Pat Brown, you said, 'They're close. Were. Not that she was involved. In his death that is, involved in *that*.' Emphasis on the final 'that.' What did you mean?"

"Nothing. That she wasn't involved in his murder. Death. Death murder."

"I understand, but you implied she was involved in something else with Pat Brown."

"Work?" Drogo's question could have been for them or himself. They stayed silent, and he finally went on. "Maybe I meant work? Ummm," he mumbled into another silence for five seconds. "Don't tell Nikola I said anything, but I think they were having an affair. Or not."

"Are you saying you know this for a fact?"

"Yeah. I was here sleeping in the stand, Zara mad again, a different night, and heard voices. I'm not actually supposed to sleep here, so can we keep that between us? Down low and that. Anyway, I peeked out, and they were in a car nearby. You know what I mean?"

"Specifically?"

"Specifically. They were *you know*, you know?"

"We do. You saw them one time?"

"There was another time too. Maybe more. As long as it's between us I think she was what is termed in polite circle as his girlfriend. Can I go? It's raining, the roads get slick. My welfare being less well when that happens."

"Thank you for your assistance. We will be in touch if we have more questions."

Drogo's pedaling started with "touch" and took him halfway down the block by the time Marlowe and Morven re-buckled seat belts.
"What led you there?" Marlowe asked.

"I know we felt there was a relationship between Pat Brown and Nikola Cassian but didn't have actual confirmation. Drogo is flaky, but from his concession stand view, sees more than most, even if unhappy talking about it. That, and his relationship with Nikola, made pushing him on it seem a good idea."

"Great idea, Morven. Very smart. Let's head back."

When Marlowe and Morven left John and Ainsley near the bleachers, the latter two were quiet for a moment, she sitting and he standing, until another siren pierced the air, causing Ainsley to leap, pirouette, and land facing the direction of the siren, barking three times before John pulled a treat from a small bag with daisies printed out it. "Ains, sit, please." She'd sat before he'd even reached the end of her name, tail stirring up dirt leisurely, before stretching to snatch the treat.

"Rest a spell, Ains? Probably not a bad idea." John often wondered if talking so much to his dog was something others, especially others living alone, did with their pets. He hoped so. "You okay sitting on the ground?" he asked. "I'll take the edge of the second level seat. High enough to view the diamond and the police buzzing around, but not so high I can't keep an easy grip on your leash."

Ainsley angled her head up to be petted and snare a second treat before settling back down, eyes closed within seconds. *Lucky dog*, he thought, adjusting the teal baseball cap he wore, adorned with a patch featuring two dogs. Staring over, he saw the forensic teams were putting up tents over Mike Ray's body and the surrounding area, scouring the ground and scene. For what? Clues, he supposed. If he could get closer, could he talk to Mike Ray's body like *Brokenwood*'s Detective Senior Sargent Mike Shepheard, glean some knowledge that way? No, he didn't believe he really could, all things considered. Seeing one body close up, back in the Case of the Nine Neighbors, was more than enough. He'd stay here, wrack the memory, get the brain charged like the Energizer Bunny. Take the time before and after Pat Brown's murder one frame at a time. *I have the order, the method, and the psychology. Or have watched enough Poirot that I should be orderly.*

Instead, his mind drifted into playing baseball, remembering trying out when he was eight for summer little league in the small Kansas town he grew up in. "Trying out" in the loosest possible sense of the word, as every kid made the team. Perhaps some kids successful in tryouts played more as they traveled to the slightly larger town nearby where the league was based, but everyone made it. When the coach—faceless in memory, only long, curly blond hair and a ratty mustache remaining—questioned him during that first tryout practice on what position he played, John could remember saying right field authoritatively, as that was the only position that immediately popped into his child self's head.

Deep in the field, watching the majority of the action from a distance, he'd hope that if a fly ball made a looping trek to him he'd manage to, via some sporty guardian angel, catch it. A rare occurrence, a ball making it out his way, and him catching it when it did was much rarer. But one time, he did catch it. Nearing the end of a season, nearing the end of a game, last inning, last out. Two on. Up one. Frightened that it'd be hit his way, and then, as if the ball itself was malevolent, *smack!* Off the bat, way up, can of corn. Every eye in the crowd pinned to the ball and him and his glove. Fear coursing down an arm, through a hand, into the glove, shaking like the archetypal leaf. Somehow, the ball was caught.

"Memory is as strange a beast as you, Ainsley," he said, causing her to raise one eyelid slowly for a second before it drifted back down. *And shows so little respect*, he thought. I'm not Poirot, making mistakes only once every twenty-eight years. I should have seen something. If there was an easy answer, Marlowe and team would have found it. People either didn't see anything or are lying, as happens in every detective show. But the lying means something as well. What did Poirot say, "Whether they try to hinder me or to help me, they necessarily reveal their type of mind." I need to bring that up next time I see Marlowe. Or not. He chuckled. They probably believe I'm nutty enough. Nutty or not, no more meandering. I'm going to sit here and wait. His musing trailed off as he stared into the vast space fly balls flew through before landing, safe or out.

A giant raindrop splattered his knee a half-inch below where the brown shorts he was wearing stopped. "What?" he called out, causing Ainsley to spring into a standing position as another raindrop hit her directly on her black button nose. She wiggled her body, starting at the tail and working up her back to her head, like a spring let go, shaking dust and two leaves into the increasing rain. "Ainsley," John shouted, "where did this come from?" He shook his fist in mock anger at the muddy sky. "Thanks a lot, rain." Adjusting his cap, he stepped off the bleacher, reaching down to give Ains a pet, pulling up his calf-high socks, a crimson stitched octopus tentacling down a ship on each. "I'll wager Mr. Hercule Poirot never had his little grey cells swamped by rain." Ainsley tugged away from the bleachers. "Got you, time to go. Let's hope we make it to the car before the heavens open." As they walked away, he gave a backward glance. "So, we have played, and the rain, he has won." His whisper wafted with his mock Belgian accent.

Morven and Marlowe were at the station after a drive that saw the sky let loose with a persistent rain like a giant hose above them with the nozzle set to the shower setting turned on for five minutes. And then five minutes later stopped, clouds breaking up like gray ships lost on a sea of blue, drifting apart. The drive also included one stop. Both detectives sat quiet in their thoughts about the case, until Marlowe gave an unnatural high-pitched, "Stop the car," causing Morven to brake and swerve into a spot in front of a small coffee stand. *Sampson's Sips the Second* its sign read.

Marlowe, voice like an Egyptologist discovering an unknown pyramid, whispered, "I had no idea this existed." Coffee and croissants (two for Marlowe) were ordered and consumed on the way back, in mostly silence, the only words Marlowe's: "Sad Ainsley isn't here for the crumbs."

Entering the cavernous detectives' room, a swarm of police worked other cases, nods and hellos tossed their way as they passed before reaching the two-desk-and-a-board corner, Nelson head down in front of the computer. He'd pinned a picture of Mike Ray to the board's top alongside the picture of Pat Brown, plus a few more Post-its, the many yellow stickies adding an abstract signaling of color to the collage of photos and notes.

"Detective," Marlowe rumbled, brushing a stray pastry flake from his jacket before sluffing it over his chair back.

Nelson straightened, sitting at attention as he glanced at him and then Morven, who'd removed her own suit coat, neatly hanging it on her chair, white dress shirt glowing as it caught sun through the window. "Welcome back, detectives," Nelson greeted them. "Busy morning?"

They nodded in reply and he went on. "Can you believe it? A second murder in as many days at the same place. Do you know the odds?"

Morven shook her head. His tone made her think he knew the fact and asked the question as a matter of course.

"They are astronomical. You've a better chance of winning the lottery. Which is like a very, very small percent chance."

"Easy on the math Olympics, we have pressing matters." Marlowe walked to the board, motioning for the others to do the same. "Two murders. Likely related. We haven't traversed too far on the first, but every trail has some puddles. Let's circle the wagons. Morven, you begin with what was found at the scene. Then, Nelson, what you've dug up. Wait, when is Mrs. Brown arriving?"

"Forty-five minutes, Detective."

"Perfect. Let's review."

The three talked the morning's scene and events, moved items on the board, talked more, then stared at the board in thought. "Interesting," Marlowe began, but before he could get any further, the phone on his desk began ringing. Picking it up, he was informed Mrs. Brown was in the lobby.

"Do you want to take this one alone?" Morven wondered.

"I think so. Mrs. Brown seemed delicate. Two might spook."

"Makes sense. Have fun." She turned back to the board as he left.

Marlowe collected Bridgette Brown in the lobby, directing her to interview room three, one of the smaller of the station's rooms. One wall was windowed, the others painted institutional gray. She hadn't yet spoken, giving him a small wave and nod when he greeted her in the lobby.

"Please, have a seat, Mrs. Brown." Marlowe took one chair and motioned her to one across from it. As she moved into the chair, he was struck by how she displayed a touch of elegance in sitting, something about the way she moved balletic. Even in plain blue jeans and a bulky cardigan the color of morning fog, she carried herself delicately but purposeful.

"Thank you for coming in. You wanted to speak with us?"

"Yes, Detective. First, thank you for returning Pat's things."

"Of course." There had to be more, but she seemed reticent. "But I sense you have other things bringing you down to the station?"

"Yes. It's awkward, in a way. But has to do with his things. I don't want you to think ill of my family." She stared at the table as if it might take over, tell him what she wanted to say.

"I won't. Anything you have to say that you believe could be important, please go on." His voice was gruff but gentle.

"I'm not sure this will be helpful, but my son, Burton, Daniel Burton is his full name, he and his father didn't always have the best relationship."

Marlowe wasn't sure where she was going but knew you often needed to give interviews a free reign, like a thirsty horse, if you wanted to find water. So, he kept quiet.

"Pat thought Burton wasn't driven, and when Burton didn't want to continue playing baseball, or any sports, Pat was hard on him. Burton's different, introspective, happier reading then whooping it up on the field. He likes reading, fantasy books mostly, and computer games in the same genre. Pat was different. The physical world was his domain." She raised eyes the color of deeply caramelized sugar to Marlowe. "I do have a point. It wasn't easy between them. Burton felt his father didn't care, which he did, I'm sure. All of this is lead-in, so you won't think what's next is, suspicious, I suppose."

"Just tell it as you feel the story should go."

"Thank you. When you returned Pat's things, I set them on the kitchen counter, then took a nap. When I returned, the phone was gone. I found Burton with it. He'd unlocked it and was scrolling through texts and pictures. I think he wanted to see if his father had kept pictures of him on it."

"Had he?"

"A few. He didn't have many, pictures or texts. He was, I'd guess, a regular deleter. Is that a word?" She'd underlined the last two sentences with a hint of scorn.

"If not, it should be. How did he unlock it?"

"He's good at puzzles, Burton, and guessed the code, which was GOD1. Pat wanted that on a license plate. I talked him out of it. Burton must have overheard."

"Bright kid. This led you to contacting us why?"

"I couldn't help myself. After retrieving the phone, I scrolled through and came across a recent text exchange, one not yet deleted and felt it might mean something. Maybe I'm wrong. With Pat, often hard to tell. I printed it out." Reaching into a sweater pocket, she pulled out two sheets of typing perfectly folded into a square the size of the pocket. Handing them to Marlowe, she said, "They're between Pat and Tom. Toomey, that is."

Marlowe nodded, unfolding them. "Mind if I take a gander?"

She nodded back, focusing on her hands, folded on the tabletop.

He read the texts, the first from Tom two weeks back; Pat's replies coming promptly.

Still waiting, Pat.

Tom, sorry for delay. Doing good work. Takes time. Lol.

Pastor, you understand I'm not waiting till eternity. Talk is cheaper than salt. take big risks, expect big returns. Not happy.

Busy ATM. More soon.

The next were from the last few days before Pat's death, starting with Tom once more:

Still not happy.

No return text from Pat Brown. Tom followed with:

PAT!! Don't mess me about.

And then:

I need the money, asap. Not kidding around.

And then:

PAT!! Last chance! I didn't make it to where I am the easy way. You don't want to find out.

Pat replied to this text, leading to a back-and-forth exchange the day before his death:

> *Tom, nice to hear from you. Not sure the problem is.*
>
> *You know Pat. The money. Given and promised. Back side's missing? You made an investment in the future, the path of righteousness. Your reward cometh with the day of judgement.*
>
> *WTF?*
>
> *There is no money now, Tom. That's what.*
>
> *There'd better be.*
>
> *Remember your political ambitions. lol.*
>
> *Don't push me, I push back.*
>
> *Lol.*
>
> *WTF? This is your last warning.*
>
> *Come to the game, we can talk. There's other opportunities. Heaven awaits.*

That was the last text. Marlowe put the paper down. "Have thoughts on what exactly their issue was?"

Bridgette shook her head. "I wasn't privy to Pat's business deals."

"This feel like one of those?"

"Yes."

"Have you heard from Tom since?"

"No. I've only talked to him a few times ever." Her mouth was drawn into a thin line, lips pressed together like a shut door.

"Sorry to bring this back up, but on the day of Pat's demise, do you remember if anyone stopped to talk to him?"

She looked up, giving a short head tilt. "I've thought about it a lot. Too much, maybe." Her hands twisted together as if they were being rung out to dry. "I remember lots of people talking to him. Toomey, for one. Miss Cassian. Mike Ray. The concession stand worker. Jack Page, maybe? Kristin? Nearly everyone but me and the kids, which had to drive him crazy, as he hated being interrupted at the game."

"Anything else you've remembered from that day?"

"It was sunny, brightly sunny. Nothing else."

"Okay. Let us know if you do."

Morven put down the pieces of paper with the texts on them, which she'd been reading. "Threatening, and appears to be some kind of moneymaking scheme between the two."

"Probably Mike Ray was involved as well." Nelson pumped a fist in the air. "Toomey got taken by those two and wanted revenge."

"Slow down," Marlowe cautioned. "Fish in the pond. Are they biting? Tom Toomey is a big fish."

"We have to bring him in," Morven stated.

"Yes. But need to flagpole it up. Innocent." Marlowe perched on his desk, reached for the olive wood bowl, removed a pen from it.

"Innocent, sir?" Nelson's curiosity was piqued.

"Captain Rebecca Innocent. Who will talk to Chief Osbourne. Will take a spell, but I'll persevere." He took a whiff of the olive bowl.

Nelson's excitement boiled. "Tom Toomey, suspect number one. Not forgetting Nikola Cassian. Second place at the mo', but with her steamy relationship ending with an abrupt break off and a firing from her job, heavily in the frame?"

"Agreed," said Morven. "She had motive for Pat Brown. But Mike Ray?"

"Fair," Marlowe said, putting down the bowl. "Let's talk more with her. Bring her in. Jack Page coming in?"

"Soon, yes, thanks for the reminder. Nelson and I can take that. Probably routine, but good background."

"Bingo." Marlowe reached for the coffee mug on his desk, picked it up, sadly remembering it was empty. "Deeper shovel on Mike Ray too. Drogo and Ford. Mrs. Ray, talk to her this afternoon. Before that—"

"Coffee?" Morven asked.

"Coffee," Marlowe echoed, moseying off like a tired grizzly, mug in hand.

Morven and Nelson picked up the smiling Jack Page in the station lobby, escorting him to interview room six, another bland room, smallish, walls painted the color of chewed spearmint gum, black ceiling.

Medium-built Jack had a face that managed a strange balance of opposites: shallow cheeks with a full smile, thin nose with wide nostrils, blue eyes with dark eyebrows, crowned by thick russet hair spiked up on top. A face that would play havoc with anyone trying to describe it to a police sketch artist, but together presenting a jangly handsomeness. His outfit edged business casual: stretchy slate pants and a charcoal and white checked button-down, sneakers made to look like loafers shaded an undefinable woodsy brown.

The detectives offered coffee and tea, which he politely declined. Informing him that their conversation would be taped caused him to jump like a rabbit noticing a big dog two feet away. He didn't say anything, just went blank a moment before the wide smile reappeared, as if the rabbit realized it could blend into the surroundings and the dog might not see.

"Thank you for coming in to talk with us, Mr. Page," Morven began.

"Happy to help." Jack sounded keen as a party guest who'd been asked to open more Champagne. "You'll have to excuse me, as I'm not sure *how* I can help, but helpful is nearly my middle name."

"You're a member of the Chapter Creek Church?"

"That's right, I am. Gotta keep the devil at bay and help those in need."

"For how long?"

"Forgive me, I'm not actually sure. Ten years now? Maybe twelve? Let's say twelve."

"You were friendly with Pat Brown?"

"Pastor Pat. What a great loss." He momentarily frowned, then the smile popped back. "He was a great man, great preacher, great helper." The frown reappeared as he removed a used tissue from his pocket, wiped eyes that were dry, put the tissue and the smile back. "It's still hard to believe." He leaned in conspiratorially. "Do you have any leads?"

Nelson sidestepped the question like a running back. "Did you always attend the baseball games of Mr. Brown's children and your other friends?"

"Baseball. Awesome sport. Fun to attend. Supporting the church meant supporting Pat, and I'm an athletic supporter, so it went together like late nights and dancing."

"But did you attend?" Morven let it hang until Jack replied.

"What? Pardon me, I must have missed part of your question. I attended most games. Many."

"But you don't have children of your own."

"Never blessed that way." An exaggerated sadness that would have impressed a professional mime crossed his face, replaced quickly by the wide smile. "Another reason I attended the games."

Nelson decided it was time for an abrupt tactic switch. "You're divorced?"

Shock, sadness, then a smile flittered in order on Jack's face. "Yes. My ex-wife, Rose. But I don't see the relevance, as they say on TV."

"Was she as involved with the church as you?" Morven sensed the man hiding something.

"I beg your pardon? Rose?" For the first time, Jack's face was clear of any emotion. "Not really. She didn't believe in the same manner as me. She didn't click with the pastor."

"Was that necessary for churchgoers?"

"It certainly didn't hurt. Not to, apologies for the cliché, speak ill of the dead, if it sounded like I was, which I wasn't. Not a bad word would I speak about the pastor." The smile returned at the end of the circular sentence.

"We've been told you didn't always speak so highly of Pat Brown."

"By who?" Jack replied. "You can't trust everyone. Not to say anything specifically bad about a specific person."

Neither Morven or Nelson said anything, letting silence thicken like overheated béchamel. Jack's face went from smile to frown to nervous, then back to smile before speaking again. "Sorry, what was the question?"

The detectives remained quiet.

He finally said, "Pat Brown? That was it. Did I ever speak bad of our pastor? I don't recall. Once or twice, maybe. Nobody is perfect."

"What would have led you to that, speaking bad of him?" Morven asked after a beat.

"While the pastor was a very friendly man, Rose thought he was *too* friendly toward her a few times and wanted me to speak to him—confront him, her actual words, stand up to him. But I'm a supporter not a divider. Descending into gossip doesn't agree with my digestion." He appeared to have eaten a frog.

"Did this contribute to your divorce?"

"Yes."

"You never confronted him after these incidents?" Nelson's tone was shocked.

"As I said, Detective, you'll pardon me repeating myself, I'm a supporter. Bringing people together not driving them apart."

"Did you notice anything odd at the game last weekend?"

Jack leaned back, curious. "Pastor dying. Sorry, that's not odd, that's obvious. Nothing else."

"Did you talk to Mike Ray?" While they didn't want to release that Mike had also been murdered, Morven felt they should bring him up.

"Deacon Mike? A saint, funny too. I'm sure I talked to Deacon Mike, never miss a chance to rub shoulders with him, to slip into the vernacular."

"What about?"

"I'm not sure I remember specifically, Detective. Probably good works, the good game, the good weather. Just talking." His smile could have cracked his face in half. "As much as I'm enjoying our little chat, I need to get back to work."

"One more question." Nelson stood up. "Where were you this morning between five and six?"

"This morning? Checking email. The early sales bird gets the commission. Why?"

"Thank you for coming in." Morven moved to the door with a card in her hand. "Let us know if you remember anything else, and we will be back in touch."

"Back in touch?" Jack's frightened tone surfaced briefly before the smile returned. "I would be happy to talk more. At another time."

11

Captain Rebecca Innocent's office occupied a corner on the floor directly above the detectives' room, and while this meant she wasn't continually hovering as a direct presence, she did make enough trips to keep all on their toes. It also meant that going to visit her instilled a feeling of traveling. Even though only one floor up, it felt to Marlowe like he headed to a distinctly other place, another country, when taking the twenty steps. He called first, every time, to ensure the travel wasn't wasted. And because he'd much rather stay working at his desk or in the field.

Not that he and his superior had a bad relationship. He didn't hide things from her, and she had an earned reputation as a straight shooter that he appreciated. But she was more administrator, with days packed full as a sardine can if the sardines were meetings around budgets, headcount, PR, initiatives carrying clever and not-as-clever names, and personnel reviews. Each stop at her office he felt as if he were a cow wandering onto the tracks of a fast-moving train. One whose conductor would stop to avoid a dangerous collision, sure, though swearing at all bovines while braking.

Taking a breath before knocking at her office, he heard a voice talking at speed inside, unintelligible through the closed door. *Might as well be hung for a sheep as a lamb*, he thought, giving a booming series of raps.

For a moment the voice inside continued, then stopped. Just as he raised a hand for a second knock, the voice said, "Enter," loudly. Marlowe gripped the bronze doorknob, opened the door, and walked in.

Captain Innocent stood behind a wide cherrywood desk, resting hands on it. She wore a complete police dress uniform without a thread out of place. Taller than Marlowe by a few inches, Innocent had a statuesque figure, intelligent auburn eyes matched in color by shoulder-length hair pulled back, set off by high cheek bones and wide, friendly mouth that could switch to scowl at a snap, her whole face displaying animatedly whatever emotion she felt. She reminded Marlowe of a classical contralto opera singer, able to hit a range of notes at various volumes.

A computer sat on one side of the desk, three-tiered letter tray on the other, the police department not yet having moved completely away from paper internal correspondence. Two wooden chairs sat in front of the desk, the only other furniture in the room being a tall bookcase on one wall filled with policing manuals and other books boasting law and order-y titles. On the wall across from the bookcase there was a 3-foot-by-2-foot photo of the City's skyline at sunset, framed in black, and three photos underneath of the Captain with the Chief of Police, Mayor, and Governor.

"Detective Marlowe. Please, sit." She beckoned him to one of the chairs in front of the desk.

"Thank you, ma'am." He sat, then she followed.

"A second murder at the same place?"

Captain Innocent never dawdles, he thought. "Yes. Mike Ray, the deacon at the church where the first victim was pastor."

"Connected?" Her inflection hovered between statement and question.

"Still early days, Captain, but seems likely."

She clicked a nail on the desk twice. "Need more support?"

"In a way. I feel that with Morven and Nelson that's enough detectives." Marlowe felt too many detectives often muddied the waters, like too much cayenne could muddy a soup's flavors.

"But?" she continued before he elaborated. "Help with forensics? More officers on the street?"

"No, the supporting teams have been very helpful. Forensics could be faster, but they're moving at pace I suppose."

"Then?"

"There's a political angle."

"Political?" Innocent leaned forward over her desk slightly.

"One of the, I wouldn't say suspects, yet, but persons of interest is Tom Toomey."

She leaned back, considering. "I see. That *is* political. Have you talked to him?"

"Briefly."

"And?"

"Short-winded I'd say. Definitely knew both victims. Was at the scene, along with others to be clear, for the first murder. Gave me a bit of a brush off."

"I'm sure he did." She laughed, surprisingly shyly. "Is there more?" Marlowe reached into his pocket, brought out the papers with the texts on them, handed them over. "Pat Brown's wife brought these in. Texts between Toomey and Pat Brown. Not friendly."

She read as Marlowe gazed at the bookshelf, noticing a book called *The A.B.C. Murders* between *Anatomy of Interrogation Themes* and *The Book of Five Rings*.

Folding the papers and handing them back, thought wrinkles mapped her forehead. "I see. Political indeed. Want to bring him in?"

Marlowe nodded once.

"Leave it with me. You want me there?"

"Not unless you want to be there, Captain."

She smiled Mona Lisa-like before emphatically saying, "Great."

They sat silently for a moment before Marlowe stood. "Thank you very much. I can get out of your hair."

He'd almost made it to the door before she spoke up. "Oh, Marlowe."

Turning, his eyebrows raised.

"I heard John Arthur from the Lucy Dixon case was at the scene."

Her ability to parse specific details while running such a large department had, in the past, made Marlowe wonder if she possessed a sixth sense or psychic powers. He'd gotten so used to this skill he wasn't even surprised at the question.

"Both scenes."

"He's not becoming a murder follower, or tracking police radio communications or some such?"

"I don't believe so. I think he's just got a knack for being in the wrong place at the wrong time. Lonely guy, more than anything."

"Don't let him derail you."

"No ma'am."

Marlowe arrived back downstairs after stopping to stare out of an upper-floor window for a few minutes. The slightly elevated view from normal altered perspective enough to make it feel different, in the same way as a dog walking the opposite side of their home street. Evening's opening hours provided a glossy blue and dusky gold backdrop, with the sky once more cleared of clouds.

Sitting down, he noticed Morven walk in behind him. "Howdy." He raised one big hand in greeting.

"Marlowe." She sat, flicking open her computer, logging on rapidly. "What's the latest?"

"Nothing startling. Innocent is wrangling a Toomey interview. Speaking of, how was Jack Page?"

"Nervous. Definitely had an issue with Pat Brown, though played it down. Not sure I see him as a suspect. However, there is something in his manner. I'll get the notes in."

"Lose Nelson?"

She looked up, smiled, fingers a blur on the keyboard. "He pleaded debilitating hunger and headed to the canteen for a snack. And, yes, I requested coffee. For you."

"You are a true partner, Morven." Marlowe arched back on his chair, putting feet on desk. Beyond the background noise of a busy station, the only sound for a few minutes was Morven's steady typing.

"Hey, wait." She spoke to herself, stopping typing. Clicked once more. Marlowe kept silent. He knew if it was important, she'd speak up.

In another minute, she did. "This is interesting. Nelson reached out to the Financial Crimes Unit. They emailed back. They had already conducted preliminary research into Pat Brown and Mike Ray. The whole Chapter Creek Church. Feeling was that dodgy bookkeeping was going on, but they hadn't yet started a full-fledged investigation. They *did* find out that Mike Ray was charged with fraud years ago, specifically bookkeeping in a way to funnel money untraced. Never convicted, so didn't show up right away in background checks."

Marlowe's chair traveled back to ground level. "That's interesting indubitably. Were both victims involved in fraudulent dealings with members of the church? Funneling money to pockets. Enough to drive an affected party to murder?"

"Maybe." She thought it over. "Could it have been Mike, then Pat found out, and Mike killed him?"

"Who killed Mike?"

"Good point. Grieving widow? Grieving mistress?"

"Not sure either seems the type, for different reasons. It's worth considering. Feels the victims were close."

"Agreed. Distraught person who found out they'd been cheated by those they think of in such a positive light, their preacher, their deacon. That could drive a person to revenge. Maybe?"

"Maybe is where we're at. But good on Nelson to get the wheels turning."

"Good on Nelson for what?" The youngest detective had walked up without either noticing.

"Nelson, welcome back." Marlowe saw Nelson had a coffee cup in one hand and reached in his direction. "We received an update you kicked off."

"I did?"

"You did. Email in your computer. But first–"

"Yes sir?" Nelson interrupted energetically.

"First." Marlowe reached closer. "Is that coffee for me?"

Morven stood in front of a tall, newly constructed condo complex, glistening steel and glass accented by a geometric pattern of graveled slate running up the side. It took up a block's corner on a far northern edge of the same neighborhood the Chapter Creek Church resided within, but far enough away she doubted Mike Ray had walked to work since moving in to a unit on the top floor. She'd called Kristin Ray earlier, ensuring she was in, and now walked up to an intercom alongside the door to the complex, buzzing their apartment.

Kristin's voice came statically out of the intercom. "Yes?"

"This is Detective Morven."

"Come on up." A persistent buzzing sounded, followed by the door clicking open. Navigating a few sparse signs, Morven discovered a bay of three elevators and soon stood in a stretching hallway with beige carpet and stark white walls, in front of a wooden door painted white with 1012 in black metal lettering.

Before she knocked, the door opened wide, revealing Kristin Ray. Less dolled up than their earlier interview, she wore a white designer long sleeved T-shirt and black yoga pants, no shoes, showing off shockingly pink painted toenails. Holding the door with one hand, she cradled an old-fashioned glass against her side with the other, a strong florally juniper scent wafting out of it. She didn't say anything. Her platinum-blonde hair looked as if a small owl had decided to nest in it.

"It's me, Mrs. Ray, Detective Morven?"

"Sure," the woman replied, backing up. "Come in. I heard the elevator. You'd think in a place like this they'd make a quiet elevator. But nope."

Morven made it inside, the door swinging shut as if magnetized. Kristin walked down a hallway, walls as white as the one outside the door but with tile floors a polished black. Passing a few doors painted black, the hall opened up to a living room featuring floor-to-ceiling windows directly in front of them, view stretching out over houses, a woodland area, and the sound separating this neighborhood from downtown, dark-blue water reflecting evening skyline.

"Sitting in here good." Kristin phrased it more statement than question, pointing to one of two white leather couches before turning her back on Morven, walking to a white sideboard. On top of it stood a colorful array of spirit and liqueur bottles like soldiers at attention, alongside twinkling glassware and a full crystal ice bucket. The bottles were nearly the only colorful item in the room, as the walls were white, free of pictures outside of one black and white photo of the Tower of London, a younger Kristin and Mike smiling in front of it.

"Sure." Morven moved to sit, pulling out her notebook.

"I need another drink for this. Guessing you're on duty?"

"Yes, that's correct."

"Then I won't offer. Give me moment." Kristin's movements were slightly sluggish, but it didn't take long to drop a few ice cubes into a glass, followed by lots of gin, a splash of dry vermouth, and a wedge of lemon. She stirred slowly, staring at the wall as if she expected it to speak. Setting down the stir spoon, she walked tentatively, sitting on the couch opposite Morven, taking a drink before setting the glass down on a glass-topped coffee table.

"Well," Kristin said, "you aren't here to tell me about Mike dying. What is it?"

Morven hadn't spoken while the drink was being made, wanting to make sure Kristin found a seat before starting. "I hoped to ask a few questions. I know it's a hard time."

"Hard enough. Ask away."

"Thank you. First, do you know why Mr. Ray went to the Hettie Pattie playfields this morning?"

"This morning? Was it?" She paused, took sip of her drink. "No idea. I didn't even wake up when he left, if you can believe it."

"Did he often leave that early?"

"Not often. We liked to sleep in."

"Had he any out of the ordinary phone calls the past few days?"

"None that I recall. We didn't live in each other's pockets. He did have a lot of calls, but the almighty pastor dying would cause that."

"I'm sure you both were affected by Pat Brown's death, but did Mike seem unduly bothered?"

"Not unduly." Kristin's creased grin was more macabre than friendly. "Mike and Pat were close in some ways, but not like brothers. More business relationship. I'm sure Mike was sad, but he believed it was a woman Pat had issues with, or a husband, and that church business would just continue. Maybe he'd find another charismatic front man. Or woman, Nikola even. Do you think their deaths are from the same person?"

"We're keeping the investigation open. Can you think of anyone who would want to harm them both?"

Kristin took another sip, swirling the drink around in her mouth before swallowing. "Mike? He was mild as milk, never wanting to get emotional, have a scene. Pat could be a hard-ass, and had a wandering eye. Mike didn't have either trait but shared a liking for money with the pastor. That's one of the reasons we got along."

"How did you meet?"

"In a bar, years ago, as people did. He wasn't initially attractive to me, but he was persistent and eventually won me over. I knew he might come to a bad end but knew he'd be fun, too. He was that."

"A bad end? Why?"

"Listen, I loved the guy, for all his faults, and don't want to say anything. But I'd like to see whoever killed him hang. He wasn't always particular how he made money as long as he made it. That's all." She took another full drink.

"Would this lead someone to kill him?"

"Money can breed anger. People sometimes believe too much. It's like a lemon. You can get one that looks perfect on the outside, you believe it will taste great, but when cut open, it's rotten. People can be the same way. Which can make other people pissed off."

"Are you talking about your husband or Pat Brown?"

"Mike was Mike. Pat was more sheen on the outside, rotten inside."

"You didn't have a good relationship with him?"

"He tried it on with me once. I laughed him off."

"Did it bother Mike?"

"Not at all. He laughed at Pat too. It didn't change their, let's call it, partnership." She'd finished her drink and, balancing on the couch with one hand as she walked, went to make another.

Morven guessed after the next drink even the tolerance-high Kristin might become less helpful. "How did Mike get along with the other people at the games?"

"Games?" Kristin was befuddled for a moment, knocking a piece of ice on the floor. "Baseball games you mean? Mike got along with everyone in his marshmallowy way. He talked to Tom Toomey a lot, but he sort of intermediated between him and Pat. Tom made this building, did you know? Gave us a sweet deal." She slipped back onto the couch, a small wave of gin and vermouth sloshing over the glass edge. "Oopsidoodle. A spill. Mike tended to clean up the spills. For me and for Pat." A tear dropped down her cheek, smearing mascara.

Morven stood. "Thank you, Mrs. Ray. This has been helpful. If you think of anything else, please call. We may be back in touch." She set a card on the table. "I can show myself out."

Marlowe had stared at the board covered in pictures and notes for too long. Nothing was clicking. Blurring instead. And it was getting late. Sighing, he faced Nelson, currently intently scrolling, clicking occasionally.

"Nelson?" Marlowe broke in to the detective's digital depths.

"Yes, sir?" Nelson wearily answered.

"It's late, yes?"

"Yeah, sort of. Not that I'm tired."

"What're your thoughts?"

Nelson looked as if gears were grinding in his head. "On the case?"

"That's a bull's-eye."

"Feels we have a lot of suspects, Detective."

"That we do." Marlowe moseyed to his desk, pulling out the chair to face Nelson, and sat down. "You have a favorite in this horse race?"

"I do, I think." Nelson's energy picked up closer to normal. "A few. I'm not sure on how it happened exactly, and I haven't interviewed him myself, but I like Drogo, for one."

"Drogo? Do tell."

"He talked to the first victim at the game and provided him with food and stuff. Could have slipped him poison, taking him off guard."

"The why?"

"I'm not 100% sure. We did find in background checks that Drogo has had problems with the law before. Only possession as a minor. Maybe Pat Brown caught him selling drugs out of the concession stand and said he'd turn him in, and Drogo decided to cut him off. And Mike Ray could have known, too; he and Pat probably told each other everything." He gave Marlowe a hopeful glance.

"Hmm," Marlowe hummed loudly. "Enough of a motive? Drogo I could see selling, smart thought. Is he a killer, twice. Worth considering. Second choice?"

"Following the Drogo family, Nikola is my second choice. She had relationship with Pat Brown, an intimate one." Nelson blushed a bit. "It seems Pat ended it and hell hath no fury, as they say."

"Do they still say that?"

"I believe they do. It could be she got angry and killed him. Or got Drogo to do it, them being cousins."

"That's a theory."

"Another thing. Did you know she had an MBA? That's a—"

"I know what an MBA is, Nelson."

"Of course you do. With an advanced degree, why is she a secretary at a church, unless involved with Pat more deeply? Or involved with whatever he and Mike were up to, financial crimes. Then either gunning for revenge when kicked out of the scheme or wanted the money for herself. But could she carry off two murders alone?" His speech came out rapid as a sprinter in the final kick of a race.

"It doesn't take a big person to carry a big grudge, as my grandfather used to say. However, I'm not sold yet. Even though your hypotheses are intriguing. More?"

"My take is Tom Toomey is too high ranking to stoop to murder, and Ash, Miss Willums, not the type. Jack Page, we don't have enough background yet. Neville Maloney didn't get on with the first victim and has anger issues."

"Back to the full corral."

"Yeah, sorry."

"We need more facts, more info. More, more, more."

"More John Arthur maybe?"

Marlowe was starting to worry somewhat about John's influence on Nelson. "Not sure we're ready for that yet. More interviews to start. Let's follow your instincts. Invite Drogo and Nikola in for formal sit-downs. Plus, I missed out on Maloney. Bring him in too."

Nelson's tone dipped asking, "Tonight?"

Marlowe smiled. "Tonight's tucked in. Tomorrow. Get on it first thing. Why don't you head out, get some rest. No kickboxing."

"None, promise." By the time he'd finished, Nelson had suit coat on racing toward the door, as if a car at a long red light finally turned green.

Before heading out, Marlowe took a call from Morven after her interview with Kirstin Ray, catching her up on the latest and vice versa. She was about to head back in, but he suggested calling it for the night. He stared at the board for another fifteen minutes, then realized the information and photos on it were coalescing into a hazy abstract collage, nothing definite, nothing he could hang a hat on, or a solution. So, taking the elevator down to the first floor, he walked outside into a summer evening pleasant as if the murders never happened. Dark sky uncreased by clouds, stars outlining constellations clearly as if freshly painted. Only one or two cars passed slowly on the street. Kids' laughter rang out faintly from a few blocks away, carrying with it that staying up later than normal, gloriously innocent reverberation only heard in summer, only heard from tired happy children.

He felt tired too. Not in the same hilariously worn-out way, but that laughter carrying on the night's low breeze made him smile. The world wasn't all full of crime. There was still joy and fun to be had for many, for most, he hoped. Without realizing the motion consciously, he'd started toward the end of the block, away from the station parking garage, making a left at the light onto the road eventually taking him through Settler's Square. And after another turn and navigating the sparse Monday night crowds—the dog walkers, those who couldn't resist the perfect evening even if the first day of the work week, the late diners who didn't want to or were too busy to, make a meal at home—after making his way through them all, he found himself at Gary's.

The bar mirrored the neighborhood's Monday summer night—a sparse but happy crowd. A group of four played Dungeons and Dragons, one bald man with a great bushy salt-and-pepper beard at their booth gesticulating wildly in a sword-thrusting manner. A couple with matching immaculate long, blond hair cuddled in on one side of another booth like two romance novel angels. A lanky man with a buzz cut wearing bright blue jeans and an avocado-hued tank top read the newspaper at one end of the long L-shaped wooden bar. Another man sat at the bar's other end, wearing brown shorts, green-and-yellow striped socks, a collared blue-and-white western shirt, and blue baseball cap. The latter was talking with smiling bar owner and bartender Gary himself.

Marlowe slipped inside the door, angling to the two men at the bar, right next to his favorite stool. "Evening, John. Gary, how runs the ranch?"

Both John Arthur, the man at the bar, and Gary turned his direction, speaking simultaneously.

"Detective Marlowe, what a surprise."

"Kit, as I live and breathe."

Marlowe raised hands. "Gents." He slung off his sports coat, hanging it on the stool before sitting on top of it. "Nice to see you both."

"You too." Gary polished the bar with a towel haphazardly as he spoke, John nodding agreement. "We were talking of you mere minutes past. Gobsmacked you're here. Figured the case and all?"

"Night was nice. Once we'd closed the gate on the day at the station, my feet headed this way."

"Glad of it. John here's been holding up your corner."

"But not by sitting on your barstool. I wouldn't dare," John said, smiling. He had a glass of pale yellow wine in front of him.

"Kind of you." Marlowe straightened. "Whatcha drinking?"

"Ruffino Orvieto Classico. Umbrian white. When Gary told me it was one of the choices, I couldn't resist. Little apple, little floral, little mineralness. Felt right for a mild evening. You know I love Italian drinks. As do you, I believe?"

"I am somewhat partial. Heck, that sounds tasty. Gary, any more Orvieto back there?"

Gary's brown-and-gray-streaked goatee moved up and down. "Multiple bottles, if needed. Let me grab a glass." He stepped toward the bar's middle, reaching for a second wine glass, then stooped to a fridge nestled under the bar. Pulling out a bottle half full, he removed the cork and began filling the glass. The two men maintained silence as the bartended worked. He returned, setting the now-full glass in front of Marlowe.

"Cheers, Detective." John raised his glass in Marlowe's direction, who returned the cheers before taking a deep, slow drink.

"All right?" Gary asked.

"Delicious." Marlowe breathed in the wine's aromas. "Like frolicking in a spring meadow."

Gary laughed. "Living up to your namesake, Kit, with that poetry." He gave the room a glance, noticed empties on the D&D table. "I'd better crack on. There's a thirsty paladin at that table. And they have a Holy Avenger longsword, so, back soon." He headed down the bar.

"Full day since I saw you?" The loquacious John was surprisingly brief.

"Was that today?"

"That full?"

"Yep. Lots happening."

"Two murders at one baseball field is a lot. Even in Midsommer, where the murders come in bunches."

He didn't say more, wearing an apprehensive look, expecting Marlowe to follow up. But Marlowe sat quietly, taking another sip of his wine. John fiddled with his glass, took a sip, and continued.

"Any updates? Guessing you were interviewing and researching suspects and witness and people helping you with your inquiries. Breaking the team into parts to divide and conquer. Setting the forensics wheels into rapid motion."

Marlowe's eyebrows raised just a touch. "John?"

"Yes?"

"We're in Gary's. It's a bar. Off-limits to case talk as a general rule."

"Right. Unless I have a revelation to drop on you here, Sherlock style?"

"I don't see your deerstalker."

"The baseball cap doubles as one." John removed his hat, put it back on backward, then forward to mimic the deerstalker's two bills. "You know, Arthur Conan Doyle never once mentioned a deerstalker hat in his writing? The illustrator of the original Sherlock Holmes stories, Sidney Paget, drew him with one."

"You don't say?"

"I do say, and see by your grin that you probably already knew that Holmesian fact."

"Do you, by the way?"

"Do I?"

"Have a revelation?" Marlowe knew John's quirks, but also knew the man often had uncanny insights—if you could shift him from the TV mystery talk.

"Sadly, none. There's something gnawing at my brain, but I haven't unraveled it yet. The two men murdered. Very different kinds of men. Mike Ray, conciliatory, pleasant, slightly whinging demeanor. Pat Brown, fiery, confrontational and charismatic. Motives on all sides, financial, passionate. There are always lots of motives. No final revelation yet. It's a tragedy, the murders, families, and church almost like a king's court in the background."

"You make it sound like *Hamlet*. Shakespearean."

"'The Russian play.'"

"Hamlet takes place in Russia?"

John affected a semi-Eastern European accent. "'No, but Hamlet is very Russian. He worries too much, complains about everything, takes too long to make up his mind, and when he finally does, it all ends badly anyway. Such is life.'"

"That's deep, John." Marlowe took another big swallow of his wine. John held a deeply serious expression, but broke into a grin. "Not really. It's actually a theory and quote from a *Brokenwood Mysteries* character, the forensic pathologist, Gina Kadinsky, who is Eastern European transplanted into New Zealand. Where the show takes place.

"I recall that fact."

"Of course you do, being a detective. She may have a point. About it ending badly."

"Let's hope the bad parts are done. And we solve this case. Sooner the better. Too much time on the trail without heading in makes for sore horses."

"No breakthroughs yet, then?"

Marlowe's only reply was to pick up his glass, take another drink.

"Looks like it. Perhaps time for an interview montage. *Brokenwood* is big on interview montages. You remember the idea, from our last case?"

The man was persistent. Marlowe admired that, even if he'd rather drink his wine in peace. "I do recall that particular Arthur theory, yes. John?"

"Hmm?" John stared at the shelves of bottles behind the bar, thinking.

"You remember, this is—"

"Real life. Not—"

"TV. No montages. Just police work."

"Any police theories to share?"

"One." John edged forward as Marlowe went on. "From this one police officer." He pointed at himself. "My theory is, this is exceptionally tasty wine. Ideal for a summer evening round the bar. Why didn't I know of it before?"

John leaned back. "No case talk in the bar. Solely drink talk. With that, it is somewhat hard to believe you didn't know Orvieto Classico, as I remember you mentioning your past Italy trips and how much you, like my wife and I, loved it there. You did say you spent time in Umbria?"

Marlowe, eyes slightly glazed at memories of the green heart of Italy, softly replied, "I did say. I missed Orvieto."

"A shame. Nice Umbrian town on a tufa. The cathedral façade is amazing, the whole cathedral, really. That façade has sculptures, bas-relief carvings, by or planned by an artist named Maitani. Scenes from the Bible. There's a Last Judgement part, and on the bottom, the carvings are hose people being sent to Hell. Frightening stuff. Feels in a way it should be required viewing for police, get a feel for the criminal element in a historic, or base way

"I'll have to see it before we get it added to the police academy curriculum."

"You should go back, see it, eat some truffles, have more wine."

"More wine." Marlowe tipped his glass, finishing the last drop, and set it back down. "More wine isn't a bad idea. One more glass."

"Agreed." John finished his too. "Then maybe you'll loosen up on talking about the case."

"John?"

"Yes, Detective?"

"No case talk in the bar."

The next morning, all three detectives were in before anyone else in the room had shown, arriving within minutes of each other around 7:30 a.m.—Marlowe first, Morven second, Nelson third. The first two hadn't gotten past muted morning greetings before he trotted in, not favoring one leg anymore. The room faintly glowed from summer's morning sunshine —another clear day so far—combining with the echoey emptiness to feel less like a routine room of desks and more, if letting imagination run, like a forest grove where the trees were squatty and four-legged. It wouldn't last, however, as by the time the three settled behind desks, other officers began trickling in, the volume of speech raising, the air itself taking on a modern crackle as computer keys began being tapped, a printer in one corner humming, overhead lights turned on, driving away sunshine.

Marlowe had left the night before after finishing a second glass of Orvieto Classico, heading out with John Arthur before waving goodbye as he walked one way and the older man another. While he'd brushed his teeth twice since the final glass, and was halfway done with a grande café Americano picked up at Sampson's Sips (along with a croissant, the only traces of which that were left in the world being three flakey crumb fallen into the pocket of Marlowe's white dress shirt after bouncing of one persistent wrinkle near the collar), on some level he still tasted and smelled the wine's spring bouquet. Picking up the olive wood bowl on hi desk, raising it almost unconsciously to hold it near his nose, he felt the wine presence expanding. *Just a daydream*, he thought, setting the bow back down. Back to reality.

Morven removed her khaki-colored linen suit coat, which matched her pants, featuring a single button and a lapel curving out like the wing of a bird of prey, set off by a pearlescent white shirt. Large, alert eye already scanned the screen of her computer, as if willing it to come to mechanical life faster. She'd spent the night before at home, sweats and T-shirt on, lying lengthwise on her comfy gray couch with feet up on one couch arm, sparkling water in one hand, notebook with interview and case notes in the other, a salad of arugula, parmesan, carrots, sprouts olive oil, and balsamic balanced on her stomach. She'd read deep into the evening, but didn't show any tiredness.

Nelson, on the other hand, sported slight dark rings under his eyes and his blue Brooks Brothers suit displayed a patching of uncharacter istic wrinkles. He'd shucked the coat, perching on the chair he'd been occupying recently on one corner of Morven's desk. Computer up, he glanced in what he hoped was a surreptitious manner at the other two A sixty-four-ounce, clear water bottle sat on the desk beside his comput er, and he'd already swilled nearly half of it since he got there, believing that increased hydration could wake him up after he'd spent a nigh tossing and turning, thinking about the case and Mrs. Marple for many maddening moments while trying force sleep, it resisting like a menta imp of the perverse.

Marlowe finally broke the silence. "Team, it's Tuesday. Normally the most common as cornbread day of the week."

Morven looked up. "But today?"

"Today we're kicking Tuesday into a gallop."

She glanced at Nelson, who was wide-eyed. "Increased cowboy talk. Must be a big day. What's first?"

"Let's get on the speaking telegraph, set interviews up. For today. Be firm. We need—" The phone on his desk rang, cutting his sentence off. Reaching across the deck and picking it up, he answered, "Marlowe. Yes ma'am. Morning ma'am."

Morven mouthed the word "Innocent" to Nelson, knowing the captain was the only person Marlowe called ma'am.

"Yes, we do still need to interview him. You did?" He grabbed notebook and pen, crooking phone between ear and shoulder as if an office contortionist. "That sounds dandy. I'll be there." The phone slipped, threating to pop out completely, and he rapidly dropped the pen to re-stick phone on his shoulder.

Nelson watched Marlowe's phone-and-notebook performance with a kind of scared fascination.

"Just me? Got it. Thank you." Setting down the phone, he grabbed the dropped pen and started jotting down notes, like a bird picking at ants on pavement. "Captain Innocent. First interview is already set."

"Who?" Nelson asked.

"Tom Toomey himself. She asked the chief, who corralled him. One p.m."

Morven smiled. "Nice. Surprising he capitulated so quickly. Just him?"

"No. He's bringing Buchanan."

"Buchanan?" Nelson asked.

Answering as Marlowe scratched in his notebook, Morven's voice carried a hint of distain. "Shane Buchanan. Lawyer. Likes to play debonair, but full of hot air in my opinion. Rolls mostly with rich clients. The man of a million objections, I heard one judge call him."

"He can be an ornery cuss." Marlowe put his notebook down. "But we'll handle. Or, I'll handle."

"Just you?"

"Condition of Mr. Toomey paying us a visit." He pulled his shirt sleeves "And he'll only come through the back entrance. Quiet demanding. But that is one interview set. Let's pin down Nikola, Neville, and Drogo." Marlowe finished the last of his coffee, tossing the cup in the trash as he walked toward the board.

"I'll call Nikola and Drogo," Morven volunteered. "Nelson, you got Neville?"

"For sure, Detective. Right away." Nelson took a big swig of water. "Well, in one moment. A question first?"

"Sure."

Leaning near Morven, he whispered, "What is a speaking telegraph?

12

Marlowe's Tom Toomey interview was scheduled for one. By chance, Morven and Nelson's interviews with Nikola Cassien and Neville Maloney were scheduled simultaneously at two. Marlowe figured his would be done by then, so he could join Nelson, as he hadn't met Neville. Then Tom was late. The front desk first received a call from his lawyer that Mr. Toomey was unavoidably detained and would be fifteen minutes behind. Two minutes after that, another call (1:20), then another (1:30), and another (1:45), like tardy baby ducks lagging behind their mother in a row. Finally, a call patched through to Marlowe where the lawyer's distinctive clipped nasally voice said they were on the way and would arrive at the station's back door, used by officers and civilian employees, no later than two.

A minute before two, Marlowe leaned onto the station's brick wall, gazing wistfully at the barn door's width of blue sky visible between station and parking lot. Two crows perched like lunch-breaking 1920s construction workers on the garage's top edge chattering, then in tandem flew off at the exact moment Tom and Shane rounded the corner. The former's wide strides kept the shorter lawyer speeding up in a comical half-jog every few steps to keep from being left behind, his full combed back mane of silvery hair fluffing with each jog.

Reaching Marlowe, Tom's put-upon visage could have shamed a bishop interrupted mid-sermon. Shane smiled coyly, saluting as he spoke.

"Detective Marlowe, wonderful to see you."

"Thought I'd see you earlier." Marlowe didn't return the salute.

"As you know, Mr. Toomey is a remarkably busy man. We are here. Shall we . . ."

"Thank you, Mr. Toomey, for coming."

Marlowe opened the door, walked past a glass-fronted reception smaller than the front entrance's, and through a metal door after a barely noticeable buzzing went off. "This way, please."

Following a journey down two hallways, one shorter, one longer, a left turn, then a right, they ended in front of the same row of interview rooms found much more quickly if coming in the front. Marlowe reached for the handle of interview room six, noticing the door to room five clicking shut.

"Wait," Tom said. "I was told I'd have special treatment."

"You get to interview with me alone. Pretty special."

"Shane." Tom grimaced at the lawyer. "This isn't what we agreed upon."

"It isn't. Detective, come now. We can call your boss."

"Call away. I can take you out front to call. I'd say it's gonna take up more of your time, and you'll end up answering the same questions, maybe in a nicer chair. It'd be like leaving a watering hole cause you don't like the rocks."

Tom sighed, shook his head at Shane and grabbed the door handle. "If this will close the loop faster, it's fine. Detective."

As Marlowe waited out back for Tom Toomey and his lawyer, Morven and Nelson prepared for their interviews. It had been decided early on that Morven would take Nikola. The two more established detectives didn't vocalize it, but by looks agreed that Nikola's manner and presence might be a difficult solo interview for the younger Nelson, who could get thrown off. They rounded up notes, sipping pre-interview cups of coffee, and bounced around ideas before taking the elevator down to the first floor to meet the interviewees in the station's main lobby.

At two exactly, they walked out of the door separating station from public, nodding to the wall-sized Officer Coleman at the desk behind a thick shielding of glass, his impressive handlebar mustache moving as he talked to an elderly gentleman wearing a pork pie hat. Seated on a bench nearby, Neville gazed at his scruffy sneakers, elbows on jeaned knees, chin balanced on hands, teal baseball hat with the Seafarers' S in gold on his head matching the satin teal and gold Seafarers bomber jacket pulled tightly around him. He had a small blue backpack on the bench beside him. Nikola bustled in as they were approaching Neville, stalking through the door opened by a man passing who'd noticed her.

She took the room in at a glance, as if waiting for someone to approach her, black hair framing the almond skin of her face via two levels, bangs and ends, crimson lips in a half-pout, eyes demarcated by black eyeliner and blue eyeshadow. The same knee-high stilettoed boots as during her previous interview didn't reach the lower edge of a crimson tweed and leather skirt separated from a white dress shirt by a golden belt the width of a fist, the gold belt paralleling a gold link chain loose around neck. Her flashily glamourous presence captured the room like a fire unexpectedly erupting, all eyes angling the same direction except Neville, who continued staring down. Her eyes flitted over the room, stopping on no one.

Morven gave Nelson a quick elbow to the ribs, as he seemed incapable of pulling eyes away from Nikola. She whispered, "Nelson, you're on Neville. I'll head off Miss Cassian."

Nelson's head whipped back like it was on a fishing line being reeled in. "Check," he whispered back, taking the last two steps to Neville.

Morven took two the other direction, tapping Nikola's shoulder.

Nikola huffed, eyes blazing. "What?" she began, before recognizing Morven, looking up at the taller women.

"Miss Cassian, thank you for coming down."

"Of course, officer… sorry, I can't recall."

"Detective Morven."

"Where's Detective Marlowe?"

"He's busy at the moment. It will be just you and me. Please, follow me."

Like a child whose toy was taken away, Nikola crossed arms as if she wasn't going anywhere. Morven ignored the stance, waking over and opening the door she and Nelson arrived through, heading down the hall forcing Nikola to jog unsteadily after her to catch up before the door closed.

Morven opened to the door to interview room two, allowing Nikola a moment to catch up and recompose before she strode haughtily in. The room's walls were green like grass gone too long without watering, the metal table and chairs stark in their plainness, lighting industrially rudimentary.

"Take a seat." Morven motioned to a chair across from the one she moved into, unbuttoning her suit coat as she sat.

"Very snazzy room here." Nikola's frown took in the room as she sat both knees facing the door. "Fashionably bleak. Did you decorate?"

"I only have a few questions. First, where were you between 4:30 and 7:30 a.m. yesterday?"

"Sleeping. Like most."

"At home?" Morven had a notebook open, as well as a typewritten page of notes.

Nelson had believed Marlowe and he would interview Neville together but as the clock ticked near to two, realized the older detective would be waiting for or interviewing Tom Toomey at the same time. He'd quickly broken out his I-POA (Interview Plan of Attack, an acronym he'd developed and was extra fond of) into a detailed series of pages, trolling notes from their earlier Neville interview and notes on the case pertaining to the man. He felt, admitting it cooly to himself, completely ready when heading down with Morven.

Once Nikola Cassian entered the room with her own kind of distracting flourish, Nelson's head had for a moment slipped into a red-tinged romantic cloud. *No one,* he thought, *had mentioned to him how pretty Miss Cassian was.* Her boots alone would have captured the young detective's attention. The combination of severe bi-level haircut, alluringly wide eyes, and well-made up lips pulled his glance toward her, along with the glances of a few men waiting in the room.

Morven's sharp elbow knocked Nelson out of his musing on whether he could ever date someone who had been a suspect in a case, followed by her saying, "Nelson, you're on Neville. I'll head off Miss Cassian." Pulling attention back to the man sitting in front of them, he nearly said, "I'm on it," loudly, but caught himself, instead whispering, "Check." *Get in the game Nelson,* he thought, clenching fists tight as a boxer being taped before a fight. He stepped up to Neville.

"Mr. Maloney?"

The man started as if caught doing something he shouldn't have. "Yes, sorry, wasn't paying attention." He stood, grabbing his backpack. "Detective, it was Nelson? Like the Seafarers' old relief pitcher from the late '90s, early 2000s?"

"I guess so? I mean, yes, I am Detective Nelson."

"Good."

Realizing after a moment they were still standing silently in the middle of reception, Nelson moved toward the door speaking rapidly. "Thank you, Mr. Maloney, for coming down to the station. We have a few more questions and felt having an interview here would best." They'd made it past the door by the time he'd finished, and were in the hallway in front of room five. "In here," Nelson said, opening the door so Neville could walk in first. Nelson followed, thinking as the door closed that he heard Marlowe down the hall.

Inside, Neville didn't move more than a few feet, gazing at the three gray and one mirrored walls like they were a painted, mesmerizing scene. Nelson scooted around him, approaching the standard metal table and chair set.

Motioning to a chair across from the one he'd pulled out, he said, "Please, Mr. Maloney, sit here."

Neville shook his head as he walked over. Sitting, he removed his cap and set it down precisely aligned to the table's edge, running fingers through thinning blond hair.

Nelson took the pages of his I-POA out of a suit coat pocket with one hand, unbuttoning the coat with the other, placing them in front of him face down. "Let's begin. First, would you like any tea or coffee?"

Neville gave a head shake.

"Good. I mean okay." The man's silent nature flustered Nelson, but he determined not to let it show. "Let's begin. First, can you let me know where you were yesterday between 4:30 and 8:00 in the morning." He frantically searched pockets while talking, looking for his notebook. Neville didn't seem to notice.

"I was sleeping until 5:30, then at the shop."

Nelson raised himself high enough off the chair to delve into back pockets. Nothing. He'd forgotten his notebook. Luckily, he'd discovered a pen in his coat's inner pocket, allowing for note-taking on the loose sheets of paper making up the I-POA.

This time, his movements attracted Neville's wavering attention. "Everything all right, Detective?"

"Perfect. Let's stay on target. You said?"

"Sleeping until 5:30, then to the shop."

"That's All the World's a Sport downtown?"

"Edge of downtown. Half-mile from the stadium."

"Anyone with you during those times?"

Tom and Shane sat on one side of the table, Marlowe on the other. He'd removed his sports coat, but they left theirs on, only unbuttoning, Shane's faux sharkskin navy number gleaming metallically under the room's light.

The lawyer crouched as if mid-spring, as Tom seemed to be checking the trio's reflection in the one mirrored wall. "First, Detective, will this be recorded? We would rather it wasn't."

"Loose lips," Tom said.

"How about I take notes. This time." Marlowe took out notebook, pen, and sheets of typing paper with the texts, smoothing them out with one hand as he set them down. "To begin, where were you yesterday between 4:30 and 7:30 a.m.?"

"I object," Shane interjected before Tom even opened his mouth.

"This isn't a courtroom, counselor," Marlowe replied.

Shane sat still, silence overtaking the room. Marlowe decided he could wait it out. Finally, Tom spoke up.

"This is a waste of my precious time. I didn't murder Mike Ray. We were close associates."

The news had hit the papers, so it wasn't surprising he knew. "It'd be helpful to have timelines."

Tom looked at Shane, then said, "I was at home with my girlfriend, Emma Dun, until 5:30. I work early, getting boots on the ground. From home, I went to the office. All morning. Satisfied?"

"Anyone else at the office?"

"Not until eight. I'm driven, not a slave driver."

"There, does that answer your questions, Detective?" Shane's voice dripped appeasement like honey. "Mr. Toomey has been more than helpful."

"That's one answer. I need a few more."

"Clock is ticking." The lawyer raised his wrist, checking his gold watch. He should have been handsome, with well-balanced features, chin not too sharp or square, aquiline nose, blemish-free skin, few worry lines. Except his eyes were small, sizing everyone they saw up like a used-car salesman about to swear a 2002 Ford is in actuality a 2022.

"You mentioned you and Mr. Ray were close associates. Business associates?"

"If the church is a business. Which it is, in a way, if you want it to grow. You have to push the envelope. Mike understood."

"Did he act as an intermediary between you and Pat Brown?"

"What does that mean?"

Shane broke in again. "Irrelevant."

"Irrelevant?" Marlowe felt one of the lawyer's tactics was throwing in words that didn't necessarily match the situation but sounded important. "You were seen having arguments with Pat Brown, also a victim. Did Mike smooth things over when those arguments arose?"

"Not especially. As I told you before, Pat and I had discussions on church matters. But not arguments."

Marlowe flipped the paper with the texts over. "I have here a series of texts between you and Pat."

"I was asleep at home." Nikola rolled her eyes at Morven. "Alone, before you ask."

"Nobody to verify?"

"Nope. You'll have to take my word. I wasn't at the playfields with Mike, if admitting that speeds this up."

"How was your relationship with Mr. Ray?"

"Relationship? You make it sound spicy, Detective." Nikola's playfulness from the interview at the church had been replaced with a flat demeanor until now, where she appeared to be attempting an air of sisterly confidentiality. "It wasn't like that with Mike. We were strictly friend zone. Not my type."

"But you *were* friends, as well as working together at the church?"

"Friendly."

"Have any disagreements with him? When you were temporarily let go, for example?"

"Temporarily let go?" Her eyes flared, relaxed. "We talked about that. A misunderstanding. But no on the disagreements. We got along fine."

"Can you think of anyone who didn't get along fine with him?"

Nikola paused, tilting her head as if playacting a thoughtful pose. "Nope. Mike tried his best to butter up everyone. It's impossible to believe someone would be bothered enough to kill him. If he *was* murdered?"

"When was the last time you saw him?"

"The last time I saw you. Same time."

"Any phone calls or other communication after that?"

"Some work stuff. What to do in certain situations with Pat gone."

"Speaking of work, how knowledgeable are you about the church's business side and finances?"

Nikola stretched her legs, flicking invisible dirt off the heel of one boot with the toe of the other. "Somewhat knowledgeable. I know there were many donations for many causes."

"You have an MBA. I'm surprised you didn't help more."

"I offered. Pat and Mike did more. And did well. Money-wise, I mean." Nikola's tone shifted again, daubed with irony. "My checks arrived on time. Honestly, I didn't have much to do with that side. But with Pat gone, probably would have had more involvement."

"Why is that?"

"Mike couldn't do it himself. My business background, I could have taken some of the weight and rewards. Hard to know what happens next."

"Will you run the church?"

"Doubt that congregation approves a woman at the pulpit. Maybe someone comes in?"

"To work with you?" Here was a motive they hadn't considered.

"If the church is there, I'd hope I would be to. I can't predict the future. Can you?"

Morven abruptly switched subjects. "How long had you and Pat Brown been having an affair?"

"My wife was at home with me, as you'd expect." Neville moved his ha an inch into the table. "I left before Dougie was up. At the shop, jus me. Why?"

"Routine procedure, Mr. Maloney. What time did you arrive at the store? Are you there that time every day?" Nelson gritted teeth, realizing he'd asked two questions at once. Not the best interview technique *Time to focus.*

"Probably sixish? I didn't stop on the way or check the clock directly." Neville stared at the white-with-black-numbers wall clock behind Nelson like he was looking at it for assurance.

"That your normal time in?"

"Sorry, you asked that before. No, not normal. We're doing inventory, which consists of long days. There's a rat problem too."

"Rat problem?"

"Our back door and bay open on an alley shared by multiple restaurants, leading to rats in the store. I wanted to get in before anyone, put out some poison. I know it's not very humane, but they've become a big problem. Sometimes you have to change the lineup."

Nelson held his pen up in the air like a band conductor. "Someone must have seen you doing this in the alley?"

"I don't believe I saw anyone. It was very early. Quiet as a baseball diamond when the visiting team has hit a go-ahead homerun in the ninth."

"No garbage collectors? Restaurant workers? They start at the crack of dawn."

"No, no one. Why does it matter? I said I was at the shop."

"If no one saw you, it means you have no alibi for that time frame No one can affirm your movements are what you say, that you were at the shop during that time."

"Why do I need an alibi? Is this about Mike Ray's death?" Neville viewed Nelson face-to-face for the first time.

"We are investigating that, yes. How did you get along with Mr. Ray?"

Putting both hands palm up in a ball-catching movement, Neville replied. "Fine. We didn't have much in common. He was courteous. I wouldn't wish him harm."

"He's the one who informed you that you would no longer be coaching, correct?"

"In a way. I knew it was Pat's doing."

Nelson felt the time was right for pushing him. Solve the case, both cases. "You admitted to being angry enough to kill Pat. Mike was the messenger, which had to make you angry. Which led you to killing both of them."

Neville wasn't nearly as startled as Nelson expected. The man again gazed up at the clock. "I was angry about coaching, as I admitted, but I didn't kill them. I'm not some kind of madman. I'm a father who enjoyed coaching his kid. Not being able to do that made me angry, but not enough to kill anyone, much less two people. As I said, I was at work yesterday morning. During Pat's death, I was up sitting with my wife watching the game."

"Speaking of the game, you were seen talking to Pat. That's surprising given your feelings."

"Talking to Pat?"

"Yes, you were seen stopping by. You weren't sitting with your wife the whole time."

Confused, Neville repeated, "Talking to?" then went quiet, dipping head to his hands.

Shane shot out of his chair, then sat back down. "Detective Marlowe, did you get the required court order for those texts from a judge? I don't think they're admissible." Tom tried to read the paper as Shane pontificated, but Marlowe's wide hands made it impossible.

"Once again, counsellor, this isn't a courtroom. And the texts were brought in voluntarily by Mrs. Brown."

"I'm not sure we should answer any questions around these texts, Mr. Toomey." Shane ran a hand through his hair as he looked to Tom, who sat quietly, staring at palms as if answers might be written there. Then he spoke.

"I've sent a fair amount of texts to Pat and Mike. Church business, as mentioned."

"These seem more personal. For example." Marlowe raised the paper, reading off it. "'I take big risks, expect big returns. And I'm not happy.' What big return?"

"I object," Shane said. "My client doesn't have to answer anything that could incriminate him, or about his finances."

"Incriminate?" Marlowe asked.

"Shane," Tom said, "shut up a moment. When in business, you sometimes need a paradigm shift to keep momentum rolling. Pat had an investment idea, but needed capital. I provided some. Enough said?"

"Let me read a bit more." Marlowe again raised the paper. "'Pat. Last chance. I didn't make it to where I am the easy way. You don't want to find out.' Sounds threatening."

Shane spoke first. "My client is a man of passion. That is all."

"Okey dokey. How about when Pat said, 'There is no money now, Tom,' and, 'Remember your political ambitions'? Was that a threat from him to you?"

"Detective, these are texts," Shane exasperatedly replied. "Emotions run high. I don't think my client can remember every text sent. And you're defaming one of the victims."

"Not defaming. Curious to why Pat Brown and Mr. Toomey exchanged threats."

Shane started to talk again, but Tom shushed him. "We weren't exchanging threats. A difference of views. It happens."

"'Don't push me, I push back.' And, 'This is your last warning.'

Texts you sent, which to me sound like threats."

"I didn't kill Pat Brown. End of story."

"See, Detective, that is that. Do we need to be here longer?" Shane made to stand.

"One or two more questions. Won't take a tic. Mr. Toomey, do you spend time on the actual construction sites you're associated with?"

"What does that have to do with anything? Wait, whatever. Yes, I do. I believe in digging deep and am not afraid to get my hands dirty. Always have been."

"Have any rat problems?"

"Detective." Shane added extra e's between the d and t, drawing it out like fairground taffy. "How can that be relevant?"

"Suppose I'm just curious?"

Tom rolled his eyes. "Yes, construction sites tend to have rat problems. We have people to take care of that."

"Using poison?"

"Whatever it takes that's cost efficient."

"All in all, seems pretty legal to me." Shane brushed his hands together as if removing dust. "With that, enough. We've gone far afield, and this after Mr. Toomey has been good enough to stop by in his busy day. I think we're done." Both lawyer and businessman stood.

Marlowe took his time, straightening the sheets of paper, putting his notebook and pen in pockets, picking his sportscoat off the chair. "We're done. For today."

"Who told you what?" Nikola went from indignation to mock shock mid-phrase, as if a doll with two faces flipping back and forth.

Morven didn't say a word. They sat in a silence for a full minute until Nikola broke it with a sardonic smile.

"You've been misinformed about any affair."

Morven remained silent, looking at Nikola without blinking. The woman tried to hold Morven's stare. The contest lasted a minute before Nikola looked away toward the mirror. She pretended to adjust a stray hair, rubbing a cheek with one hand like she had a toothache.

"So you know. Where from? Oh, it doesn't matter. About a year."

"Was it still going on when he died?"

"Not exactly. He'd stopped it. When he told me my services weren't needed at the church."

"Guessing that made you angry."

"You'd guess right. I worked hard to get my position at the church. And with Pat. Dealt with some crap, too. Bastard didn't even care."

"Do you keep in touch with Drogo regularly?"

"My cousin? Random. Not as much as when we were younger. Some. He's a goof, but fun. Why?"

"Just doing background."

"Did he tell you about me and Pat? Probably. Dork. Cops scare him."

"Which made you angrier, losing the job or the breakup?"

"That's an odd question." Nikola considered. "Not sure it matters. The job. Guys are everywhere, getting another wouldn't be hard. Pat never promised me he'd get divorced or some nonsense. Wouldn't have worked for the church. They had become intertwined."

"Losing both was like losing twice. I get it. Twice the anger."

Nikola's lower lipped slipped forward, giving a childish pout. "I suppose."

"You'd broken up and lost your job. Both via the same person. Then you go to his kid's baseball game. What did you talk to him about?"

"Didn't we go over this with the other detective?"

"It's odd you'd go to the game, much less talk to him, with what you've just said."

"You're persistent." She sighed. "I wanted to go to ensure I had Pat where we *had* to talk. I tried to convince him to take me back. That I would be in his best interest."

"Threatening him?"

"Not threatening. Convincing. I can be very convincing." She smiled coyly. "Guys are easy, often."

"Did he go for it?"

"Not immediately. Wavering. Which is why I wouldn't have killed him."

"Did you bring him food or a drink at the game?"

"No." She shook her head, rapidly at first, then slowing like a car pulling into a parking space. "Wait. I didn't take him anything, but I did refill his cup. I took a cup he'd been drinking Dr. Pepper out of, which he loved, and got it filled with sangria. That was his norm: start with soda that Drogo usually brought him, then switch to a drink. Maybe he thought if I got it filled no one noticed. If my fingerprints were on his cup, that's why. But I didn't kill him, even if angry. And I had no reason to kill Mike. We were going to run the church together. Now, can I go? I'm answered out. Unless you want to book me?"

Morven stood. "I can escort you out, Miss Cassian. We'll contact you as our inquiries continue."

"Whatever." She winked bawdily at Morven. "But next time, I want to be grilled by Detective Marlowe."

"Sorry, Detective Nelson. I remember talking to Pat now. It was about Gerry's swing." Animation colored Neville's voice. "I noticed that Gerry, Pat's youngest, kept doing a minute double-clutch motion before extending his swing. A twitch. Nothing most people would see. I guessed Gerry himself had no idea, like many players. I decided to tell Pat what I noticed."

"Why? You didn't like him."

"That's true. I admit that. Gerry I like. Nice kid, in the main. Not a bad ballplayer. Could tighten his attention span, like most kids." He smiled. "Quick on the basepaths. Accurate. I didn't care for Pat, but that didn't mean I didn't want the best for the kids."

"How was Pat's reception?"

"Didn't speak much. Nodded. Said thanks. I went back to my seat."

"That was your only contact with him?"

Neville nodded, gaze over Nelson's shoulder, as if he was rewatching the game.

"And that was the only time you left your seat?"

"No, I didn't say that. I talked to Dougie, too, through the fence."

"What about?"

"I told him about Gerry. Figured he'd pass it on. He's got some coach in him. I talked about his play too. I wasn't the team coach, but remain Dougie's coach-dad. It had been a good game. Until, you know."

"Pat Brown's death?"

"Yes."

Nelson's usually rapid-fire follow-ups faltered. There was more to ask, Nelson was sure. He flipped over papers, caught John Arthur's name in his I-POA notes. The rest of the game. If anyone knew what happened, Neville might. Why not, he decided.

"Mr. Maloney, you seem to pay close attention to the games."

"I do. That's why I go. That and supporting Dougie."

"What happened in the game from the top of the first to the top of the third?" Nelson said, pen alert.

Neville brightened visibly, smiling at Nelson. His whole posture changed talking about the game—shoulders un-slumped, hands moving like players rounding the bases. "First to third inning? I actually have my scorebook here." He reached into his backpack, pulling out a dark green wire-bound notebook, and flipped it open. "Here we go. Top of first. Torrent scored two runs. Back-to-back doubles, two singles. One hard hit to third, causing an error. One a looper over Dougie at shortstop. Ground out, short fly out, fly out. Bottom half, three straight strike outs. Solid young pitcher for the Torrent. Hard to find at this age."

Neville took a breath, Nelson writing furiously.

"Second inning. An interesting one. Started with a strikeout, then the second batter up, full count, strike thrown, catcher loses the ball. Batter sprints and slides into first. Bus-sized cloud of dust. Safe. Completely threw off our pitcher. He walked next two up. Then, grand salami time. Grand slam. Felt it was coming. After that, Dougie talked to the pitcher, and we finally got the next three outs, two pop-ups and a strikeout. Back on track. Bottom of second, Reign time. Fly out, ground out, single, single, then Dougie hit a swell rap to right, scoring one. Followed by another strikeout. Top of Third for the Torrent. They worked a walk, then hit into a double play. Finalized that half of the inning. Reign up, bottom of the third. First— Wait, you wanted up to the top of the third."

Nelson continued to write. "This is perfect. Very detailed."

"I go to the games to watch the games."

Putting pen down, Nelson interlaced fingers, stretched palms out. "You'd miss it quite a lot if you weren't able to go."

Neville gloomily watched his own hands. "I can't imagine it."

"Do you think you'll start coaching the team once more, with Pat Brown gone?"

"I hope so. I've missed it. Can I go?"

"For today. We may want to question you more." He stood, buttoning his coat. The other man picked up his hat and tucked it on his head, following Nelson out the door.

13

It was another beautiful summer's day, not too hot even at afternoon's midpoint, faultless sky blue as the idea of a robin's egg. A breeze wafted in off of the sound on the city's western side, coming in from the ocean farther west, traveling over neighborhood's built from tall brick and steel apartments, from houses of all shapes and sizes, coffee shops, bars, restaurants, stores, and offices. Relentless, the breeze wound around them all, including John Arthur's house with its bright yellow door, that particular house empty, pushing eastward to the Hettie Patty playfields, where it rustled the hair of John himself, sitting once more on the bleachers. The breeze caused him to reach up and reposition his blue baseball cap, tucking in a few hairs that slipped out.

    He'd spent the morning in his usual way. Getting up at seven, scratching Ainsley as she stretched on the bed, having jumped up to his from her lower bed next to it. Then feeding her before taking their morning walk, three block south (west side of the street Mondays, Wednesday, and Fridays, east side Tuesdays and Thursday, another direction entirely on weekends), a block west, three blocks back north. They both knew every house on the walk, where every dog on the blocks lived, when the friendliest dog-friendly inhabitants might be outside pulling weeds, wanting to take a break to pet Ainsley. Routine, as John happily told anyone who'd listen, being good for dogs, but not mentioning it was also needed for him—daily tasks taking place at daily times. Since his wife Marlene died in a car accident unexpectedly, the routine kept him moving.

Which meant after the walk, during which they'd seen six rabbits, providing Ainsley with no end of doggy delight as she raced each one's direction, stopping to smell voraciously where they'd been, he'd continued the routine. Teeth brushed and flossed, shave, shower. Breakfast of cut apples, walnuts, coconut. A few side apples pieces for Ainsley. After that, reading. Today, rereading the classic *Murder on the Orient Express*, a Poirot collage of Ustinov, Suchet, and Branagh mustache-ing his imagination as he read. Routine like a ladder, climbing from one day to the next. If he didn't stick to it, he felt himself at times as if the ladder had been kicked from under him, for a moment floating in air, not attached to anything, not yet falling, ready to fall. That moment when everything feels unmoored, anything can happen, and what does will probably not be positive in the long run. *Perhaps a murderer feels like that*, he once thought, *before they make a decision that's unchangeable*.

In the hours, days, months, and year after she'd died, he'd felt that unmooring, and still often did. Walking from empty room to empty room, Ainsley trailing behind. The heater would go on, pushing air into a back bedroom causing an unbalanced knickknack—she'd loved them; collectibles from Italy, from England—to topple off a shelf. He'd run into the room, hoping while knowing it was impossible that she'd somehow be back. But she wasn't. And so the routines continued. Ainsley up again at 10:30, both heading to the backyard for ball throwing, then back inside for more dog napping. He tried to avoid watching TV in the mornings, but sometimes broke that routine. The silence, even with Ainsley's occasional snoring, too much. He talked to her a lot, inside and out, neighbors who once wondered now used to it. The silences still multiplied.

When too much, no matter what time of day, he'd break routine, turn on one of his favorite mysteries. Routines were sometimes made to be broken. Rewatching a classic *Midsummer* or *Poirot, Death in*

Paradise, *Father Brown*, or *Brokenwood* kept the silence at bay. Even when who did it wasn't a question, well-known voices filled the house, voices he and his wife listened to time and time again. The shows entertained, made the rooms less empty, silences less daunting, the ladder again resting safely against the roof. And there were always new shows to watch to test his crime-solving skills, to learn from, to keep him sharp.

Today, for example, he'd had a lunch of leftover homemade hummus with mini-peppers for dipping while watching a British mystery new to him called *Mrs. Sidhu Investigates*, starring Meera Syal as a crime-solving chef and caterer whose food business keeps taking her into crime scenes. It also featured one of his and his wife's favorites, the usually somewhat villainous Craig Parkinson as a world-wear DCI who at first finds Mrs. Sidhu annoyingly involved and then comes to rely on her. Solid mysteries, pitch-perfect acting, slightly different slant on the mismatched duo, food tasty enough that you wouldn't want to watch it hungry. *A perfect antidote to a day about to slip into doldrums*, he decided.

He was into the third episode, about a software company CEO strangled at his desk, when someone was described as 'one of those toasts that always lands butter-side up.' Amazing phrasing. Like the best shows, there was a phrase each episode, oftentimes multiple ones, that stuck in the head and demanded repeating in conversation. Actually, this particular phrase could be used for Pat Brown. Until his untimely death. The first murder victim at the playfields had what appeared from outside viewing to be a fairly charmed life. His chosen profession, or vocation, a success, expanding larger and larger like the rings of a rapidly growing tree. Family. Financial security. People providing enough adulation to fill a church the size of a small stadium. Butter-side up.

Yet, he'd been murdered, followed by his closest confederate and church partner. Both at the same place. Continuing to watch, petting Ainsley, John's mind wandered along the murderous pathways of the last few days. He'd admitted surprise that day of the first murder, finding himself involved in another criminal case with Detective Marlowe and eam. But the world of television mysteries, a world he found himself inhabiting, took over. He'd watched so many, maybe all that watching was or a reason. Maybe he was *supposed* to help solve this crime, along with the past one. "You can," he said out loud, Ainsley opening one eye, "learn a lot from TV."

Thoughts swirling around his head, John decided to break this day's routine. Instead of taking Ainsley for an afternoon weekday walk around the neighborhood, he'd put her walking harness on then bundled her into the car. Thinking about the case on the couch, TV in the background, feet up, wasn't a bad way to shift the facts. Movement, as many detectives have shown, wasn't essential. The mind worked anywhere. However, that last visit to the playfields had been interrupted by another of the City's random summer showers, rain descending like unexpected guests at a party. It'd be worthwhile to revisit it again.

Which is how he found himself back on the bleachers where Pat Brown had sat. They'd walked the park closer to the high school, Ainsley overjoyed at meeting two seven-year-old boys playing a very focused game of tag amongst picnic tables and trees, happy to stop and pet her for a minute. Then meandered far away from bleachers, the dog's nose down smelling a million smells: squirrels, rabbits, raccoons that arrive at midnight to scoop up misplaced snacks, kids, parents, ice cream remnants melted into soil, chip crumbs too miniscule for the human eye, gum molded to bench undersides, other dogs of countless shapes and sizes, crows pecking bugs turned up by landscapers wielding rakes and weed-trimmers. They traveled the bricked edge of the school, close then farther away like truants, up past playground swings and slides to the farthest baseball field, then back past others before arriving at these particular bleachers. The playfields mostly vacant, waiting for the weekend like so many people. Only the boys they'd seen, a couple sharing a sandwich balancing on a teeter-totter, and a father pitching over and over to his daughter taking swings, a day off from work John hoped they'd remember long after the sun went down. They also ran into the groundskeeper, who stopped to pet Ainsley a moment as she smelled his cart voraciously, John amazed by the string, tape, leather bands woven together, bolt nuts on them slightly glinting in the sun, bungie cords, rubber bands, and more encircling the cart's handles, as if they were utility belts.

Sitting on the bleacher's metal slats, he concentrated on the game that day of the murder, the two victims, what he'd picked up from Marlowe and team, stream of consciousnessing events, faces and facts as if stirring a minestrone. One which needed more salt and spices in the way of facts. He'd call Marlowe later, try to pick his brain, even knowing the friendly detective wasn't keen to share. And rightly so, John knew, as he wasn't a detective. Just an American who watched British mysteries.

Sighing, he stared past the fence over the field, where a single Steller's jay creased the sky. A wooden "thunk" from his left broke into his reverie of crimes and potential criminals, the noise causing him and Ainsely to jump, his slight, hers larger, accompanied by one of her peculiar high-pitched barks. He noticed a thin, ponytailed man exciting the closed concession stand. "Drogo Oates, I believe," he said to himself.

Drogo wore old jean shorts, frayed edge long and ragged enough it'd be called fringe if they were sold in a boutique, plain white T-shirt, and green flip-flops. He held a thin box with Poole's Paradise Pizza in cursive red script on it next to a palm tree and an anole lizard. Not noticing John and Ainsley, he removed a slice of pizza out of the box, stretched arm high to the sky and then down to the ground, showing a level of flexibility many aspiring gymnasts would envy, before sighing and taking a bite of pizza while mid-stretch.

"Good morning," John called over, Ainsley straining leash, tail wagging with the hope this new person would be one who liked meeting dogs.

"What?" Drogo looked their way, startled, dropping the box but holding the slice.

"Just saying good morning."

"Got it. Morning. Still waking up." He took another big bite, nearly finishing the slice.

"Drogo, right?" John walked toward him, Ainsley by his side on a tight leash.

"Do I know you? Is that dog friendly?"

"Ainsley? Very."

"Great. I like dogs. But you never know, you know? Best to check." Drogo squatted, reaching the hand with the remaining pizza high above his head, the other hand at Ainsley, which she promptly licked before moving quickly in to lick his face, which Drogo found amusing.

"Ainsley," John chided gently. "Enough licking."

"Licking dogs are okay with me. Probably extra cheese to lick in the stubble." He continued to pet her, Ainsley eyeing the pizza remains. "She's a good one."

"She is. We've never met, but my name is John Arthur. I knew of you from past games, when I'd come to see my nephews play."

"Lots of games." Drogo finally stood, snapping the last bite of pizza into his mouth, Ainsley gazing up.

"Have time to sit?" John motioned back to the bleachers.

"No, I'm busy. Well, not really busy. Sure, why not."

John sat, Drogo sitting about a foot away. Ainsley carefully made her way between them, balancing her sixty pounds on the metal seat.

"We were here the other day, too, when the incident occurred." John felt Drogo's fortuitous appearance, almost like a lesser-known guest star in a television mystery walking past police detectives on a coffee break, was too opportune to miss asking him a few questions.

"Incident?"

"Pat Brown dying?"

"Yeah, that."

"Strangely, we were here the morning of the other incident too." He might as well admit it up front, John felt.

"Mike Ray dying?"

"That's it."

"You a cop?"

"Not a cop." John shook his head regretfully.

"Shamus?"

"Not that either. Fun word, shamus."

"I guess so. You must have bad timing, being here both times." Drogo petted Ainsley.

"I suppose we do. You were here for both too?" Drogo nodded, ponytail slowly bouncing along with the nods. "Which makes sense, as you work here. Anyone else you noticed at both?"

"No. No one at first. Two joggers. Then a single jogger. Then the detective with the mustache. Marlowe. Old Ford, he's often here. Lonely guy. A red car. Black truck. Maybe a delivery van? The pretty lady detective. Mike Ray. But he was, you know, dead at the second one. Other cops. I notice a lot. Except when sleeping. Which I was, between us, at the second scene. In the stand. Girl trouble. There were others probably, but that's it."

"Ah." John tried to sound knowing, though it'd been a long time since he'd had relationship trouble. "Anything else you remember from that morning?"

"The detective made me hang around forever. Ford, too. He didn't mind. Not a lot to do but keep everything here clean. I keep them full and hydrated, Ford keeps them clean. He's like family, watches out for me." Drogo moved his arms as if directing bleacher waves as he started to ramble, Ainsley watching hands as they moved. "The detectives nearly hit me on my bike. Bet they didn't report that. It was a mess. Rain, cops, people in white."

"I'll bet. Did you know Mike Ray?"

"Somewhat. He came to a lot of games. Not someone I'd hang with. Ordered tons of candy bars. A lot of one type, rather. The 100 Grand. Seemed to love it." Drogo's stomach growled. "Guess I like it myself. He used to get grabby with his wife, you know, personal spots, sitting on the top row. Thought no one could see. But I see things. I'm not just some counter jockey."

"Of course not. Anything out of the ordinary from the first incident?"

"Nah. Same old Saturday. Kids wanting stuff, parents giving it to them, or not. Then they start crying and get it anyway. Same thing like every day there are games. Until the dying."

"Did you serve Pat Brown?"

"Serve? Wait on him more like it. I always delivered him chips and a Dr. Pepper right off, or Nikola, my cousin, like third cousin, hassled me."

"Really?"

"Yeah, it's hard work, concession stand manager. She and Pat were close. Close-close, you know? She said when they started being close that he couldn't be distracted from the game, he was too important.

She scares me. He scared me some too. Seemed threatening for a man of God. Once when I didn't hop to it when he used to come up for chips, before I knew about him and Nikola, he didn't think I was quick enough and said he'd get me fired if it happened twice, that he knew the park commish. This job is hard, man. I need a rest now and then."

"Makes sense. That day the same as always?"

"Same as. Wait, not exactly. I was busy, and so Nikola took his drink and chips to him. Told me I needed to speed it up. I was gonna take it, but didn't."

John sat quiet for a moment. "Pat also drank sangria that one of the moms brought. Did he come to get a fresh cup?"

"That's a weird question."

"'A man is dead, these are important questions.'"

"Hunh?"

"Sorry, TV show quote. The cup?"

"Nah, he usually used the same cup far as I know."

"Check. See anything, anybody acting differently than normal that day?"

"Yes. This mom from over at field three came for a sandwich. We don't have sandwiches. Everybody knows that."

"Anything at this field, these bleachers?"

"I can't remember anything, but there's something strange every day. Keeps me busy. You know, John, this is a wild job. You got kids coming up, parents, spills. You run out of candy and have to make a sign that says *I'm out of candy* and people still ask for candy. It's like they don't notice what I do at all. It's so busy an elephant could stomp past, stop, breakdance, and I wouldn't see it. That's how it is."

John stared into the space where a high fly ball would have landed if traveling from home to the second basemen's glove, blinked three times fast, then smacked his hands together. "That *is* how it is. Drogo, you are a genius."

Drogo grinned. "I am? I guess you could say that. No one else has, but sure."

Standing, John reached out his hand, which Drogo took, shaking it rapidly. "We have to go. Come on, Ains." Ainsley stood and stretched her head toward Drogo. He dropped John's hand, which he had been continuing to shake at the speed of a paint-mixing machine, and gave the dog a hearty scratch.

"Thanks again, Drogo," John said. Heading to the car, he heard Drogo back on the bleachers.

"A genius. Glad someone finally agrees with me."

At the station, interviews over, Marlowe, Morven and Nelson took regular positions in the far southeast corner of the big detectives' room. They'd compared interview notes, highlighting particularly interesting aspects, Marlowe reminding them it was frequently the little facts, the potentially overlooked turn of phrase from a witness or footnote from forensics, that spurred mental horses on to solving a crime. They were in a bad box at the moment, he'd said, like a cattle drive in a thunderstorm, but they'd find their way with persistence and by keeping the cattle together. Nelson followed Marlowe's cowboy-hatted inspirational speech by saying the past, the deep past, regularly solved the crime, bringing up John Arthur and Mrs. Marple, which he'd continued to watch at home. He scanned his notebook for quotes he felt might be helpful, before noticing the other two heading off in the direction of the canteen. Morven glanced back, smiling, motioning him to follow.

They arrived back at desks restocked with late-afternoon provisions: two cups of coffee precariously carried in one hand and a bag of salt and vinegar chips for Marlowe; a bottle of Carsely all-natural sparkling water and apple for Morven; a can of Bloom's Mighty as a Mayor highly caffeinated beverage and slightly aged chocolate chip cookie for Nelson. Seated, they began the painstaking process of inputting interview notes. Not a favorite task by any means, but detail roundup, as Marlowe called it, underlined the recent things said by suspects and made it easier in the long run to make an arrest and secure a conviction.

"To the computers," Morven said. For fifteen minutes, only the occasional swallow, crunch, and tapping of fingers on keyboards came from the two desks, accompanied intermittently by a mistype-driven "Drat" from Marlowe, the word like a mistimed cymbal's clang in the midst of a symphony, causing the other two to rotate eyes.

The rest of the room was louder, full of a diverse mélange of officers working up their own cases, chatting about suspects, bouncing facts and theories like so many basketball passes, moving incident boards from one desk to another. Occasionally a voice rang out clear as a bell within a guttural background rumbling. The whole crush of voices melded eventually into a sound collage out of which certain words bubbled up: burglary, assault, arson, criminal, lawyer, coffee, paperwork, quitting time, doughnut, beer, Seafarers, captain.

The end-of-day voices behind and beside them were loud enough that none noticed when Dr. Jones Peterson arrived. He stood, hands in pockets of his white lab coat, blue scrubs on beneath, folder wedged in his shoulder's crook. Then, grabbing the folder with his right hand, he raised arms high, boldly exclaiming, "Long live the king."

Marlowe and Morven looked up, startled, and Nelson jumped out of his chair, his hand in a saluting motion as if expecting an actual king's arrival.

Recovering, Marlowe said, "Doc. Nice of you to stop by."

"I was passing," the short in stature, if not in presence, pathologist replied.

Nelson returned to his seat, shell-shocked. Next to him, Morven said, "It's not every day we see you in this room, Doctor Peterson."

"Stopping by an officer's desk is something I enjoy, though rarely do. A custom more honored in the breach than the observance. Today, however, as I was near and knowing full well the depths you three are wading within, decided it was my duty, as well as a pleasure."

"Always a treat, Doc." Marlowe leaned back. "What's the latest?"

"Ah, Marlowe, never time for the niceties. Tis true that words without thoughts never rise to heaven, or even the floor above. I do have a few updates, if the time now be auspicious?"

"We're all ears, Doc."

"Mike Ray. As surmised at the scene, death caused by blunt force trauma, leading to an internal hemorrhage. Said trauma caused by blunt instrument approximately 2.5 inches from the shape of the blow. No particle remnants in the wound."

Opening her hand to give a visual of the size, Morven said, "Perhaps the size of the thick end of a baseball bat?"

"Very astute, Detective. I would think that accurate as the moon thinks of the sun."

Nelson raised a hand.

Marlowe hid his grin at the classroom motion. "Yes, Nelson?"

"Did you know there were only like 360 murders by blunt instrument last year?"

"Did not. Doc?"

The doctor ruffled pages in the folder. "Like an oracle, Detective Nelson, you are correct. And I did."

"More on Mike Ray?"

"He was healthy for his age. No other injuries. He'd had only coffee when looking on morning's face."

"Other DNA at the scene?" Nelson spoke up without the hand raise. "Not necessarily my purview, but I've spoken with forensics briefly, and they didn't mention anything specific found yet."

"Thanks, Doctor," Morven said. "Can we ask a question about the first victim?"

"You speak, and I shall respond to the best of my abilities."

"Had Pat Brown been drinking Dr. Pepper as well as sangria before he died?"

"That offense is rank, the Dr. Pepper. But yes, Detective, curiously, he had both in his stomach."

"Do you know, and this again may be off your purview, if the cup found next to him contained both?"

"I wish that information was in my memory locked, but it is not. However—" He set the folder down, fished a phone out of his pocket with his left hand, swooping up his right hand in the stop signal toward the detectives. He dexterously made a one-handed dial and started speaking into the phone.

"Yes, Johnny? Still remain on stage?" The voice on the phone chattered, but they couldn't make words out. "A query: the main cup in the Pat Brown case. Sangria and Dr. Pepper resided in it? I know, I feel the same on the bastard soda. Sure, holding." His right hand went down as he spoke to the detectives. "Johnny is checking. Forensics manager Johnny Airess."

The phone began chattering, the pathologist's right hand silencing any response from the team before he spoke. "As if my ears were twitched to heaven. Right-ho Johnny. It will sp g indeed. Thanks muchly." Tucking phone back into a pocket, he said, "No. The cup closest only contained the alcoholic beverage sangria—no Dr. Pepper—and strychnine."

"Interesting," Marlowe replied. "We've found no fingerprints other than Pat Brown's on it, correct?"

"That's correct," Morven confirmed. "I'm sure forensics gathered all cups and trash from the scene."

"Worse remains behind most times, but here, all was gathered, yes. Why, if I may ask?"

"Probably a tough task, but we should find all cups that contained only Dr. Pepper and fingerprint them. One has to be Pat Brown's."

Doctor Peterson nodded sagely as Marlowe continued the thought. "And perhaps also has the murderer's on it. Good thought. Request that ASAP. One more question, Doc."

"Ask as if angels could speak."

"Strychnine. Is it available readily do you know, outside of for medical professionals?"

Doctor's Jones face could have doubled for Melpomene, the mask of tragedy. "You can't imagine…"

"Not you, Doc. Curiosity only."

"I will make myself another face then." He smiled. "Strychnine. Poison fruit. Derived from the nux-vomica tree grown in southeast Asia and Australia. Able to grow in other climes, mainly avoided. Nasty stuff. Not used for medicine anymore, by the way, outside of rare unproven treatments. Outlawed in the main, but utilized still in outdoor pest control occasionally. Older bottles of it still show up, too. Residing on the back of back shelves."

Marlowe's mustache bobbed. "This has been a helpful drive-by, Doc. Lots of fat to chew."

The doctor picked up his folder, tucking it once more under his arm. "If this is to be—"

"Or not to be! I know that one," Nelson interrupted

Chuckling, Doctor Peterson walked off, saying, "He wears the rose of youth upon him. Farewell, farewell. You know where to find me."

14

The three detectives reflected a moment. Afternoon had exited offstage as they'd talked with the Doc, day slipping on early evening like a tight jacket, slowly, one sleeve at a time. The big room's cacophony distilled down from a roar to a murmur, a handful of higher-proof conversations continuing as officers filtered out for the night, heading home to families, or to bars and restaurants for an after-work beer or cocktail. Some to Luther's London gym for a post-work workout. Different ways to relieve the day's stresses.

Marlowe's team remained silent until he spoke. "The doc is his own breed of cattle. Worth listening to, and this time, giving us some paths to trod quickly."

"Agreed," Morven said. "Calling Johnny Airess in forensics about cups found at the field for one."

"Yep. Big task, but might as well request. Dr. Pepper and fingerprints. Probably not a combo the Dr. Pepper folks would use in marketing."

Morven laughed. "Nope. I'll get on that, seeing as he's still in the office. Another I thought of?"

"Do tell."

"Talking to Ash Willums again. She had the sangria. Did she notice Pat Brown switching cups? Or someone taking him a new cup?"

"Very smart, Morven. Detective Nelson, can you get on that?" Nelson was taking notes while they spoke. "Yes, sir," he replied. "I can call her ASAP."

"Dandy." Marlowe reached for the olive wood bowl as they fished phones out of pockets, Morven walking toward the board while punching buttons so they didn't talk over each other. As if on cue, as Morven and Nelson began talking, Marlowe's desk phone rang loudly.

He grabbed it before the second ring, moving surprisingly fast to avoid extra background noise during their calls. "This is Detective Marlowe. Mr. Arthur is calling for me?" He considered whether to send his friend to voicemail, knowing he could ramble and not wanting to derail. But decided as they were on calls, he might as well join the party line. "I'll take it."

The corner became a frenzy of questions and replies, some friendly, some emphatic, a grin or two thrown in while talking for Morven and Marlowe, a blush on the cheek spreading like fire for Nelson. None of the three concretely grasped what the others were saying, each focusing on their own calls, Morven near the board, Nelson hunched over the desk, Marlowe facing the station wall and window, the antique phone's base in his lap, receiver on ear. Nelson finished first, followed by Morven. Marlowe last, after a few "sures" and "maybes" and a final "I'll be in touch."

"Well, those calls together was exciting as rooster with socks," Marlowe said. "Loud as it'd be trying to put those socks on, too." He took a sip of cold coffee. "Who's up first?"

"I'll go," said Morven. "Pretty straightforward. As you'd expect, forensics is digging through everything found at both scenes, but it's going to take some time. A scientific process, Mr. Airess said, finding himself very amusing." She rolled brown eyes slightly. "He did let me know they didn't find any unexpected DNA on Mike Ray. Hairs from his wife, nothing suspicious. They're sorting items discovered nearby the bleachers, ground, concession stand. Nothing matching the dimensions of the blunt instrument the doc talked about it has been found."

"How far did–" Marlowe began, but Morven finished his sentence.

"They take the search?" He nodded, she continued. "To all the fields, the playground, the park-like area adjacent to the school, and the inner edge of the greenbelt. I've requested they go deeper into it, and research the park. Feels like that blunt instrument should be around, unless it was removed somehow. He grumbled but said if we had the budget, he'd get on it."

"I'll call the captain and get the thumbs-up. Sure it'll fly. Anymore?"

"That's it from forensics."

"He ask you out again?" Marlowe's mustache moved like a boat on a big wave as his smiled stretched wide.

Morven's eye roll went up farther. "Not directly. I sensed it coming before hanging up. Nelson, how was Miss Willums?"

The blush that had faded from Nelson's cheeks as Morven talked rebloomed. He stuttered, "She, Miss Willums, was fine. Helpful."

"How so?" Morven asked.

"She said she remembers perfectly that she didn't give Pat Brown a cup. Nikola brought the cup to her to be filled. She says while she couldn't be sure as she didn't watch him every moment, she doesn't remember seeing anyone take him another cup. And that she is sure as shooting—her words—she didn't give him a second cup. She always gets the cups from Drogo before a game, taking back to him those not used. Except this time, he gave them to an officer."

"Good call asking her about where she gets the cups. Smart thinking, Nelson."

Marlowe's praise caused Nelson's blush to deepen. "Thank you, Mr. Detective."

"Did she call you Nellie?" Morven kidded.

"What?" Nelson sputtered "Well, she did. I said Detective Nelson. She stuck with Nellie." He decided he'd better change the subject quick. "Detective Marlowe, who were you talking with?"

Marlowe, sniffing his olive wood bowl, looked up. "John Arthur. A surprise? I can't decide."

"Did he solve the case again?" Nelson's Arthur awe was evident.

"Easy. If he did, he didn't tell me. Might be more police work needed."

"Yes, Detective."

As Marlowe didn't follow up, Morven asked, "What did he want?"

"He wondered, curiously, how far into the past we'd gone with everyone on that original list he provided. Said he'd talked to Drogo who gave good insight. That seems improbable. Asked if we've found the second murder weapon. I told him we were following all lines of inquiry, which he likes to hear, and which he said he'd take as a no. Then he asked if Dr. Pepper was found in Pat Brown's cup. Sometimes he is uncanny, I'll give him that."

Morven smiled, running her hand under the desk edge. "He doesn't have us bugged, does he?"

"Seems he almost does at times."

"Was that all?" Nelson seemed disappointed.

"Nearly." Marlowe stared out of the window, catching a sliver of sky between buildings. "Asked if we got a breakdown of the baseball innings he missed day of Pat's death."

Nelson said, "I have that, can I send it to him?"

Marlowe mulled. "Can't see why not. Got his email?"

"Sure. On it." Nelson began to type as Morven spoke up, "Mr. Arthur has a lot on his mind. Doesn't seem he provided the usual amount of TV quotes."

"He quoted me part of a poem. That count?"

"From a British mystery? Which one?" Nelson stopped typing, grabbing his notebook.

"Don't think it was. Called "Antigonish." Know it?"

Seeing dual shakes, he recited, tilting head back. "Yesterday, upon the stair, I met a man who wasn't there."

"That sounds familiar," Morven said. "Did he say why he brought it up?"

"No, just laughed. Crazy as a javelina with lockjaw, or insightful as a crow. Hard to tell."

"That was all?"

"Oh, you know. Said he was working the little grey cells and wanted to talk more tomorrow. Which reminds me. It's getting late. Let's get notes in, update the board, then skedaddle." He tipped his coffee mug completely over above his mouth. Not a drop remained.

"First," Morven spoke before his mug found the desk, "more coffee?"

"Right as rain, Morven. Coffee-scented rain."

If someone told Marlowe as he left the station an hour and a half after the conversation with John Arthur that the next morning he and his team would once more be at the Hettie Patty playfields, he'd have first refused to believe them. Then decided either that they were trying to imply the place was cursed, that he was cursed, or that another murder had taken place. An event which might bring him back to muttering about curses. Yet, that was where he found himself.

The night before, he'd almost ambled down to Gary's before heading home. It'd been a long day and a conversation with the genial English bartender and a drink tended to provide the ideal counterbalance. His steps started that direction, but only a few feet before backtracking to the parking garage. The night sky hadn't reached full dark, faint shafts of light dimming west to east along the horizon. A few cars passed like birds without a flock, a far cry from the bumper-to-bumper mid-weekday scene. People laughed from the direction of Settler's Square, or he daydreamed they did. A delicious smell of fried food—French fries, mozzarella sticks, falafel, onion rings—drifted up like a fast-food fairy tale. He wavered, then moved toward the garage. *Better the drink you dream about then the drinks that tire you out*, he'd thought.

On the way home, nose influencing wallet, he stopped at Sykes' Swell Dogs, picking up two veggie dogs with onions, cream cheese, jalapenos, and mustard, with a side of fries swimming in melted cheddar. Once ensconced on his living room's fluffy orange upholstered sofa, feet up, one hot dog in his left hand, the rest of dinner balanced expertly on his stomach, he'd opened a well-thumbed poetry anthology in his possession since high school. As he remembered, "Antigonish" by Hughes Mearns was in it. Eating the first dog, he read the poem slowly, then read it a second time consuming half the side of fries in a few bites. Switching to the second dog, he flipped some pages, stopping to read a poem called "Skunk Hour" by Robert Lowell before flipping back to read "Antigonish" once more.

"John," he said to no one, "I'm not exactly sure where you're riding with this poem, but it does echo where we're at, I suppose. Close-ish to a murder, but not close enough." Sitting the book down, Marlowe picked up two TV remotes. He turned on the TV with one, the DVD player with the other. *Time to take it back to the corral*, he thought, pressing play to start an episode of *Gunsmoke*. He watched one episode vaguely, the two murders circling his brain like so many wild broncos, making concentration hard, clicking into a second when his eyes began drooping. It had been a long couple of days.

The next morning, his phone rang as he brushed teeth. Quickly rinsing, spitting, and wiping a towel over face and bald head, he picked it up without even looking at the number on the screen.

"Marlowe here," he said.

"Good morning, Detective, hopefully this isn't too low in the dawn digits for a call."

"John," Marlowe recognized the older man's voice. "You're awfully peppy."

John laughed. "Ainsley gets me up when the sun sneaks in. Summer, that's early."

"And?"

"You gave me your cell number before, so figured it was fine to call."

Marlowe sat on the couch as John talked, longingly gazing at a picture of Kitty actress Amanda Blake on the cover of one of the *Gunsmoke* DVDs wearing a shirt with frills at collar and cuffs and sporting a high bouffant hairdo.

"I wanted to catch you before you went into the office. I wondered if you and the team would meet me back at the Hettie Patty playfields this morning, first thing. I could be there in twenty minutes. I'll leave Ainsley at home. You can call Detectives Moven and Nelson. Or I can, but you'd have to give me their numbers."

The man's fizzing enthusiasm wasn't contagious, but was admirable. A hint of a grumble laced Marlowe's single word reply. "John?"

"Yes, Detective?"

"We're pretty busy. You know, two murders."

"I know. And you haven't had coffee yet, I'd wager." In the background, Marlowe heard Ainsley's high-pitched bark. "Ains, quiet. Marlowe's on the line." Ainsley quit barking. Marlowe picturing her staring at the phone. "Sorry, dog walked by the house. Back to it, no coffee?" Marlowe's silence was his only reply. "I'll take that as a yes. Here's the thing." He paused dramatically. "I have a theory."

"You have a theory?"

"You sound like Inspector Neele. 'You have a theory as to who put the taxine into Mr. Fortescue's marmalade?'"

"What?"

"I'll play Marple." John switched into a poorly done, high-pitched English accent before Marlowe could interrupt. "'It isn't a theory. I *know*.'" Back to normal voice, John said, "Did you blink? Inspector Neele was a blinker."

He tried to avoid it, but Marlowe actually blinked, while at the same time unconsciously pulling his left earlobe, a mannerism only unveiled in moments of surprise. He nearly asked who Inspector Neele was, but wasn't awake enough for one of John's TV asides, instead saying, "You know what?"

"The murderer. Or, I don't know exactly, but I'm pretty sure. We need to get back to the fields."

"You can't just tell me on the phone? Or at the station?"

"I could, but I'm not 100%. Returning to the scene of the crime happens in enough British mysteries that I know it's key to the final answer."

Marlowe didn't reply, rubbing his head. He'd missed a spot with the towel. If only John wasn't right so often. "Okay, John, you win. We'll meet you there. Two conditions."

"Amazing." John's one-word reply contained more joy than a birthday toast.

"First, stay in your car until we arrive." Marlowe figured with a murderer running around, best to keep John out of harm's way. They'd had a scare on the previous case.

"Check. Not sure why, but check. What else?" John had an inability to see that his deductions made him a target. Probably the TV watching.

"You have to bring us croissants. Lynley's is fine, if open."

"Easy enough. Happy to."

"And, John?"

"Yes, Detective?"

"I'll take two."

Marlowe put on burnt-brown loafers, a matching belt over less-burnt-brown slacks, and suspenders the shade of basil in the sun too long with diamond-accents over his white dress shirt, then called Morven. Already up and nearing her car, she displayed hesitance about the playfield plan, making the point the whole team probably didn't need to be there for Mr. Arthur's theory, no matter how helpful he had been in the past. They were busy, with the cases heating up. Marlowe agreed, then gently gave his reasoning. They'd spent yesterday in the office. It'd be a positive to visit the scene. Mr. Arthur did tend to prattle on about TV too much, but his instincts also tended to hit the bull's-eye. She came around, saying she'd pick up Nelson if Marlowe rousted him into readiness.

Nelson's hello answering the phone came amplified, crackling with energy, as if the hand not holding the phone was plugged into a wall socket. When Marlowe began mapping out the morning visit to the playfields to meet John Arthur, Nelson didn't allow him to finish, saying, "Let's go," followed rapidly by, "Apologies, sir, it's very exciting." Marlowe laughed it off, telling Nelson he'd need to polish his spurs at a gallop as Morven would be picking him up in ten minutes.

Stopping at Sampson's Sips for a double cappuccino, Marlowe pulled into the now-familiar parking lot at 8:00 a.m., the lot as barren of cars as a cloudy sky is of stars. Only one, a black Honda Fit, parked near the concession stand. Pulling to it and backing into the adjoining space, he saw John sitting on the hood, head bent, eyes closed like a monk praying.

"John," Marlowe said, breaking open the quiet morning.

"Detective." John stood, rubbing eyes with his knuckles. "I was deep in my mind palace, didn't even hear you pull up."

Marlowe got out of the car, reached back to pick up his sports coat, then changed his mind, leaving it. The sun already blazed. Instead, he grabbed his baseball cap, settling it on. "Thought we mentioned staying in the car until we police arrived?"

"We did. My mistake. No one here." John swept the lot with his gaze. "Seemed safe."

"Best to take precautions. Even the safest trail can have a hidden prairie dog hole."

"'Ah, but when Arthur himself is involved, he too is dangerous.'" John's Belgian accent rang true as a broken Champagne flute.

Marlowe grinned at the idea of the older man being dangerous. "Fair enough."

"We will see the others?"

"En route. Couldn't resist Arthurian theories for breakfast."

"Arthurian? I like that. Perhaps too regal?" He went on without waiting for an answer. "I'm no king, but I did bring croissants." He grabbed a white bag from the car and handed it to Marlowe. Opening it, a buttery aroma tumbled out and up. Reaching in, Marlowe grabbed a croissant and took a bite. Flakey, crisp, soft, perfect.

"Forgiven for forgetting to stay in the car?"

Nodding, Marlowe took another bite right as Morven's Neptune-blue Kia Sportage pulled in. She and Nelson excited simultaneously, he trotting around the car's hood as she walked over to the other men.

"Good morning, Detective Marlowe, Mr. Arthur. Beautiful day." Morven wore a terracotta-colored suit with a single closed button on the jacket over a white shirt, one that would appear too elegant for the morning if she didn't exude such a controlled, casual air.

Before they answered, Nelson broke in, as if worried he wouldn't get to give salutations. "Yes, good morning, Detective and Mr. Arthur. Thank you for calling us here." While his tightly fitting tailored blue suit, over white shirt and matching blue tie, had creases that looked like they could cut skin, there was a brown stain on the pocket the size of a dime.

Mr. Arthur waved, quiet for once, as Marlowe welcomed the team. "Morven, Nelson, morning. Know it's daybreak, thanks for obliging. John's brought us croissants. And theories."

The two detectives gathered around Marlowe, grabbing croissant and napkins. Morven returned to her car to snag two bottles of water, one for her and one for Nelson, reminding Marlowe he still had coffee in the car. A few minutes passed as they munched pastries, small talking the morning sun, last night's Seafarers surprising win (a walk-off-walk in the 10th), asking John about Ainsley, and watching two kids who'd arrived at the park at the lot's far end carrying kites painted with owls in hopes that the breeze, feather-light, might pick up. It could have been a group of friends meeting at the corner café for a weekly catch-up.

Finally, Marlowe said, "John, these croissants are better than biscuits, but I believe you had more than pastry in mind."

"Correct. Shall we move over to the bleachers?"

"Why not." Marlowe brushed croissant flakes from his shirt.

They walked to the bleachers in groups of two, John and Nelson in front, Morven and Marlowe trailing behind. Soon, they were seated on the metal bleachers where Pat Brown had sat, gazing out at the immaculate baseball field. Infield dirt raked smooth from bases to pitcher's mound to home plate, outfield grass a green ocean calling to be rolled around in, white chalk lines between bases and home so straight Euclid would be proud. At the field's edge, Douglas Firs like stretched wooden sentries on the edge of the greenbelt. Even the metal fencing separating field from spectators and bleachers themselves sparkled, not a stray gum wrapper or shoelace evident. They noticed Ford David when sitting, off two fields down pushing his cart of tools and trash, and Drogo's bike chained to the back of the concession stand.

John stood up, and while Marlowe and Morven looked bemused, Nelson's eyes gleamed. "Are you starting the monologue?"

Smiling, with a tip of his baseball cap, John took a breath, bringing his hands together before speaking. "I hadn't planned on doing a detective monologue, or summation, with you standing in for suspects as in the Case of the Nine Neighbors."

"Mighty kind of you, John," Marlowe said.

"You're welcome. However, as we're here, let me say that I've always thought, because I've learned it via many mystery episodes set around sporting events, that the specific baseball game being played the day Pat Brown was murdered was important. So I thought we might re-enact that on the diamond."

Nelson jumped up, giving a short fist pump. "Yes."

Marlowe and Morven stayed sitting, as Marlowe said, "Hold up there, rein it in. We don't wanna muss that field up, John. And time, you know, is short."

Nelson looked like a kid at a county fair who'd been given an ice cream cone, only to have the ice cream fall onto the dirty ground.

John smiled. "I felt that might be pushing it too far. Let's just sit, then. And take it back a step. Arthur, he will begin." He paced before them while talking, Nelson sitting back down in front of him, Morven and Marlowe up a level.

"Before we get to the game, which is part of the all-important how, let's turn our gaze quickly to the first victim. Pat Brown. Charismatic pastor. Well-to-do. Beloved by many, as evidenced by the success of the Chapter Creek Church. But not by all. This leads to the who and why. From what I've learned, mostly by talking to you, but researching some on my own, those two lists aren't short. Why? Financial reasons, pointing to people like Tom Toomey and our second victim, Mike Ray. Revenge, leading to Nev Maloney or even his wife, or a wildcard like Jack Page, who you've told me a bit about. Jealousy, leading to the wife, or to the pastor's once-time love affair, Nikola Cassian."

A door slammed shut, causing John to pause, as Drogo excited the concession in a huff buttoning the top button on his jean shorts, rounding the building corner, hair flying freely behind him.

"Hey, man," he said to John. "I didn't tell you things to stitch up my cousin. Nikola's no–" Drogo noticed the detectives sitting on the bleachers. "Oh. Cops. It's you, Marlowe and Morven and… don't know your name, man, sorry."

"Drogo." Marlowe stretched the name out. "Taking up residence in the stand again?"

"You know. Girlfriend trouble. Just tonight. And last night."

"Were you eavesdropping?"

"What, not me. But I did *hear* John. That's not illegal is it?"

"Nope."

John spoke up. "Actually, not bad that you're here, Drogo. Mind staying? If okay with the Detectives? I won't say anything out of school."

Marlowe nodded. "It's your show, John. I'll butt in if necessary."

John brought his hands together again with a bow. "Perfect. Drogo, mind sitting?"

Drogo looked slightly confused, but not much more than normal.

He wiped eyes with the bottom of his ruby-red T-shirt, then sat on the first bleacher, five feet from Nelson.

"Thanks, Drogo. The detectives are allowing me to monologue. I was just saying that Pat Brown wasn't well-loved by all."

Drogo nodded. "You can say that again."

"I think I just did. Anyway, many who were at the game the day of his death had issues, let us say, with the victim. He wasn't a kind man, but was one who inspired loyalty. How then was the crime committed? It was a day most ordinary, *n'est-ce pas?*" John's momentary poor French didn't cause the detectives to blink, but Drogo squinted hard as if that would help him understand. "A day like any other at the ballpark. And no one saw anything odd, say someone adding something to Pat's drink. Unless I'm missing something?" The last said as an aside to the detectives, an actor talking to the audience offstage. On their head shakes, he continued.

"There's one fatal flaw in that train of thought, however." Marlowe perked up with this. "Every baseball game is different, not like any other. I have felt the game was important from the beginning, as I said. It turns out, I am right." He beamed. "Once I had the full progression of in-game events, I realized, with the help of a history of watching TV mysteries, you can—"

"Learn a lot from—" Marlowe interrupted John, only to be interrupted himself by Morven.

"TV."

"That's it, detectives. You're learning. I realized the actual in-game play-by-play, plus a mystery TV trope I call The Scenery, some call it Beneath Notice, caused people to miss it when something odd *did* happen. Pat Brown himself missed it even as it happened directly beside him, resulting in his murder. And Mike Ray's murder."

15

"The murder was ingeniously planned *and* spur of the moment." John continued pacing as he talked, raising a finger occasionally as if a teacher underling a particular point around diagramming a sentence. "Which made it tricky. Let's start with the game. There were three key moments. Thank you, Detective Nelson, for providing me with notes on innings one to three, as well as information on a few attendees." Nelson beamed, Marlowe briefly frowning. "The second inning. A slide into first. Not normal, but it happens. Rarely. That was followed by a grand slam. Very exciting. Very odd."

Marlowe's and Morven's looks were more curious than spellbound, but both Nelson and Drogo couldn't take their eyes off John. "I arrived in the middle of the third. If I *was* like Poirot, I would call that a key moment too. But the next was the bottom of the third, when Gerry Brown, the victim's son, hit a three-RBI triple, with another photo finish slide at third base. That should have told us everything, yes?" Seeing four uncomprehending faces, he continued.

"Bottom of the sixth. Tight game. I believe it was Nev Maloney's son who hit what appeared to be a home run, which was when Pat Brown's distress was noticed. A distress that led to his death. Enough said?"

"Not quite enough," Marlowe replied. "Remember, busy day. Croisants only buy so much time."

"There are croissants?" Drogo asked, to no reply.

"Right, Marlowe, staying on track. Staying on the base paths. My point: during those key moments, events happened that nobody noticed. Or noticed, but didn't understand the importance enough for it to stick."

"What events, Mr. Arthur?" Morven asked. "Adding poison to Pat Brown's drink? I know people are watching the game and get distracted by exciting plays, the ooh and ahh factor. And we've been told Pat Brown was known to be very focused on the games. Even with that, I can't see how exactly he would not notice the addition of poison to his drink. The murderer would have to take the lid off, add it, put it back on."

"Very astute, Detective Morven. A fact which puzzled me as well. And I was there for much of the game and tend to notice things. Or try to, at least. A conundrum. But not unsolvable with the help of an episode of Poirot. Now, Marlowe." He saw the detective mopping sweat off his head with his hat. "Forgive me, but I have to have a TV aside." Marlowe nodded.

"When speaking with Drogo here the other day, something he said sent me to solving the case."

"It did? I said something important?" Drogo said.

"He did?" Nelson said at the same time.

"Both correct," John clapped hands together. "Very important. You said, 'They don't notice what I do at all.' And it clicked."

Marlowe leaned in. "Poirot say that?"

"No, Poirot, he is always noticed, as he might say. After talking to Drogo, I still hadn't completely worked it out, but that phrase 'they don't notice what I do at all' stuck. So, I went home and watched an episode of Poirot, "The Yellow Iris." Based on an Agatha short story and which she, interestingly, eventually rewrote in a way into a novel called *Sparkling Cyanide*, not even starring our immaculate Belgian. It is—"

"John?" Marlowe sighed audibly.

"Stay on track. "The Yellow Iris" is a perfect example of the TV trope I mentioned, The Scenery. It plays off the fact people tend not to notice certain strata of workers. In that show, it's waiters. In others, postal workers, utility folks, counter help, and on. People are so used to seeing those employment genres that they begin overlook them. They become the scenery. They can do things in front of others and not be noticed."

"Hold on. Wait." Drogo stamped his feet, standing. "Are you saying I—" He glanced over John's shoulder. "Hey. Hello, Ford."

John turned, backing up a step as Marlowe stood, saying, "Mr. David. Didn't hear you come up. Sorry if we broke into your work day." He touched Morven on the shoulder while talking, and she smoothly slid off the bleachers.

"No problem, Detective. Heard voices. Wanted to check on Drogo." Ford's voice came out slow and soft, like a morning mist off the sound of an August day in the City. "You can't imagine Drogo had anything to do with the murders? He's a good kid. At heart."

"No," John said. "It wasn't Drogo. Because it was you, Mr. David."

Everyone but John and Ford moved. Nelson jumped into a crouch, Marlowe stepped cautiously down to the first bleacher, Morven edged nearer Ford, and Drogo ran his hands through his hair repeatedly. John and Ford just looked at each other.

"I wonder?" Ford considered. "The guilty should take the punishment, as they did."

"You're saying you did it?" Marlowe was only a foot from the man now.

"I'd like this man to say more. I'm curious myself. We met the other day, but I didn't get his name."

"Me, too," Marlowe agreed. As Ford didn't seem to be moving, he gave John a nod. "And he's John Arthur. Who should continue."

"Of course. The guilty party often becomes part of the monologue. In *Death in Paradise*, for ex —"

"John?"

"Back to the day of the first murder. When there was that slide at first, you were nearby, Mr. David, and went to clean the base and base path. My surmise is you stayed close during the games Pat Brown attended ed." Ford nodded sedately. "Then you waited. When Gerry Brown hit that triple, you walked past as you would, moving toward the next place to clean up, and switched cups as Pat stood watching intently, the poison *already* in the cup. Nikola then came and took the cup, got it filled with sangria, returned it to Pat, who drank it and the poison. You continued cleaning up third base and the field and went on with your tasks, no one noticing you. A bold plan."

"Bold?" Ford replied. "Cautious, more like. You said waiting. There was years of it."

"I can imagine. The plays on the field had to be perfect, to position you in the exact perfect place at the exact perfect moment. The rare first base slide, followed not long after by a hit sure to distract Pat at third. You must have planned a long, long time."

"Years. Carried a cup taped inside my can here." He knocked against the side of the trash can he wheeled around everywhere he walked. Morven moved closer, but the man relaxed his arms. "For an eternity it felt at times. Like you said, no one notices me."

Marlowe scratched his chin. "This is unexpected. Mind stepping a step away from the cart?"

"Not at all." Ford smiled, but it was as if the words were coming from deep in a canyon.

"Want to tell us why you killed Pat Brown?"

"Let him tell it." He pointed to John. "He seems to know all."

John nearly went into a Poirot quote, decided it wasn't appropriate. Ford's demeanor went past defeated criminal looking for gain. There was tragedy in the craggy forehead wrinkles. Like Lear, John thought. "Let me try. It has to do with the woven leather cords wrapped around the left handle of your cart. I thought those were bolt nuts on them, but they're gold beads. And it's actually a bracelet."

No noise except far-off kids' laughter answered him. The detectives and Drogo all stunned. Finally, Ford agreed with a short nod. "It was your son's, right?" John pressed. Ford answered with a low moan.

"John," Marlowe said. "Can you explain?"

"Sure. Ford's son was Dan David, who you might know as Dan Jesse, the young man who committed suicide at the Chapter Creek Church."

"Suicide? He was murdered." Ford spoke clearly, plainly, faster. Beside him, never averting her eyes, Morven texted. "Not that they'd soil their hands. Not them. But they killed him. He believed that man, the pastor, was so divine. Perfect. My Dan started attending the church. He'd had some tough years, was looking for some light to guide him I suppose, a purpose. The pastor was it, Dan felt. A man of God doing good work, helping people, showing them the path to being better. Dan gave him everything: time, adoration, money. He and I fought about how much he gave, and he walked out of our house. I knew that man was a louse. Dan eventually discovered Pat and Mike were skimming most of the money they took in for supposed charities. Broke his heart. He was a good kid. Left me a message apologizing and telling me. Then he killed himself. But they killed him. And my wife, who died soon after she heard about Dan. They needed to be punished. Retribution." His head dropped to chest like an anchor was attached to it.

"How'd you figure that, John?" Marlowe asked.

"The leather around the handle of Ford's cart, for one." John said. "I noticed Mike Ray and Pat Brown wore braided leather watchbands. Nikola wore a braided leather bracelet, too, I noticed it at the game. All with gold beads, though those on Ford's cart are awfully dusty. Tied them together."

Nelson finally shucked off his shock. "But in Marlowe's interview notes, Mr. David told him he didn't have children. And in the articles I read about the suicide, he was always Dan Jesse."

Ford appeared lost in memory, so John replied. "I sadly wasn't at Marlowe's interview. The last name became the final piece of the puzzle. When I decided it had to be Mr. David, I did some scrolling on the church myself. Found a short article about Dan's death. Dan Jesse. Dan David. It made sense."

"How, Mr. Arthur?"

"Like Gerry, I'm the son of a preacher man. Due to growing up in the church, I suppose, those two names, Jesse and David, just set off alarm bells in my head. I did some research, and in the Bible saw that David's dad was Jesse. A religious person like Dan, if they were going to change their name, it clicked. I'm sure as you kept digging, you would have discovered the name change." Nelson nodded, but Ford spoke first before any of the detectives.

"Like he had a new dad. But I was his dad." Ford's voice came out earthy. "And I didn't lie. I didn't say no children period, I said no children in our house."

Marlowe heard cars and sirens coming into the parking lot. "Fair enough, Mr. David. Mind if I ask about Mike Ray?"

Ford pointed at John, who replied. "I can keep going. Mike Ray was as guilty to you as Pat Brown." Ford gave another slow nod. "You enticed him here early that morning. Not sure how."

"Implied Dan had given me hard information about their scams."

"Makes sense. He showed. If I had to guess, knowing some about him now, he'd think you were looking for a payoff, not revenge, and wondered how much, or even if he could talk you out of it. No one was here. You used a bat?" Another nod. "And then didn't report his death until you'd hidden it. If I had to guess, you dug a hole in the greenbelt beforehand, then buried it." Another nod. "Might need to bring that up with your forensic team Marlowe."

Marlowe rolled his eyes.

Two marked police cars pulled up, four uniformed officers jumping out. Morven gave them a relax gesture with both hands. "Anything else to say, Mr. David? We have some officers here to take you in if not."

"No, nothing. They deserved it. I'm not sorry."

As Morven, Nelson, and the officers walked Ford to one of the cars, Marlowe and John huddled near Drogo, who was sitting on the bleachers with his head in his hands. The atmosphere at the field, so charged with electricity moments before, seemed as if the plug had been pulled.

"You okay, Drogo?" John asked kindly.

Drogo's eyes were red and wet. "I dunno. What just happened? Ford, I felt, you know, he was my friend. I can't. It's too weird."

"He was your friend, Drogo," Marlowe said, putting a hand on the man's shoulder. "Sorry you got pulled into our… whatever this morning was."

"'Every murderer is somebody's old friend,'" John said.

Drogo wiped his eyes, looking at John. "You're right. I guess. Or, I don't know. It's been a hard few days."

"It has. Maybe you should call your girlfriend, let her know how you are. Or your cousin."

"She is my cousin. My girlfriend. Not close cousin. Like fourth."

"I was thinking Nikola."

"She's not my girlfriend, man. She's my cousin."

Smiling, John moved to Drogo's other side. "I remember now. Maybe call your girlfriend, then call Nikola."

Standing between the two, Drogo breathed out an extended breath, as if releasing the morning's tension. "Yeah, good idea. You two." He looked from one to the other. "Not sure how you do this murder stuff." He walked off.

"Glad it wasn't him," Marlowe muttered.

"Not the type. Memorable supporting character, though, I must say."

"John?"

"I know, not TV."

"Every murderer is somebody's old friend?"

John smiled, gazing up at the blue sky, which hadn't changed one tint since they'd arrived, still shining over the immaculately raked, trimmed, and lined baseball field. "That's actually from a movie." They headed oward their cars while talking. "But it *is* a Poirot movie."

"Is it now?"

"Yes, *A Haunting in Venice* starring English actor Kenneth Branagh s Poirot. He's more an active Poirot than you'd expect, leaner by maybe wo stones than the traditional portrait of our Belgian detective. Very arrowed in the movie, which takes place . . ."

They kept walking, and soon were far from the bleachers.

Marlowe and team worked long hours the next few days. Bringing in Ford David for the two murders didn't stop their part of the investigation like he end of a TV show episode. Instead, the tasks continued at speed—onducting interviews with Ford and his lawyers, rounding up remaining vidence, liaising with forensics, inputting data and information, chatting with the district attorney's office. The list was lengthy. And tiring. During he interviews, Ford went into a nearly muted state, freely admitting he was responsible for the "retribution," as he called it, but in as few words as possible, void of emotion. It was as if he had been a river pushed along by is hatred of the two victims, now dried up to only muddy drops.

The man was a murderer, twice over, but Marlowe couldn't help the orrowful feeling that surfaced inside his head during interviews. Driven mad by grief, Ford carried himself like a character in a Shakespearean ragedy. Knowing how long he'd stewed, seeing Pat Brown and Mike Ray t the games, waiting so many interminable innings, days, months, years ntil the perfectly timed moment was chillingly pathetic. Ford did have few lighter moments, as Drogo repeatedly stopped by during the interiew process asking to see the accused. These visits were the only time Ford's face changed from unmoving granite, a wry smile creeping across he man's face as Drogo gossiped about people at the playfields, babbled bout girlfriends and cousins, or complained about police and the world t large. Small infusions of humor in drawn-out depressing hours.

By midafternoon the third day following that last trip to the play fields, Marlowe sensed the wear and tear on psyches. He'd demanded Morven and Nelson close laptops. "Enough" he said. "Let's call it. First round's on me." He'd thought they might try to skip the drinks, heading to exercise routines, naps, dinners, dates—lives outside of the station—but both had enthusiastically given him the thumbs-up. It wasn't so late that a round would cut Saturday evening completely off. He'd shuffled them to Gary's so he could make a last phone call to Captain Innocent apprising her of where they were and that he'd called it for the day.

Which is how he found himself walking alone down 1st Avenue, the center street of Settler's Square. Surprisingly quiet for a weekend afternoon. Only a handful of cars driving past, a few people on one corner huddled around a street magician dressed in red and white clown make up, a mountain of a man in a green tank top walking three Chihuahuas Marlowe pivoted around, and three teens on skateboards, who whizzed past him as he arrived at Gary's.

Walking through the door, he was greeted by The Kinks song "The Village Green Preservation Society" from bar speakers and a short, high-pitched yap.

"Ainsley, shhh. Gary doesn't like barking," John said. He was sitting at a table with Morven and Nelson, Ainsley pulling Marlowe's direction as John held her leash. "Hey, Marlowe, you're here."

"I am." Marlowe stopped near the table to reach down and pet Ainsley, who instantly after lay back at John's feet and fell asleep.

"Marlowe." Morven smiled. "I gave John a ring. Felt he should be part of the post-collar drinks." Not only had John helped solve the case she knew he and Marlowe had become friends.

"He should at that." Marlowe sat, noticing Morven and Nelson both had nearly empty pint glassed in front of them. "You've been busy."

Before they replied, Gary appeared at the table. He'd been arranging bottles behind the bar, where the only other patron sat on a stool nursing a tall, bubbly highball the color of fog. "Kit," Gary chimed, "'bou time. Peelers all here. They've one on you."

"Gary," Marlowe said. "Quiet one?"

"So far, my friend. Feels the case must be moving the right direction."

"That it is." Marlowe's reply was underlined by enthusiastic nods from the table.

"Then a drink is in order."

"On me, even. What'll y'all have?"

"We should have a celebratory toast," John declared. "Prosecco?" He knew Marlowe loved Italian drinks of all kinds.

"Afternoon bubbles." Morven laughed. "Perfect with me." Nelson and Marlowe nodded agreement.

"Bubbles it will be," Gary said, "and water for Ainsley." The bartender went to assemble the drinks.

Nelson, surprisingly quiet and thoughtful since John arrived, spoke up. "Mr. Arthur, do you mind a question?"

"Not in the least, Detective. I might have one or two myself. Oh, wait." He glanced at Marlowe, who'd been bending down to pet Ainsley. "Marlowe? Guessing this might be a case question. I know your thought about case talk in the bar."

Marlowe pulled himself back up tableside. "As it's almost solely us here, one or two is okay. Quiet ones, though, Nelson."

"Will do, sir," Nelson whispered. "I've been wondering about the leather bracelet connection. When did you notice that, Mr. Arthur?"

"From the beginning. I just didn't know it was important." All three sported questioning looks, so he continued. "I noticed the curious leather watchband on Pat Brown and should have made more of it, as a leather band, even with the gold beads, was surprisingly unostentatious for someone who wasn't afraid to display affluence."

"Then when did you know it was important?" Nelson asked.

"After I decided Mr. David was the murderer. Or during that process. Reasoning backward in a way. Understand?"

Marlowe grinned. "Not sure we do."

"Reasoning backward? Sherlock's deductive process? You know the result, then go backward on the steps that led to it. I knew Mr. David had to have done it, then went backward in my mind collecting the facts tying into that deduction."

Nelson raised his hand, causing Morven to nearly spit out the last swallow of her beer laughing.

"Detective Nelson?" John said teacherly.

"Was that in a particular Sherlock Holmes show?"

"In the books. *Study in Scarlet* I think."

Before anyone spoke, Gary arrived with a tray balancing four flutes full of the Italian sparkling wine and water for Ainsley. He passed them out, placing the dog's bowl under the table, saying, "Cheers, mates. Congrats too."

They passed thanks to the bartender as he strode off, picking up the used beer glasses before leaving.

"Well," Marlowe drawled, holding his glass out in the middle of the table, "we reached the end of the trail. Here's to it." They clinked glasses, took sips, leaned back. "Any questions for us, John?"

John's golden eyeglasses twinkled from sunshine streaming through the bar's windows. "Two. First, when you solve a case does Marlowe always buy the drinks?"

They laughed, as Marlowe said, "I believe he does. And?"

John paused dramatically. "How long before our next case?"

"John." Marlowe took a slow sip before continuing. "No case talk in the bar."

AUTHOR'S NOTE

The names, characters, and situations represented in this novel are, of course, wholly invented. Except those names and characters from cited television shows, movies, and books. And Ainsley the dog, who is definitely based on a real dog, one that is giving me the "take me on a walk" look as I type.

I'd like to once again give a huge thank you to Ainsley for her invaluable assistance in writing this second book featuring Arthur and Marlowe. Also, giant thanks to my wife Natalie, for her insistence on having a second book written – like the first, it was given to her as a birthday present. Also, even more thanks to Jon and Nik, for all their help and assistance in making this book, and to Elizabeth White, the world's finest mystery book editor. Thank you, also, for reading it. My guess is you've read the first The American Who Watched British Mysteries book already, but if not, I hope you enjoy it, too.

Printed in Dunstable, United Kingdom